GLINT & SHADE:

ANTHOLOGY

VOL. ONE

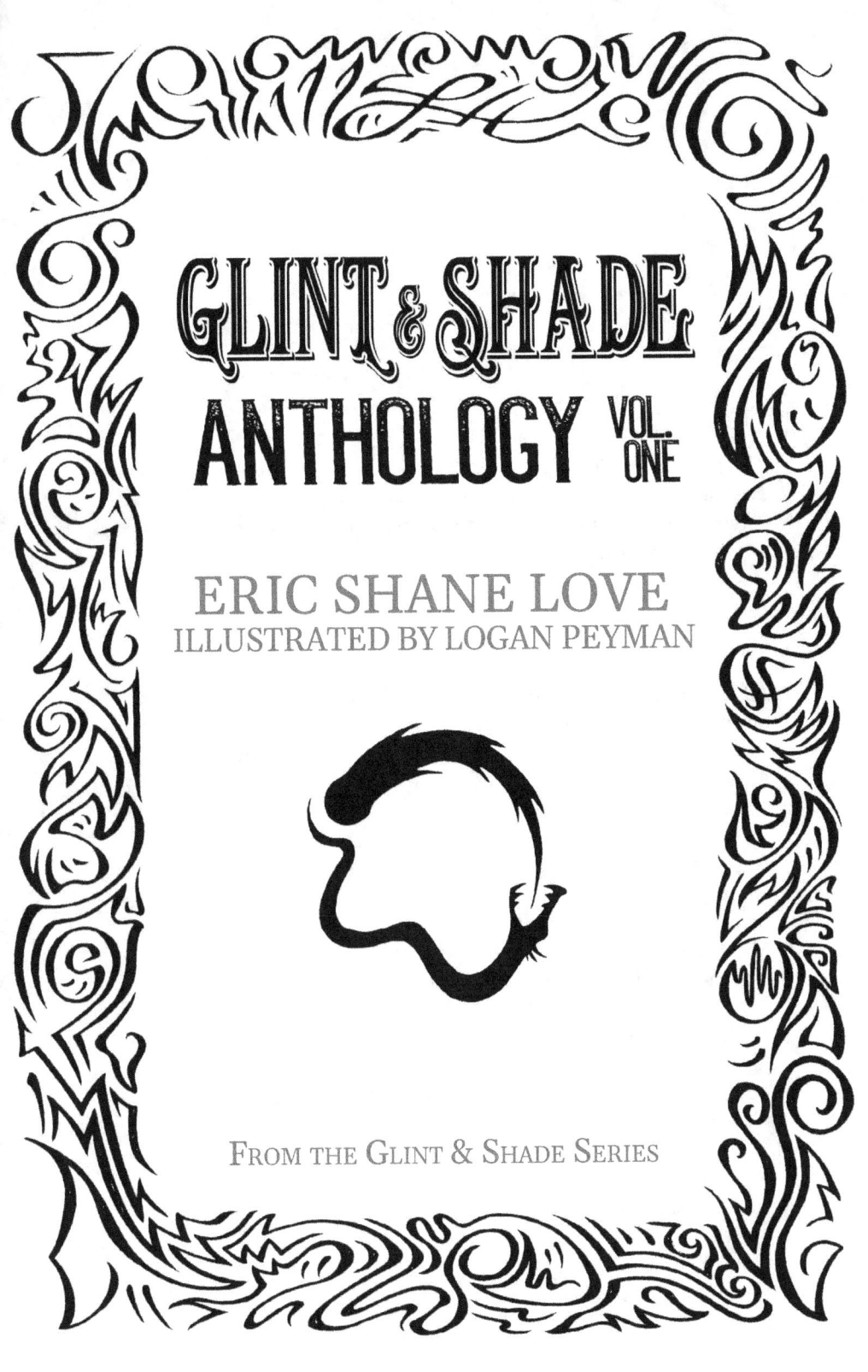

GLINT & SHADE

ANTHOLOGY VOL. ONE

ERIC SHANE LOVE
ILLUSTRATED BY LOGAN PEYMAN

FROM THE GLINT & SHADE SERIES

This is a work of fiction. Names, characters, places, and incidents either are the product of the author's imagination or are used fictitiously. Any resemblance to actual persons, living or dead, events, or locales is entirely coincidental.

All rights reserved. No part of this book may be reproduced or used in any manner without written permission of the copyright owner except for the use of quotations in a book review. For more information, address: eric@ericshanelove.com.

First paperback edition October 2023

Book design by Anja Scholte
Maps and illustrations by Logan Peyman
Author portrait by Philipp WL Günther

Trade Paperback   979-8-9853173-6-7
Ebook   979-8-9853173-8-1
Audiobook   979-8-9853173-7-4
Also available for Kindle

www.ericshanelove.com

INTRODUCTION

While writing the *Glint & Shade* series, I often get sidetracked down streets adjacent to the main story, through hidden coves or inside secret huts . . . things that aren't, strictly speaking, crucial to the story. But for me, these things are inescapable. I believe songs and stories, fairytales and superstitions, religions and politics give a culture its soul and define its character. The meals prepared in home kitchens, what people do together when the work is done for the day, the way birthdays and holidays are celebrated: these are details that give the tapestry of a culture texture and life. They inform those on the outside what to expect. They are often the shorthand by which people communicate, perhaps even without realizing it. These details are the reality of a community. And these are the details I cannot help but chase while I write because they tell the truth about the people in my stories, providing an authenticity that a world relies on to transcend fantasy and become believable.

World-building is something I enjoy immensely, so long as I honor the truths and limitations of the world I am inventing: otherwise, the new world is inauthentic. Its fabrication then becomes revealed beneath thin coats of glossy metaphorical paint, and that will not do. As I build this world, I look to the fabric of the daily lives of the people inhabiting it to make it honest. Not just the characters I know by name, but also their neighbors. And strangers, both across the mountain and across the world. I've spent most of my life—even as a child—studying the world around me. How people interact with one another based on invisible barriers created by our differences: religious beliefs, politics, personal backgrounds, racial differences, sexuality, economic inequality, prejudices, and so on. How potent these surface factors can be in making us see others in a particular and often poor way. I'll give you an example.

Around the age of seven, I remember looking at a girl in my class named Judy. We sat across from each other. Judy was an ugly girl. She had red hair and freckles. Everyone knew she was unattractive, even Judy . . . except one day, I watched her as she focused on her assignment. She had lost herself in an art project, if I remember correctly. I was shocked at what I saw, as if I'd never seen her before. She was happy in her work, unbothered by the other children in our class because her artwork made her forget the rest of us. Would Judy not want to hide her unattractive face? Her fiery hair and freckles? And if so, how could she forget we were all there, potentially watching her? I had my own insecurities, and I never seemed to forget people "saw" me. How could she work without, so far as I could see, even a hint of self-doubt? As I watched Judy, I saw beyond my preloaded expectations. Beyond what my prejudices and the collective attitudes of my peers told me to see.

Judy's freckles stretched across her cheeks and nose like a star field. I've even used this imagery in this series: perhaps Judy inspired it. Her freckles were beautiful, and I'd never noticed. She had dimples, and somehow these made her smile come alive in a way mine did not. She didn't have boring blond or brown hair, like me and practically every other white kid in my class. Her hair was red, and as the sunlight poured in through the window behind her, it set it on fire. It was glorious. I kid you not: I never saw Judy the same way after that. I could not understand why my classmates thought she was ugly: Judy was beautiful. And yes, it is possible—perhaps even probable—my imagination has altered or exaggerated her description in the many years since, but so what? The experience resonates inside me all these years later, and that makes the telling true even if the details are not. Revelations such as this taught me to pay attention, to stop and really look at the world around me, including the individuals inhabiting it. This kind of observation is also what made me jealous of the black girls in my class because they could adorn their hair with colorful beads that rattled like music when they moved. It made me wish I knew the lyrical language of the Indian kids in my class, or envious of the Hispanic boys with their beautiful dark skin, hair, and eyes. I looked at myself in the mirror: I was so boring. Somehow, as a child, I saw all of our differences as being the secret ingredients that made my world—and the culture I grew up in, specifically—wonderful. That made us as a people—one people, I tell you—exciting. Our differences did not separate us. Our differences made us glorious, and I was fortunate to be raised by parents who often celebrated these differences rather than criticized them.

I once heard the expression, "Unity isn't sameness. It's diversity in the right places." I heard this at church camp as a child—a man named Bubba declared this truth while speaking to a bunch of stinky camp kids— and it never left me. I would now take it a step further: our humanity does not make us divine . . . our diversity does that. This is why, when I found Eliot on the page, he looked nothing like me. This despite the fact that the first two books in the series are based on a dream I had in 2001, and in that dream, Eliot *was* me. There are practical reasons within the story that account for the color of his skin, but even without those reasons, I would want this world populated with people who don't look like me. Who don't think like me or behave like me. Otherwise, it would be so very boring and unrealistic.

So long as I have written stories, which has been since elementary school, I've been interested in the kinds of nonverbal, intangible interactions that make us humans who and what we are. How natural disasters or calamity can unify us, but variations in skin pigment can turn us into enemies. How our faiths can draw from us our very best or our very worst, causing us to either transcend our humanity or be stripped of it. How tiny and finite our minds can be even when we believe ourselves free thinkers and seekers of truth. You know people like that, don't you? Yes, of course you do. We all do . . . but are you certain you aren't one of them? Am I? That's the challenge: our own personal truths can be the most difficult to sort. The reality of our own shortcomings as thinkers is nearly always the most obscured. This is something I devote quite a bit of energy to in my personal journey: sorting my truths or attempting to. I do not want my default to be assuming I am right. If I always begin with that assumption, I am not challenged to think harder and better. If I am not challenged, how will I learn? And if I do not learn, how can I grow? I try to take in the world around me first without judgment, in particular when I interact with those who come from a different background or perspective than I do. This last happens as often as I can orchestrate it. I prefer surrounding myself with people who cause me to take a second and third look at how I perceive my world. Otherwise, if I surround myself with only like-minded people, it reminds me of soaking in bath water I'd shared with my cousins as a child.

People fascinate me. What motivates people fascinates me. I think we can learn so much about a culture by listening to its songs and reading its literature. By watching its movies and TV shows or scrolling through a For You page on TikTok (for hours, obviously). Truth comes out of our slang words. In our tabloids and shock jock radio shows. Among our sacred sects of religion, politics, and fad health crazes. Even our lies reveal so much truth about who we are. I can't help but search out those kinds of truths and revelations while building the world of the Glint. But all of that cannot fit inside a single series of books. In most cases, when I reference a story or a song or a bit of folklore in my series, I have an elaborate idea—and often a complete picture—of what those things are. Many times, those stories exist as complete tales. Those songs I've actually sung while sitting at my piano. Those terms have an entire world of meaning and value. I understand why people celebrate their holy days the way they do in this world. I know about their superstitions. Heck, I know about the origins of their superstitions. How historical events blurred into myth through the ages and were eventually fired in the ovens of time to become glossy morality tales taught to children. But again, I cannot fit all of that content into the series.

That's where this and future anthologies come in. Some of these stories existed in one form or another even before I finished the first book. At least one existed before I began it. Still others began as dreams. Others were glistening threads I wove into something bigger. And some of what you will read was originally part of the main books in the series, a gleaming jewel of two or three lines or perhaps a paragraph or a page. These little pockets of story give us glimpses at the motivations of characters we get to know well throughout the series and launch us into histories and experiences beyond the books. These scenes may reveal much about characters that I love and whom I hope you are coming to love as well.

4

Every few books, I'll offer one of these anthologies. This one has elements that relate to the first two books in the series, *The Scarecrow Hunters* and *A Greedy Shadow*. It also contains stories and songs referenced in the third book, *The Singing Bones*. So if you are wondering where this first anthology fits within the rest of the series, it snuggles right in between the second and third books. It loves a good cuddle, after all.

After many of the stories, you will find an author's note. They give a bit of insight into what led me to write the story or how it grew into its final version. Where it came from, who inspired it . . . that kind of thing. However, the author's notes are not required reading to understand or enjoy the stories. Most of these tales can stand alone all by themselves. Others are bridge chapters, or what I call springboard scenes, that link one book with the next in the series. And at least once, you will find an alternate telling of a chapter you've already read, assuming you have read *A Greedy Shadow*. Only here, it will be from another character's point of view. But the entries herein can be read and enjoyed without reading the main books in the series, though I hope you will read them, too. I have so much to show you, after all. If you enjoy this kind of anthology, remember there will be more to come. Also, I would encourage you to check out the terms at the end of the books or on my website: www.ericshanelove.com/glossary. Obviously, you can look up a word from the text you may not know, but if you are like me, looking up one term will send you along a seam of clues leading to a larger bit of fabric. Remember, it's a tapestry . . . and tapestries are made up of little bits and threads.

Thank you for joining us. Now, I'll let you get to it. Happy reading.

I

PART ONE: STORIES

These short stories relate to the first three *Glint & Shade* books, but they can be read and enjoyed independently of the series. Apart from a few words here and there that are specific to the world in which the stories exist, I've tried to keep these as self-contained as I am capable. But know this: there will always be hints at parts of that larger tapestry peppered throughout these tales. Keep in mind there is a lot to be gleaned from a culture's literature, and one of these stories is a folktale that exists within the world of the Glint. Remember, too, some of the folken you meet here, you might see them again.

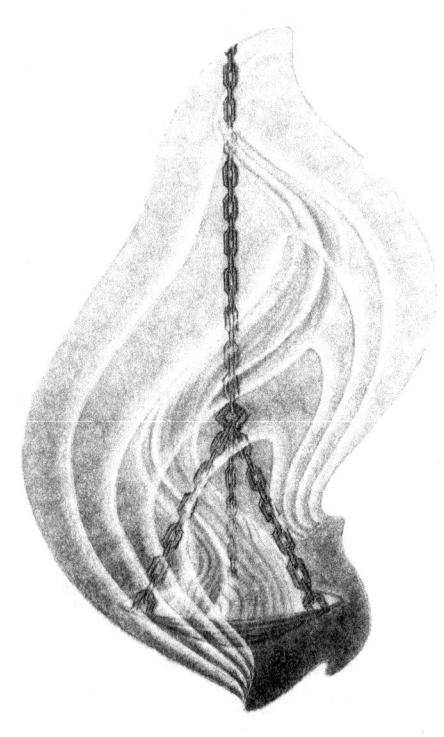

KOLINGA

"Storm's almost here . . . ."

Natty paused. Her burning match hovered just above the wick of her candle, but her eyes were on her apprentice, Breme. "And?" she asked.

"It should be here within the hour, I think," Breme said.

Natty lit the candle, then blew out the match and tossed it on a table. "And did you not trust me? Did you not believe me when I said a storm would come?"

Breme did not answer. He knew his mistress well. Her question was part of her pageantry. Part of establishing a mood for what would come later. The effort and its effect were for the benefit of their guest. Most of it, at least. Natty was made up of sharp edges and blunt objects, after all. Rather than responding, Breme pulled the double doors of the small wooden cabin shut. The storm would come soon, but only when Natty wished it. Already the water of the Barren was frenetic, its undulating waves sloshing chaotically onto the dock. The wooden structure swayed in the wind. Gray hemmed in the cabin from sky to sea. Inside was little better, though the candles offered a cheerful light.

"Are we safe?" the girl asked, having arrived just after dawn that morning. She had peculiar questions for Natty. She was a peculiar girl.

Natty huffed. "No one is ever safe," she said. As she turned to set a kettle near the fire, Breme saw she was smiling. She was enjoying herself, at least.

Breme had been with Natty since just after he was born. Destined for servitude, Breme had been made a eunuch. Perhaps this should make him sad, but Breme wasn't. His mistress was mother and friend and confidante and protector and superior and lover to him. She was everything he needed or wanted. To anyone outside their little isolated world, the two would seem very odd. That, too, was part of Natty's pageantry.

Looking through the cabin's dirty glass window to the water surrounding them, Breme understood the girl's worry. Natty's cabin was a square wooden structure built on a deck in the middle of the Barren, one that reached well past the lake's forsaken shores. Walking the dock to the cabin took no less than a quarter of an hour, and that when rushed. Few people were willing to brave even the shores of the lake, much less trespass so far past the breakers, to visit an old hag's cabin.

Natty was not a sorceress, as people suspected. She was a seer. And an Edön. As a khamun who specialized in neutralizing dark energy, she was unafraid of the Barren. She might have been, if she had been able to know fear. But her capacity to be afraid had been culled by her cumatu. And her cumatu was why they had a guest just now. The girl wanted Natty to tell her all about the kolinga—the coming-of-age rite specific to Natty's people, but similar to cumatus from other regions. Specifically, she wanted to know how Natty's kolinga had changed her when she was young. And how Natty had changed the kolinga in return.

For his part, Breme was appropriately afraid of the Barren. The Lost Lake, as some folken called it, was a desolate salt lake haunted by the ghosts of the souls it had eaten. No one ventured onto its waters save for the Skie-Len, and that barbarous group, like the rest of the Skree, bathed in death.

The girl trembled. Natty sat in a chair and motioned to the floor in front of her. "Have a seat," she said. The girl appeared reluctant at first, but she did as instructed. "We will be fine," Natty said. "Do not fret yourself. This cabin is enchanted. The storm is not."

The girl did not relax, but neither did she complain. Breme brought over a small table and placed it next to Natty's chair. On it was a bowl filled with salt, a vial of crow's blood, the skull and dried feet of a bat, and a pungent cloth that glistened with the entrails of a large frog. Set dressings . . . . The salt was for cooking. The crow's blood was left over from their supper two nights earlier, the bat parts all that remained of Natty's pet, Girta. And the entrails were the scraps of what would be their supper later on: Natty loved fried frog legs. But the girl did not know Breme had set the table with the trappings of Natty's kitchen. Nor could she guess this was all part of Natty's show. The pageantry worked. The girl appeared unnerved. Still, she did not complain. For all her fear, she was stoic.

"Now, what exactly would you like to know?" Natty asked.

"Tell me about your kolinga," the girl said.

"My ko," Natty mused, scratching her chin. At sixty-three years, she was not a terribly old woman, but she had an ancient soul. This made her seem much older than she was. This, too, Natty used to her advantage. No one expected much from an old hag. "That was a lifetime ago. What do you want to know?"

"Everything," the girl said.

"Very well," Natty said, settling back against her chair.

Breme took a seat on the other side of the room. He could see both Natty and the girl from this vantage. In particular, he could watch the girl. This was the task given to him by his mistress. "And what should I look for?" he had asked. "You will know," she had said. He was told to watch the girl's eyes. Breme was not a seer, but Natty had initiated a bit of his training with the sight. He had only twenty-five years; there was time yet to gain some skill. He could not say for sure—and Natty would not lay things out so cleanly—but he guessed whatever it was she expected him to find while watching the girl, it would come from the sight. So he watched and listened. He would enjoy the show.

"Every girl's kolinga began on the day of her first bleeding," Natty began. "The weeks leading up to it were ordained by a series of ceremonial events. Each girl was sequestered away from the main population. They were prepared for what would come with ceremonial food and garments. It would not be easy, after all." Natty waited, apparently to see if the girl would ask another question. She did not. Natty went on. "But I think you understand the simple mechanics of the kolinga, don't you? Hmph," she grunted, nodding her head. "And I think you know the kolinga is no more.

I think you know I burned it to the ground, aye?" Still the girl said nothing. Natty nodded. "Then let me get to the bones of the story."

Outside the cabin, the wind buffeted the structure. Inside, its joints creaked and popped. The two doors that opened onto the vast expanse of gray water rattled in their frame. A thunderbolt split the sky, its belly bounding over them in thunder moments later. The cabin shook. Breme, despite all he knew, was terrified. The girl must be as well, but she hardly reacted. Again, Natty nodded.

"Yes, let me begin . . . ."

Like most girls from Ti-Fleek Lustrė, I was aware of the kolinga my entire life. Having been born in the mountain region surrounding Lustrain, I could not help but wonder over the mystique of the ceremony. I could not help but wonder if I would be chosen. I did not know as a child there was no choosing: we had each one been bred for it. We had been made for the kolinga . . . little more than crops to be harvested.

My people were a superstitious bunch. I suppose living in a world within sight and smell of the Barren makes us strange. We were quite safe from the Skree. I was taught this safety came from living in the mountains, that the Skree preferred easier villages to plunder. I believed this then. Of course I did. I was only a child. But even as far back as then, I sensed the truth of things. Or some of it, leastways. But I suppose I'm wasting your time. Let me get to the point.

Some of my earliest memories are of crafting my kolinga gudwat, the ceremonial gown we wore. They're made of the finest fabrics and adorned with colorful braids, intricate needlework, polished gems, and carved beads. They are things of immense beauty. The better to draw in unsuspecting girls, I see now. For many years, I worked on my gudwat. The gowns were revered as the most sacred garment of our people. The kolinga was the most sacred event in our culture. Every little girl longed to be chosen. Every little girl was lied to.

In the weeks leading up to my kolinga, I wore only simple colorless robes. Each morning I drank special broth reserved for girls awaiting their ko. For each meal, I ate foods blessed by our khan, meats sacrificed to our gods; I drank wine poured from ancient vats that were said to have been crafted by the Monkshood themselves, those dumas who first forged the bonds of allegiance between my people and the earth we lived on.

This contract, as it was, led to the kolinga: the act by which the girls of the cluster would join the Mothers. This is what we called the collective khan who raised us, our spiritual superiors. They who held the positions believed to have once been established by the Monkshood. The Mother Khan, our high priestess, served me the sacred foods. My ko was the final step from girlhood into womanhood, and what little girl doesn't want to become a mother?

When a girl's ceremonial cleansing began—the week-long period of preparation leading up to her ko—you could almost watch her outgrow her girlhood. I so wanted that for myself, but I was not like the other girls. And you knew that already, aye?

The broth they fed us was laced with poison meant to dull our senses and bring us, slowly, into a mild stupor. To take away any lingering wish to remain autonomous. To begin our molding into Mothers—but not in the sense us girls believed. When finally the day of our bleeding came, and we donned our gudwat, we felt queenly. That was the intention, I believe. To make us feel like queens.

A kolinga might last up to several days, perhaps even a week. More in rare cases, I suppose. But most required no more than a day and a half. When a girl emerged from her ko, she was given a new name and a new room. No longer was she a girl of the cluster, now she was a Mother. I never emerged from my kolinga, not in the sense meant by the Mothers, but I did receive a new name. One I chose for myself.

Like many girls, I came to our cluster around the age of six years. I spent the next eleven years perfecting my gudwat, anticipating my ko, and fantasizing about what it must feel like to become a Mother. When it was time for my preparation period, the Mothers sequestered me from the other girls. I drank the bitter broth and ate the blessed food. I wore the plain, undyed garments provided to me by the khan. But I was no good at this process: I was too excited. My Mother wore out her cwen rod on my backside that week. The cwen rod, the Mothers said, was a tool for making queens. I admit: I was never the queenly type, though I did not see that then.

On the morning of my first bleeding, the Mothers stripped me of the plain garments of my preparation. I was older than most of the girls when they had their kolinga. I was late, but my Mother assured me this was no real concern. A girl's bleeding comes when it comes. The Mothers bathed me with spiced water and oils. They gathered my hair in a tight knot. They dressed me in my gudwat, adding the final touches to its glamour from their own chests of trinkets and treasures. Ribbons festooned with flowers and herbs they wrapped round my neck and waist. Then they prepared the path for me, a path I would walk alone.

Back and back, many a many ago, when the land was still fertile and its temples still stood, the cluster had been built on a sacred patch of ground that literally exhaled its mysteries like hot breath. Heady clouds of smoke and mist puffed out from some ancient and secret oven in the heart of the mountain, the ground riddled with vents. Atop one such vent, the Monkshood built a hut. Around this hut, they built another. And around this hut, they built yet another. A hut within a hut within a hut . . . this was the most sacred ground of our cluster, in all of Ti-Fleek even.

In the time of my ko, the mountain's breath remained . . . no doubt it still does. I walked the long corridors of the sacred huts, feeling the weight and pull of what was happening—I felt my kolinga in my chest. I felt it in my head. Looking back, I know most of what I felt was the drugs they'd given me and the spells they'd cast to limit my thinking. Do you know the purpose of the kolinga? Its true purpose, I mean. Not the lies force fed us children. Please indulge me a moment to explain. Then I will get to the part of my story you wish to hear. I promise . . . .

The kolinga was a tool for stripping the girls of Ti-Fleek of their essential parts. A way to form them into the collective known as the Motherhood. Of course, motherhood is a cruel allegory here. The kolinga sterilized the girls. As a child, I'd never wondered over this, that none of the Mothers were actual mothers. That none of us girls were born in the cluster. Even now, I cannot say for certain where us girls came from. I have no memory of my earliest years. But I suspect we were harvested from the surrounding villages. Perhaps from Lustrain itself. A girl coming to the cluster, and especially a girl who was *chosen* for the kolinga, was venerated above all in Ti-Fleek.

The Mothers were a homogenized lot. To us girls, their sameness made them feel superior, but that was our brainwashing. That was us girls believing the lies they fed us. The kolinga was meant to make us each, to the last one, just like the one before her. Just like the one who came after. It was meant to take from us what made us unique. Our individuality. Don't misunderstand: the Mothers were strong. Very strong. Perhaps stronger than most men or women. They were considered protectors throughout the mountain region, and for good reason. They could be warriors or healers. Skilled in the arts of the elhwith. In magics and potions and seeing . . . all of the things, both of dark and light. But my preparation did not take. For as I have said, I was different.

My Mother, for every girl had a Mother we were conscripted to, brought me to a large wooden door carved with runes and words from ancient lynthian scrip. The letters ornate. She left me there to find the rest of my way on my own. When I opened the door, the handle was warm in my hand. Beyond it was a courtyard surrounded by a high wall, and in the center was a large yet unassuming hut. The path leading to the hut's entrance was strewn with flower petals, precious metals, and jewels mined from the mountain. I walked this path, my eyes on the ground before me. As I got closer to the hut, I saw the petals were withered. The air was warmer there. The door to the hut had no handle, so I pushed against it with both hands. The door was hot, but not unbearable, and it swung open with little effort.

I stepped inside. The door closed. Incense assaulted my nostrils and burned my eyes. Something in the substance must have quickened my menstruation, for then I felt my bleeding intensify. The pain had been dulled by their drugs, but not eradicated. And now it, too, quickened. I gasped as a pang rippled through me. I did not know it, but this was perhaps the first hint that my kolinga was not working. That I was not susceptible. The air inside the first hut was hazy with incense, and I was eager to pass from it into the next. Upon reaching the door to the second hut, I placed my hands on the wood and pushed. It, too, opened easily. It, too, was hot against my palms. Hotter than the first. I stepped through, and the door closed behind me. Candlelight illuminated the third and last hat. The light danced along its walls, wreathing it—the sacred of the sacred, the naval, the womb—in a soft amber glow.

This womb—the innermost hut, if you prefer—was not large, no bigger than a carriage, but it was taller. Around its base was a trap filled with fragrant oils that bubbled and hissed from the heat. I felt my gudwat sticking to my skin, my hair coming loose in wet clumps and falling around my shoulders and down my back. I swayed on my feet, as much from the heat as from the drugs and spells. I did not want to touch the inner hut's door. I feared how it might burn. But that was why I was there, to go through that door, so I touched it. Tentative at first. Then, as before, I placed my palms flat against it. It was hotter than the previous doors, but it did not scald my skin. Instead, it vibrated, and my palms tingled with the kinetic energy of what was beyond the door. I pressed. It opened. I stepped inside. It closed behind me.

The sacred of the sacred was filled with steam, but rather than being fabricated by the Mothers, as in the first hut, with their tinctures and incense, this steam was from the earth. Before me was a pool of mud glistening with a colorful sheen as it boiled and exhaled steam. The steam rose and lifted through an opening in the ceiling. I suppose that alone made this holy place bearable for me to stand. The air was thick and sulfuric. It stank and burned my eyes and throat.

I walked to the pool's edge. What should happen next? I wondered. There was no adornment in the sacred of the sacred. No carved walls. No tapestries as in the other huts. No runes. No lynthian scrips. No tables for incense or traps for oils. Only the mountain and the plain walls of the hut and the sky above. So I sat on the stone of the mountain, on a smooth round that made sitting more comfortable.

Then I waited.

I do not know what would have happened next had I been a normal girl of the cluster. I believe the Mother Khan would have come. I believe she would have administered certain rites. But with me, no one came right away. By the open sky above, I counted the passing of time. I cannot say for certain, but I believe time ebbed and flowed inside the sacred of the sacred. Mayhap it did not only move forward, but also side to side. Perhaps even back. How could I know this? Because I changed. I grew hungry, then full. I grew tired, then restless. My hair went from wet to damp to wet to dry. My clothing, too. My gudwat glistened with perspiration, then crackled from dry heat . . . but the air was far from dry. By the time someone arrived to tend to me, I counted seven rotations of the sun. A week had passed, or so it seemed. But who can say when time is squirrelly? And when someone finally came, it was not our Mother Khan.

The dumas did not come through the door as I had. Rather it came from the mist. And I call it an it because it was sexless. Unlike the golden skin of my people and the other girls of the cluster, its skin was pale but inflamed around the eyes and ears. Its every opening seeped fluid. And I did see every opening, for it was naked. As plain as the sacred of the sacred was, this body was ornamented, covered with runes and lynthian words—I felt the spell of these without needing to understand them—and scars that I swear looked for all my world like the agonized expressions of lost girls. The eyes in the dumas's skull were black pits, though not bereft of life and movement.

I stood. The dumas approached. Neither of us spoke. Then it touched me. That is when I poisoned the kolinga.

I had not meant to. I wanted my ko. I wanted to become a Mother. To live on in the cluster. Like any girl, I dreamed of one day becoming the

Mother Khan. No part of me had entertained anything besides. I had no aspirations of being ousted or of complicating the cluster's venerated ceremonies or of rending the very fabric by which the cluster existed. Of breaking its foundations. Even so, something happened when the dumas touched me. Something issued from me into it. I felt it bolt from me into the flat palm of the pale white creature. I felt it snap the dumas's thread of life in two. I could only watch as the creature stumbled backward, one step, then two . . . . I could only watch as it toppled into the pool, the look of shock on its face so evident, it stole away my breath.

Then the mountain trembled. I heard cries coming from without, followed quickly by hastened footsteps and battering. I could just make out some of what the voices were saying. The Mothers were trying to get in to stop whatever was happening. They were too late, of course. I did not know this. Mayhap they knew but refused belief. Mayhap they yet hoped. Either way, I tried to assist them. I pushed against the door to open it, but it was solidly fastened to the walls. It would not budge. I tried to pull, but there was no handle. I dug my fingertips into its seam, ripping my nails from my effort, but the door would not move. A glut of steam issued from behind me, and I turned to see the pool vomiting its hot breath into the sky. The trembling mountain began to shake. The ground beneath my feet cracked. The mountain yawned as if waking. I fell to my knees and clung to a bit of jagged stone. I could not escape, nor could I avoid the chasm if it opened further.

And open further it did. I did not fall into it, not at first. But everything else did. No, that isn't true. Nothing fell . . . .

The walls making up the sacred of the sacred splintered. Piece by piece, they were sucked into the mountain's maw. Then the candles and their sconces from the second hut. The oils and floor tiles. The ceiling. All of this was sucked in. Then the outer hut, its door first. Then the walls. Then the Mothers. Then the cluster girls. Then the cluster itself. I watched in horror as every scrap of the cluster, from kitchen to washroom to altars to holy artifacts, was eaten by the mountain. And only after, and I say this true, did it come for me. Mud wrapped itself round my legs, then my waist. My gudwat burned away in the acidic flow. My skin blistered red but did not break. The mud was hot, but not harmful. It seared away the hair from my scalp, however. All hair from my body, in fact. When at last the maw took me into itself, I was naked as a newborn rat.

I did not fall into the mountain. I fell into the elhwith. I spiraled end over end. All the while, I felt my kindling . . . . This is what I came to call it

19

after. The secret birthright hidden inside me. Hidden from me, leastways. My life's blood dripped from between my legs. It was not a heavy flow, but it felt pulled from me. And I felt a tremendous beast awake within me. It stood up and began walking around inside me. It was fantastic and frightening and fevered. The beast was me—I was the beast. It was silver, with a simple curved horn that grew from its skull, right at the base. This curved up and over its head. Nostrils flaring wide, the beast panted wild with wonder and hunger. It was built like a bull, only it wasn't quite like a bull. Its hooves beat against the . . . the what? There was no floor, but there was resistance. This, too, was me. I was resisting the beast. I was resisting myself. In my mind's eye, I saw the beast turn toward me. It stared at me with its eyeless face. Then it kicked, and I broke open.

Light flooded in. The sound of bird song and wind dance. Of wild forest things and creatures from the depths of the sea. Of gods and devils. My skin glittered with the dust of stars and the milk of moons. My eyes burned with the salt of suns. My belly stirred with the nectar of worlds unknown to me. My lips tasted flesh. My tongue tasted sweat. My throat swallowed bitter fluid. And I stood in a vaporous tent of silver. I walked forward. The beast walked forward as well, its horn teasing the way.

"Ada-handura," it said. I did not understand. I could not. "Ada-handura, doesah."

I turned my eyes to look above. Had it told me to? Yes, I believe so. I had told myself, but in a tongue I did not know. Above me, I saw a dark sky. Through a thick scrim of rain-heavy clouds, I saw starlight twinkle. Then I saw a great white light burn away all other light and all other darkness. This light—a comet, I realized—fell from the sky, a dark, serpentine shape riding its tail. It crashed into the mountains. The earth exploded. Silt and salt filled the air. A crater opened. I fell backward.

I spiraled end over end once again. I smelled death and felt both hope and hopelessness. When my feet found solid ground—or leastways, imagined solid ground—I was walking a path paved with glittering jewels. Every color was present, many I had never before seen. Many I have never seen since. I sensed many of these would kill me outside of this place. These made up a circular path of gleaming light, and in the center was my silver beast. It danced with others like it, only these came in many shapes, sizes, and colors. Gold and silver and topaz and lapis lazuli and crimson and violet and more and more and more. Above this was a sky made of forests. Below, a sea made of stone. To my left were mountains made of hooves and horns. To my right, fields made of feathers and scales. In front of me was a vast storm. It churned as if to destroy the planets, but from within its cyclone emerged more beasts. Behind me, I heard singing. I turned to look. A star field glittered there. Each star winked at me. Each sang my unknown name.

I kept walking. As I did, my feet sank into the light path. Up to my ankles, then my shins. I kept walking. By the time I sank to my waist, I knew what would happen next but not what would happen after. I kept walking. Up to my naval. Then to my breasts. Then my shoulders. My chin. My eyes . . . .

I went through. This time I did not spiral. This time I did not fall. I simply was. All around me was velvet darkness. All that I had seen before was now in my throat. Then in my chest. Then in my belly. My silver beast—myself—pawed at the darkness. This was a comfortable place, but I knew I could not stay. Or rather, I should not. But the choice was mine. I tried to walk. There was no ground. I tried to swim. There was no water. I tried to fly. There was no air. Instead, I thought. That is when the darkness swirled. My thoughts were the catalyst that sent it scampering. That is when the voices collated. I had not noticed them before, but I heard them now: the many voices of stars. Utwah, they said. Kola, they said. Lightfoot, they said. Arant, they said. Aric, they said. Then they pushed me forward. Then they laughed. Krea, they said. Natty, they said. Oro, they said. And of these last three, I knew I must choose.

"Natty," I said without understanding.

"Natty," the voices said in return. The name given to me at my birth fell away from me then.

Then I fell. Not end over end. Straight down. I was twisted like a dish rag. I felt my body contort as I fell, as all the poison of the cluster was rung out of me. I cried out in pain and alarm. I was coming undone. I do not speak in hyperbole: I mean I came undone. I mean I was refashioned after. I had been reduced to parts, and those parts put back together again.

The hot wind grew warm. The warm wind grew cool. The cool wind grew cold. The cold wind became water. The water lapped at my skin. Its salt dried my lips. I slid as if a throat of darkness swallowed me. After a time, slivers of nearly green light speckled the walls and ceiling. Then darkness took me again. Not evil: sleep.

I did not dream. Or rather, I had no further dreams. For mayhap all I had experienced so far had been nothing more than the delusions of a drugged girl. I think you know the truth of this. I think this is why you came. I had not dreamt. I had had no visions. I had slipped between this world and the next. I had found myself in the elhwith during my own awakening. I had fallen through a slip and witnessed what had happened within me, and more besides. Only now, when I woke from slumber, I was not in the elhwith. I was not in myself. I was in a vast underground lake. The vaulted sky-rock above pulsated with pale green light. The dark water around me glittered with glowing white fish. They buoyed me. They kept me afloat. They kissed me with their tiny mouths. I tasted the lake on my lips: it was salty. It stretched so far in every direction, the horizon glowed in a steady, perpetual ring.

How was I meant to escape this place? This subterranean vaultine? I did not know. I cannot say how long I floated. But in time, sleep took me again. When I next woke, months had passed. I was no longer on the mountain. I was no longer below it. I was on the shore of the Lost Lake. Its waves crashed around me. My gudwat was tattered, but there. Months had passed, aye. But inside me, it had been years. Not years forward, years back. And not years only: ages. I saw the Coming. I witnessed the Fall. I experienced the quickening of my birthright. And do you know what I learned?

The cabin trembled in the wind like a leaf on a tree. Despite himself, Breme had become captivated by Natty's story. He'd never heard it before. He knew his mistress. He could tell when she told true and when she told false. When she elaborated. Embellished. Or lied outright.

This story was truth.

Breme shook himself, coming back to his task. The girl remained seated, stoic as before. Unmoved, apparently, by Natty's tale. Natty stood facing the window, looking out on the storm that now raged. Mist from the lake crests smeared the window. Rainwater beat against the roof. The wind howled. Natty turned back to the girl, but before, she looked into Breme's eyes. *Watch,* he heard her say in his head. So he did.

"And do you know what I learned?" Natty asked the girl. The girl did not answer. Natty smiled. "No, of course you don't. That is why you are here. To learn why your pact is failing. To learn why your kohlas is splintering. Yes, you want to know why. You need to . . . ."

Breme, now watching the girl, gasped. For just a moment, the girl was gone. In her place was someone else. A witch, perhaps. The dark outline of an antiperson. Two glowing orbs where eyes should be. And Breme, even limited as he was with the sight, understood he was seeing past a glamour. In a blink, the antiperson was gone, and the girl was back. She remained stoic, yet a hint of surprise twisted her grimacing mouth. It was that word Natty had spoken: kohlas.

Breme had heard this word before. Natty had never explained it, but Breme had come to understand through the little she had said that it was a similar cumatu as the kolinga. Only the kohlas was for another region, outside the Ti-Fleek Lustrė. Beyond Ausrost's borders, Breme assumed, in some distant part of Carde-Meridea. He knew no more than that, but he had no doubt that word had an effect on the girl whose glamour had been pierced through by it, if only for a moment.

"I have seen you," Natty said. The girl did not reply. "I see you now."

In a flash, the girl was on her feet. And yes, she moved quickly. But there was a flash of light as she did, as though her glamour once again had weakened. She lifted her hands in front of her and began shaping her fingers into a spell, but Natty was ready. She threw a candle, shielding the flame against the wind as it flew. The flame quickened. The candle struck the girl in the chest, her robe feeding its fire. She was instantly garlanded in flames . . . but this did not penetrate past her glamour, Breme saw. Through the flames, he saw glimpses of her true self.

The girl opened her mouth to shout a spell, but Natty was ready. "Khal-ee—" the girl began, but Natty had thrown another candle. This one melted to liquid wax and covered the girl's mouth. It hardened there, a lock with no key. Natty threw back her head and laughed. She circled the girl. The girl's wary eyes followed Breme's mistress. Breme watched, fixed and fascinated.

"Who is this boy?" Natty asked. "Who is this boy who threatens your kohlas, hmm? That is what you wish to know, but I do not know. Your dark woodsmen do not know. What magics make him resist your intentions, I do not know. What makes him resist his kohlas, I do not know. But what I do know is this: your Dragon is a false god. Your Dragon is no god at all."

Wind filled the cabin. It pitched Breme from his seat. This was not Natty's wind. The girl screeched, but not through her mouth. From her throat. She screeched into the cabin. Into the whirlwind she had birthed. Natty laughed.

"Yes. Yes! Bring your storm, witch!" Natty cackled the laugh of a madwoman. She threw back her head and screamed laughter.

The girl lifted her hands now. One palm faced outward. With the other hand, she formed a circle with thumb and forefinger. Breme felt his mind itch. He felt his throat compress. From the girl, many emotions emanated. At the fore, anger. Close on its heels, fear. But not far behind this, he felt love and wonder. And he knew this was for the boy, whoever the boy might be. And he heard two words: scarecrow hunter. Then three: my scarecrow hunter. Then one: no.

His body crumpled into a knot and flew against the wall. The wind inside the cabin beat against him. It bruised his skin. But Natty still laughed.

"Do you think your wind frightens me?" she screamed. "I am sister to the wind. I am daughter to the sky and the earth. I am kindred to the beasts of the deep. I am brother to the animals in the fields. Cousin to the mountains. Friend to the sea. I am Edöné. And you think to bring wind against me? You are a stupid, wretched bitch, aren't you?"

The girl's mouth flew open, the wax shell splintered, and the flames encircling her glamour sputtered as light from within pierced its way through. Again, Breme saw her eyes. Only now, they smoldered. She screamed in a language Breme did not understand. The itch in his head grew fevered. But still, Natty laughed.

"Tell me his name!" she screamed, stepping closer to the burning girl. "Tell me the boy's name . . . ."

The girl reached her flat palm forward, as if to slap it against Natty's chest, but Natty caught her by the wrist and pulled her close. They stood nose to nose. Wind and flame and scalding light and furious sound spun around them in a cyclone, but Natty did not sway. She did not waver.

"Tell me the boy's name, or I will pluck it from your miserable head," she said. The witch—for there was nothing else this girl could be—screamed. She screamed a name, but Breme could not understand it.

Natty understood. "Eliot," she said. "Now, thank you, bitch. And I must give you a message: the mountain is angry. The world is angry. The earth, the wind, the fire, the salt . . . they are all angry over what you have done. And they are not kind like me."

Natty released the girl. Natty fanned her arms. The double doors of the cabin flew open. The storm outside blew in, smothering the storm inside. The girl's eyes grew wide. A thunderbolt ripped an open wound into the sky above the Barren and surged inside through the open doors. It wrapped a fist around the girl. Her hold on Breme relented. He gasped as the lightning snatched her away into the darkness beyond the cabin.

The storm outside continued, but inside, the cabin grew calm. Natty closed the doors and returned to her seat. "Eliot," she whispered to herself.

"Good for you, boy. Good for you. I send you strength and clarity . . . you will need both."

"Mistress?" Breme said. He came to her, kneeling beside her chair. She put a hand against his cheek and smiled.

"All is well," she said. "Or soon may be."

Breme shook his head. He believed his mistress. He always believed his mistress. She had saved him, after all. She had loved him well. But Breme could not understand all that had happened.

"What did you see?" Natty asked him.

"Her eyes shone," he said.

"Aye, they did . . . for a while, leastways." The woman's own eyes glittered. Breme put his hand on her arm. Natty turned to look at him. Again, she stroked his cheek. She leaned and kissed him gently on the lips. "You did well, Breme."

I did nothing, Breme thought. But he held his tongue. He did have a question about her story, however. "Was it your Edönic quickening that ruined your kolinga?"

Natty smiled. "Aye. It spoiled me for it."

He nodded, not truly understanding. Another question came to him. "You killed her?" he asked. "The witch?"

Surprise flooded Natty's face, but then it melted into amusement. "No," she said. "I am not allowed to kill her."

"But lightning—" Breme began.

"She is powerful. I could not kill her. I lack that authority. She would never expose her vulnerable underbelly to someone like me," Natty explained, but Breme could not understand.

"The boy?" he asked.

Natty's smile was enormous. "Yes," she said, "the boy . . . Eliot."

"She wants him," Breme said. "She loves and fears him."

"I know," Natty said. Then she sighed. "I will want my supper soon, Breme. Spanking witches is hungry work."

Author's Note

An important step in writing this anthology was to show the kolinga, a cumatu similar to the kohlas but from another culture and involving girls. There is a purpose for all of these cumatus. You will discover that purpose later in the series, unless you see it taking shape already.

One thing I love about the world of the Glint is that no one power is stronger than all the others. Natty is not necessarily stronger than the "girl." We cannot assume Natty is stronger based on this story alone. Had this confrontation happened outside Natty's cabin and in the girl's—how shall I put this?—jurisdiction instead, perhaps Natty would not have been victorious. But Natty is at least a counterbalance to the darkness inside the girl. To the intentions of those who initiated the kolinga and kohlas. Like the balance of the force or the wheel of Ka, good and evil herein are not black and white . . . the same as within you and me.

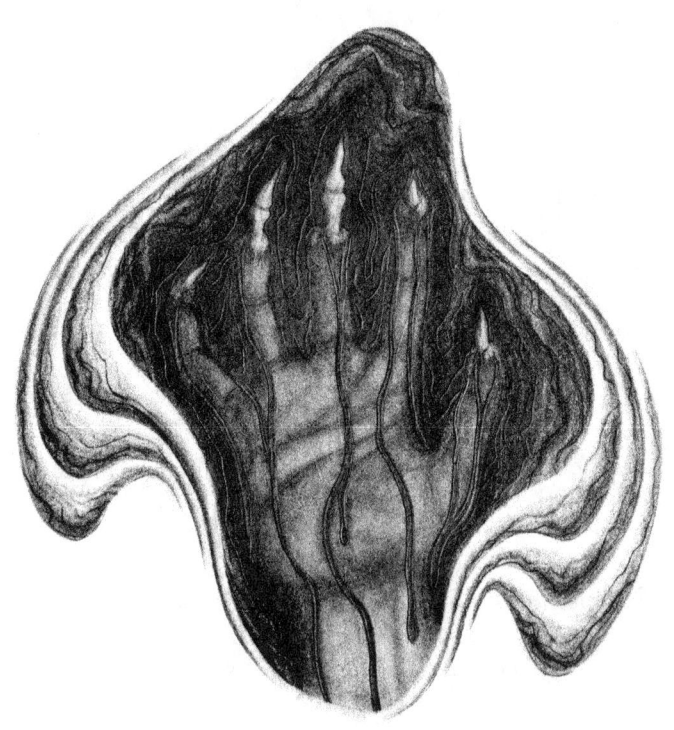

NOWAYS PLACE

Cicadas buzzed in the waist-high grass, a symphony on the duality of nature: chaos and order. The wind played the accompaniment, turning the brittle grass into an undulating stringed instrument as big as a village. Cal-En slapped at a biting insect on the tender flesh of his neck, almost without noticing. This place had mesmerized him since first he found it. It flooded him now with hope and promise and expectation. In the southern distance was the near endless prairie, the Border Lands beyond it. Valleen and the Carde border was a few months to the southwest, Traigen a little farther to the southeast. Due north, and perhaps only a three-month stretch if a traveler was unseasoned—less than two for someone like Cal who knew what he was doing—was the wealth of Ausrost: Lustrain.

"Aye," Cal mumbled, his excitement burning a red-hot core in his belly. "This would be the place then."

He removed the bristly blade of long grass he'd been chewing from his mouth—a favorite practice he'd had since childhood—and tossed it inside the dark mouth of the well. This well, nestled in the shadow of the Lusty Mountains and surrounded by grassland, was perfectly situated between three of the most important villages in Ausrost—indeed, in all of Mor-Thandak—Valleen, Traigen, and Lustrain. The well, abandoned a lifetime earlier, it seemed, is what had drawn Cal to this place.

He'd been sitting on the idea for months before he mentioned it to his wife, Juss. It first came to him when he was part of an expedition into the Lusty Mountains. His mind had marinated on it for the duration of that excursion, but he'd mentioned nothing of his idea to his comrades. He wouldn't want them to steal it. The idea was that good. The first time he mentioned it to another soul was weeks after he'd returned home, during an early afternoon visit to his favorite pub in Valleen. He was in between jobs just then but still had a few coins rattling around in his pockets: coins he could spend however he liked—he'd earned them with his own sweat, after all. He'd been nursing his fourth ale, working up the courage to return home to his ramshackle single-room lodging he kept with his wife and two small children. The lodging house was rat-infested and stank of filthy river water, and his family lived in a room barely larger than a stable stall. Every time his wife lit the stove, the tiny quarters became insufferably hot, even in mid-winter. And he couldn't remember the last time he and his wife had a go of love business. It was impossible to rut with your wife when there were always two small sets of eyes watching.

But all of that could change soon. It would change, Cal reasoned. But he had to think through every detail first. He had to be prepared for every eventuality. And he had to be ready in every conceivable way before broaching the subject with his wife. She would not be easy to convince. Thus, Cal first tossed out the idea to Rayford—the barkeep at the Wet Eel Inn and Tavern. Lodging at the Eel was far too expensive for the likes of Cal and his lot, but the swill Rayford kept in a barrel was more than drinkable and had only a nominal impact on Cal's wallet.

"Thren, aye . . . ." Rayford did not seem impressed.

"Aye, Thren," Cal said, his words blending in the middle. Eel swill did that to him. "There's a well there . . . . Lookit. Valleen is, what, a four months' hike."

"Four and a half at least," Rayford barked without looking up from the glass he polished. "Mayhap five."

"Four, I says," Cal barked back. "Traigen maybe four and a half the other side." Rayford scoffed; he did not agree with Cal's estimate. Someone from the end of the bar shouted, "Five, easy," but Cal barreled forward, undeterred. "Yer missin' the point, Ray. Lustrain is just north of the well—"

"Just north, he says." Rayford laughed. "Just a little jaunt in the foothills, says he. It's a three-month trek through rough mountain terrain, and that if the weather's nice." Again, he scoffed. "Just north, he says . . . . That swill is meltin' yer brain, Cal. No one goes to Lustrain that way."

Cal ignored the interruption. "I say true: it will be the Throm of Ausrost." Now others at the bar joined Rayford to laugh at Cal's optimism. "Fuck the lot of yehs," Cal said and took a deep, final swig from his glass. He tapped the glass with a finger, and Rayford refilled it. "Lookit, they's nothin' either side for months and months. Ever'body in Ausrost and Carde—and ever'where else, for that matter—gots to come right up to it 'fore hiking into the mountains to get to Lustrain. And ever'body got to get to Lustrain, aye?"

This was true. Lustrain was the seat of wealth in all of Mor-Thandak. At some point, every village, city, stronghold, or landholder would have business in Lustrain. Or with someone who had business in Lustrain. The Lusty Mountains were crisscrossed by two roads meant to get people in and out of the village. Cal's objective was straightforward: provide an outpost just south of a quicker route. No matter no road existed that way yet.

"I'll just put up a ways place, right there at the feet of those Lusty Mountains. A nice little holdover for weary travelers . . . and I'll stuff my pockets with teegs and lusts."

A good-humored cheer went up the length of the bar, more at Cal's expense than to celebrate his idea, but he didn't mind. Let them laugh now. They wouldn't laugh forever. Someone at the end of the bar—same as before, Cal guessed—shouted something about Cal buying a round for the bar patrons since he'd have fat pockets soon enough, but Cal was unperturbed. He only smiled and took another long swig.

"Let's say yeh have the right of it," Rayford said, wiping down a bit of spilled ale on the bar. "Seems to me like a great plan. But how is it you're the first to have it? Wouldn't someone have thought it up 'fore now? And if that well is there like yeh say it is, who's to say no one tried yer plan already? Tried and failed at it?" Ray glanced around the room at his compatriots, all of whom seemed to be encouraging the barkeep. He smiled. "Yeh never striked me as bein' the smartest trap, Cal. No 'ffence meant."

But he had meant to offend, Cal knew. They all thought he was a joke. A drunkard who couldn't keep a job. A slackard who looked for excuses to avoid his wife and kids. They thought him a deadbeat. He'd been called a trap and a milly his full adult life. But Cal-En would have the last laugh. Yes, he would. And when he was a rich man, he'd come back and buy the Wet Eel. Then they would see.

He was so caught up in his thoughts, and so committed to his most recent draw from his glass, that it took a few moments for Cal to realize the laughter had died down to an awkward rumble before petering out in a series of coughs and grunts. He looked at Rayford, but Rayford was studying a series of scratches on the bar. Then Cal felt a hand on his shoulder.

He turned to find himself a breath away from a man so old and decrepit, it seemed a miracle he still had the strength to breathe. Cal often saw him in the Wet Eel. Come to think of it, the old man must have lived in the tavern, for Cal had never seen his corner chair empty. Neither had he ever seen the man interact with anyone in the bar, or anyone in the bar interact with him—save for delivering the codger his drinks, that is. Yet here he was, his watery, bloodshot eyes so close to Cal's, he thought one slight slip and they might kiss. Cal did not want that. The man stank of piss.

"Someone did," the old man croaked. "Someone thought of it 'fore you, aye. And a good idea it were, aye." The man wobbled, his eyes skittering around the room as if he might find the rest of his thought scattered there.

"Who did what?" Cal asked, almost tipping off his stool in an effort to put distance between him and the drunk old codger. Perhaps this should be his last drink, Cal thought. One more could make finding his way home, climbing the three flights of stairs, and crawling into bed too much like work. Well, perhaps this drink, and then one more. But none after that.

"It were a proper village once," the old man said. Cal had forgotten the man had been speaking. The swill in his head was making it harder for him to focus on any single thread. With effort, he turned his attention back to the old man. What was this man's name? Cal wondered. Had he ever known it? "It were a village till it were burned to the ground."

"And why'd it burn? Poor plannin', sounds like to me." Cal nodded at his own logic, seeking affirmation from Rayford and the other patrons, but everyone else in the room appeared to have moved on. So Cal looked back at the old man. His watery eyes had never left Cal.

"Brogden burned it," the man said.

"Lookit," Cal interrupted, "Brogden don't burn—" but the old man went on.

"To kill the evil in it. But alls they managed was to trap it. To trap the evil in that well of yers . . . ."

Cal watched the man for some sign of jesting, but it didn't come. Cal laughed, shaking his head. "Yeh mean to tell me yon well once were surrounded by a village, that Brogden burned down the village to root out some evil, but instead, they trapped the evil inside that well?" Cal cackled when the old man nodded. He looked up and down the length of the bar, desperate to find someone to share his mirth. But no one else laughed. None of the others even smiled. They weren't looking at Cal or the old man. They were each one studying their drinks.

"Leave it be, boy," the old man said. "Fer yer own sake. Leave it be. Thren's well is haunted, and worser than that. It's tainted, dark. It's spoilt." He patted Cal's hand, turned, and shuffled out of the bar.

Cal shook his head. "What was that?" he asked, confused. Rayford refilled his drink without asking. "I mean, what's his story? Crazy old codger needs to lay off the ghost stories, I reckon." Again, Cal laughed, but the sober way the bar remained quiet made his laugh thin and unconvincing.

"In all the years I've run this tavern," Rayford said, "that old codger, as you called him, ain't never said more'n two words at a time." He held Cal's eyes for a long moment before continuing. "He come from Lustrain way. He grew up near Gro-Len. Mayhap you should listen to him. Mayhap he knows somethin' you don't."

But Cal hadn't listened, and here he was, at last, standing beside the well. It felt like the well had called him here. His wife and kids—along with her insufferable younger brother, Nathan—would be along in two short weeks, three at most. And by then, Cal would have the beginnings of what would become a fair-sized farm. They would live in tents at first, while Cal and his brother-in-law built the main house. Or something with a roof, at least. They could put up a house in a matter of days, but in time, Cal would build his family a mansion. Later would come a barn and a series of cabins. Eventually, he'd build an inn, complete with an alehouse and restaurant. In a few years, he may even have a few other permanent residents, pokes hired for protection and ranchers to work the land. Cooks and cleaning folken, too. Maybe he'd even set up a smithy. In the meantime, he would build a perfect ways place for travelers to and from Lustrain to lay over. And he would grow rich.

The following days moved slower than Cal thought possible, but somehow more than two weeks passed. The calm and quiet—something he'd longed for back in Valleen—was enough to make him itch all over: he missed his wife and kids. This surprised him, but they should arrive by week's end, if his estimate was correct. Until then, he would continue his efforts. He had erected a makeshift fence, enough to keep in the two goats who'd made the trip with him. Burp and Glut, he called them. Every couple of days, he'd move the little fence and let the goats go after a new patch of earth. They did a decent job with the grass, but it grew so thick and tall in some places, Cal had to break out his scythe. His hands were blistered tip to heel, but he supposed it was all part of the process. At least there was an endless supply of fresh, sweet water in the well. The old codger had been dead wrong on that account: the well water was far from spoiled. It was delicious.

Cal had accumulated a rather large pile of cut brush and grass to burn, but the days were so hot, he could not bear the thought of a fire. And the nights were for resting. And celebrating. But he guessed he might spare an hour or two later to burn down the pile. There was an endless supply of things to burn, or so it felt. But just now, he would manage a few more rows with his scythe. There would be tilling to do, and planting. Come autumn, they would have a nice garden. For now, his stores were enough. And his wife was coming on a wagon stocked with grits, flour, dried meat, and salt, more than enough to get them through the summer. Besides the heat and effort, Cal thought it best to wait for his brother-in-law before breaking ground for a garden. The boy would have to earn his keep, after all.

He uncorked a bottle and took a drink from a leather wine pouch. It wasn't great wine, but it served the function. He took another sip.

"Now's as good a time as any," he declared, recorking the skin. Cal wasn't afraid of work. No, sir . . . but he believed in efficiency. And he believed in well-placed energy. An afternoon such as the present one required a bit of gracious repose, and that alone would be worthy of setting aside his scythe blade. But as it happened, there was a nice cloud cover rolling in and hovering just at the edge of the mountains: just enough cool to make a fire, even a big one, manageable. Burp and Glut would continue working on the grass. He would light the bonfire and nurse his wine pouch.

It was the next afternoon when his wife arrived with her brother and the children. They found Cal covered in ash, head to foot, and nothing but charred earth for as far as they could see. Burp and Glut, gods rest them, were crispy in death. The tent and Cal's provisions had been consumed in the blaze. Cal alone had managed to avoid being turned to ash, or nearly. The well remained unscathed.

"Lookit," Cal said in response to his wife's scowl and his brother-in-law's imputable glare, "the grass needed gettin', so it's got. Aye? No sense wastin' the summer doin' a job it took a single evenin' to do with fire. I mean, I didn't intend on burnin' the tent, but I were about it all by myself. I mean, where were you? Had you two got here one day earlier . . . ." He threw his hands into the air in an exaggerated shrug. They would never see this his way, he knew. And he saw no sense in parlaying with two people who'd already made up their minds.

"Cal-En Ferret," his wife said, "where will we sleep?" Her voice was level. Reasonable, even. But Cal knew her tricks. He would not be pressed into an argument over this.

"Juss," his brother-in-law said, coming to stand beside his sister. "Mayhap we should go back. There were that village no more'n two days back."

"Three," Juss said.

"Three days then. It seems a bit crazy to stay out here in the middle of—"

"Just shut yer fuckin' gob, Nathan," Cal spat.

"Cal! Your children!" Juss's hand shot out to point at their kids, her eyes burning hotter than the fire had. Helen, aged eight years, and Brok, aged six, were both covered in soot. Brok's nose was snotty, and Helen's face tear-streaked. Cal shook his head and hurried to them, scooping them up into his arms.

"Lookit," Cal said, "yer pooey is makin' somethin' nice. And tonight, we get to sleep underneath the stars. Would yeh like that, Helen? How 'bout you, Brok?" The children nodded their excitement. Cal looked back at Juss. "It's okay, sweet Juss."

"Sweet Juss," his wife spat. "Nothin' sweet out here. This land's forsaken."

For a few moments, Cal, Juss, and Nathan surveyed the land surrounding them. None spoke. Cal saw both carts Juss and Nathan had brought: one, stacked with lumber and tools to build the house, pulled by a mule, and the other, bearing casks and bags of supplies, by an old mare. Cal knew this little fare represented all the wealth they presently owned— besides the well, of course. The last of their money was spent procuring the mule. The carts and supplies had been another matter. Nathan had taken out a loan from the regentry in Valleen. For a while, he'd been infatuated with the Head Regent's grandson, or the grandson had been infatuated with him—Cal couldn't remember which—and somehow that entitled Nathan to a loan. The same loan the regentry had refused Cal. Had in fact laughed Cal out of the building over. But no matter. If all he'd had to do was rut with the rich man's grandson, Cal guessed he might have given the boy a go. But thanks to Nathan, there'd been no need. And repaying that loan was a matter for Nathan to sort, not Cal.

"It do look like we might grow a pretty garden here about," Nathan said.

"See?" Cal nearly shouted, feeling a sudden camaraderie with his brother-in-law. "That's it, Nathan. That's what I been sayin'. Alls we need is to get good and started."

"Cal-En," Juss said, taking her husband's hand. "I want to believe in this place. I want to believe in you. We came this far, and I want to give it a go. But I need to know it'll not all end in tears."

"Or flame," Nathan added.

Cal smiled. "Lover, I give you my word. This time next year, you'll be sittin' pretty on your front porch, sippin' honey water and watchin' all the folken puttin' coin in our pockets, drawin' water from that there well. You'll see."

Juss looked at her husband. He wanted her to see what he saw, to feel what he felt. The possibility. The promise. It was like a fever in his bones . . . but the best kind of fever. This plot of land—forsaken by all others for the sake of pitiful superstition—would make them wealthy. He wanted her to feel that promise, to catch the fever in her own bones. He would need her. They would need each other. Nathan, too. There was lots of work yet to be done, but so much to look forward to. So, so much. Juss's expression softened.

"That's my girl," Cal said and, moving Brok to the same arm as Helen, used his free arm to gather Juss in close. Helen squealed, and Brok giggled.

"Okay," Juss said, a smile creasing her features at last. Cal kissed her cheek, then her lips.

"Where's the goats?" Nathan asked.

"Let's stretch out a tarpaulin," Cal said, ignoring his brother-in-law. "We can break ground on the house tomorrow. But tonight it looks like rain."

The house was a simple affair, not unlike their room back in Valleen, only twice the size. One corner had a wood-burning stove. Beside this was a table and benches for family meals. It wobbled, but they'd built it from scratch. There was a young forest not more than a half-hour walk, so there was a bounty of wood to be had. But neither Cal nor Nathan had the skills or tools for proper planing. Still, the table was a table, and the benches were sturdy. On the other side of the room was a small bed. In truth, the bed was a straw mattress laid on the hard-packed earth of the floor. A curtain cordoned this side of the room off from the other side. The kids had pallets in the room's center, and Nathan slept in a hammock stretched out beneath the porch roof. It wasn't glamorous, but it kept the rain off. And it had taken only a month to build.

Nathan had proved himself to be a workhorse. He'd hitched the mule to a plow and was preparing ground for their garden. Juss had been busy mending Cal's shirts and pants, and keeping a keen eye on the kids. She obsessed over them, or so Cal always thought. He had spent the days since the house was built poring over his notes. He had endless ideas. After the main house was built—not the dreary little cabin they all shared now, but a proper mansion!—he would focus on the barn. Visitors would likely have tents in the early days, but Cal could always rent out stalls in the barn. And he needed a place for his own mule and horse. Eventually, he would build cabins for visitors to rent—simple affairs like the house he currently called home, at the beginning, at least. But in time, he wanted his inn and tavern to draw people from all across Ausrost because of its splendor. After that—and this was key, he imagined—he wanted to build a road through the mountains to Lustrain. Nothing elaborate, but better than the handful of deer tracks that currently provided the way. Just enough to make the journey faster and safer . . . and his ways place would be the best starting point.

He wouldn't do the work himself, of course. He would sell the idea to others who would. But like any good idea, it had to be studied. Inspected. Twisted inside and out to find the weak spots. Planning such a venture required quite a bit of work and concentration. So much, in fact, Cal needed a nap every afternoon to recover. He was just slipping into one of these when Juss came bounding inside the house.

"Cal," she demanded as she came stomping in the door. Already Cal hated her tone. "Nathan needs you, 'member? You promised to help with the stones."

"Woman, can't yeh see I'm workin'?"

Juss put her fists on her hips in that way Cal hated, and her lip twisted like it always did when she was about to launch into a tirade.

"Cal-En Ferret, yer about as useful as Glut and Burp just now." Then she must have had an idea because she scoffed, shaking her head. "Except at least they don't eat no more. Yeh might think about earnin' yer keep."

"Earnin' my— Lookit," Cal began, but Juss was gone. She hadn't given him the chance to point out this entire venture was his idea. That their imminent fortune would be his doing, mostly because coming was his idea. In one sense, he'd done all the work that should be required of him: perhaps Juss and Nathan should carry the enterprise for a change. He was spitting mad, and he hated getting so angry. He didn't want to let her get to him. She didn't understand him. She likely never would. He'd never be able to sleep after her outburst, he knew. He'd promised to leave the wine alone, at least during the day. Just then a nip seemed the only way he might salvage his nap, though. It took more than a nip, but the wine helped, and soon enough Cal was asleep. But Juss's words must have crept into Cal's head, somehow. For he dreamed about Burp and Glut.

The goats were grazing, only the grassland was ash. Still, they munched and munched, content the way only fat goats can be. They bleated back and forth, and Cal smiled. It was almost as if they talked to each other. He heard their chewing and breathing and realized there was no wind. No sound at all other than the goats.

"Eat them all," Burp said.

Cal shook his head. He'd thought he heard the goat speak.

"Not all of them," Glut said. "Not yet."

"Who told you to talk?" Cal asked. Now that was a question for the ages. It was both the dumbest thing he could have asked but also the only thing to ask.

Burp and Glut looked at Cal. Were they smiling? Could goats smile?

"Who told you to burn?" Glut asked.

Cal's heart nearly jumped up his throat and out of his mouth when Juss came in through the door, screaming.

"What did you do?" she yelled.

"What do yeh mean, Juss? Calm down. Yeh pert near scared the life out of me." And this was true: Cal felt his entire body vibrate with fear.

He'd been dreaming about his idiot goats talking, and now here was his wife, screaming to raze their little house. Cal took a deep breath.

"What did you do," Juss asked again, this time moderately calmer.

"What are yeh on about?" Cal asked, confused.

"The well." Juss said this as if it explained everything. It explained nothing.

"Woman, I cain't read yer mind." Cal stood, uncorked the wineskin, thankful there had been more wine on his wife's cart—his cache had been consumed by fire—and took a drag. "Slow down and start over. What about the well?"

Her fists were on her hips again, and her lip turned up in a sneer. Gods, he hated that sneer. Then she turned and stalked away, so Cal followed. They came to the well. The bucket lay on the ground, turned on its side. Bones spilled out. Bones blackened from fire and soot.

"What the . . . ," Cal began, but swallowed the words. "The goats?"

"Aye, the goats, Cal. In the well. In our drinkin' water."

Cal looked at his wife. His bewilderment felt eternal. He looked around. Nathan was busy working on the far side of the camp, his shirt wrapped around his head and his chest and back smeared with sweat and mud. Cal looked for the kids. He didn't see them.

"Where are the kids?" he asked.

"Yeh mind tellin' me how those goat bones ended up in our drinkin' water?" Juss snapped.

"Juss, where's Helen and Brok?" Cal asked again. Nathan had buried the goat bones, and deep. Cal had watched him do it. There was only one explanation to this mystery: the kids must have played a game, dug up the bones, and dropped them in the well.

"Are we 'sposed to drink spoilt well water now?" Juss asked.

"Spoilt?" Cal said, remembering the old man's words back in Valleen. "The well's not spoilt, Juss. Gods confess it, calm down. Yer fit to splittin'. Where are the kids?"

"They's playin' in the woods," Juss said, dismissing his question. "But I need to know why yeh put the bones in the well."

Cal spat. "Why the fuck would I put bones in our well? Think about it, Juss. Think about it fer one second. That don't make no sense, do it? Na, it don't."

Juss's fists were on her hips again, her foot tapping in the dirt to add further annoyance. "Then how'd they git there?"

"Helen and Brok," Cal said. "Obviously."

He picked up the bucket, dumping out the bones, then used his shirt tail to wipe out the bucket. "It's not too bad," he said. "Mayhap they's not in the water, only in the bucket?" He hadn't meant to make that last a question. He'd meant to state it as fact, to calm the woman down. His wife, like other females, was prone to fits of extremity. It took a firm hand to reel it in once one of Juss's fits got wind in its sails. But he was baffled: how could the kids dig up the bones with no one noticing, especially with his wife's dedicated eye?

He looked again at Nathan, suspicion blossoming behind his eyes. Juss and Nathan came from good stock. It was what first attracted Cal to Juss. She was curvy in just the right places, with a pretty face and big breasts. Instead of breasts, Nathan had muscles. But otherwise, he was as pretty as any girl. Cal had hated him for this. And now, he wondered if, like his sister, Nathan might just be capable of extreme fits. Would he sabotage their well? Would he not want their venture to succeed? No, that didn't settle. It was Nathan, after all, who had a sizable loan to pay back in Valleen. Then who? He hadn't done it, despite what his spiteful wife might believe. And she seemed unlikely to have done it.

No, it had to be Helen and Brok. There was no other explanation.

Cal lowered the rope into the well and drew up a bucket full of water. He sniffed this, his wife scowling at him all the while. Then he dipped his cupped palm in the water and sipped. It was sweet as ever, cool and untainted.

"It's fine," he said. "See for yerself." He extended the bucket to Juss. She clucked her tongue and stormed away.

Nathan was up early; he was always up early. That boy didn't realize they had all summer to get the work done, Cal guessed. Why anyone would be up with the sun made no sense to Cal, especially since no one was beating down their door for a cool sip of water from the well, or for a place to stay overnight, either.

Which was a funny truth: Cal had seen no one on their way to or from Lustrain all summer. He supposed this made sense: until now, there had been no reason to come this way. Most folken couldn't know about the well. Otherwise, Cal would have had a harder time laying claim to it. There must be countless ways to enter the mountains, he knew.

Part of their task would be to educate travelers to and from Lustrain about their holding, inviting them to the farm. How else would they make any money? But one thing at a time, and just then Cal had to deal with Nathan.

"What now?" Cal asked, stepping onto the porch and squinting at the already too bright morning sun.

"It's the horse," Nathan said.

"What about her?"

Nathan waved his hand for Cal to follow him. Cal did, to the far side of the patch of ground the boy had been clearing, over a small rise, and down into a culvert. Here was the old mare—dead, of course.

"Well, I'll be bloody damned," Cal said.

"What do yeh think?" Nathan asked.

"What do yeh mean, what do I think? I think she's dead," Cal retorted, pissed off that he couldn't make it through one single day without some horse shit calamity befalling them.

"Well, yeah," Nathan said, "but how? I don't see no snake bites. No foam around her mouth. No sign of a struggle. It don't make no sense."

"Yeah, it do," Cal said, sitting his rump on the dusty rise of the land. "It makes perfect sense. I cain't win for some reason. The gods won't let me."

"You think the gods did this?" Nathan asked. "And you think it's all about you . . . but of course yeh do."

"What's that supposed to mean?" Cal asked, but Nathan wasn't listening.

Cal looked back over his shoulder toward the house and the well. After the fire had burned the brush, the grass had sprouted back almost overnight. With daily afternoon storms, it had grown lush and green. But the rains had slowed, and the days grew suffocatingly hot. Already the green had started fading from the grass, being replaced by brittle brown. Of course it was.

"Would you look at that," Nathan said, and Cal did.

"What is it?" Cal asked. Nathan tried to lift the horse's head to turn its neck, but it must have been too heavy. "What is it, Nathan?"

"Well," Nathan began, but got distracted. He was pressing along the horse's neck as if feeling its contents. Cal remembered a game he'd played as a child. They'd called it Guess and Gander, though he'd never understood precisely what that was supposed to mean. But the game was simple: he and his friends would take turns hiding a secret thing in a sack.

Then the other kids would use their hands to feel what was in it, guessing based only on the shape and feel of the thing. A silly game, come to think of it. And no less silly being played with a horse's throat.

"Well, what, Nathan?"

"It feels like . . ."

So it was Guess and Gander, after all. Cal snorted.

". . . a bone."

"A what?" Cal asked, certain he'd misunderstood. "There cain't be no bone in the horse's throat. Horses don't eat bones, Nathan."

"Only one way to find out, I reckon," Nathan said.

He took out his knife and used the blade to pry open the horse's mouth, then he reached inside.

"Gods dammit, Nathan," Cal said, "please tell me yeh aren't 'bout to stick yer hand down that horse's—" but Cal could only gag out the rest of his statement.

Nathan pulled his hand back out of the horse's mouth, a bone gripped in his fist. Both his hand and the bone were coated with frothy horse spittle, but the bone was charred black.

"Yeh've got to be fuckin' kiddin' me," Cal spat. "There ain't no gods dammed way."

Nathan held the bone up for Cal to see. No doubt about it: the bone had once belonged to either Burp or Glut.

"Well, those damned things won't stay buried," Cal said. "Why'd yeh reckon that is?" Nathan looked at Cal but didn't answer. "Oh, fer fuck's sake," Cal said and stormed back toward home.

Summer spread herself thick like a wool blanket over their camp, the rain truly behind them. There hadn't been a cloud in the sky for weeks, and the ground was dusty as graveyard secrets. Like charred bones, Cal thought with a grimace. The heat was unbearable most days. They opened all the windows in their little house to allow air through, but the wind seemed only to spite them. Most days Cal spent the hottest hours sprawled out beneath the canopy of shady limbs in the same forest they'd collected wood to build their table. And every day, Juss gave him hell for going. No one could be expected to work in this heat, Cal reasoned. Never mind Nathan kept at it with the garden plot. He was obviously a little crazy. But that suited Cal just fine. No need for Cal to pitch in when Nathan was more than capable on his own, and they only had the one plow besides. Anything else would just be idle work, and Cal didn't believe in idle work.

He was dozing one afternoon when footfalls woke him. He sat up on his elbows to peer into the dim light of the forest. Sunlight burnished the grassland into a bright blur, but Cal made out a man's shape just inside the tree line.

"Nathan?" Cal said, rubbing his eyes. "That you?"

"Aye," Nathan said, stepping deeper into the shadows. Closer, so Cal could better see him. "Cal, we need to talk."

"No, we don't," Cal said, plopping back onto the ground.

"Cal, we do. It's Juss . . . ."

Nathan didn't say any more for several moments, long enough for Cal to wonder if he had left. Or if Cal had dozed off. He stirred himself up to his elbows again to see Nathan still there. His shirt was wet at the neck and beneath his arms, and a red bandana wrapped around his throat. Again, Cal noticed the boy's pretty features. It made Cal want to punch his pretty face. Cal had a good ten years on Nathan, but Cal looked—and felt—much older than thirty-two years. Nathan's big girl eyes, on the other hand, made him look younger than he was. The fact that Nathan was strong as a bull ox and stubborn as a mule when it came to work only made Cal hate him more. The way his lips always seemed to sulk reminded him so much of his wife, he doubted if he could tell them apart by kiss alone if he was blindfolded.

The idea made him sick. Nathan had no business here, he thought. Nathan had no business being pretty like his sister, putting twisted ideas in Cal's head.

"Get on with it," Cal demanded.

"She don't like it here," Nathan said. "Juss, well . . ."

"Well?"

"She don't seem to take to it, is all," Nathan stammered. "I hear her cryin' a lot."

Cal rolled his eyes. "She's a woman, or had you forgot that?"

Now it seemed it was Nathan's turn to roll his eyes. He sat. "Cal, we need you."

Of all the petulant, dull-witted, nonsensical arguments Nathan could make, the least likely of all would be this. Or should be, Cal thought. "No, Nathan," Cal said, his voice honey laced, "you *need* to stop complainin'. You *need* to finish your tasks. But you *want* me to do everythin' for you."

Nathan shook his head. "I'm not talkin' about the work, Cal."

"Then what?"

Nathan was on his feet again, pacing in the shade of the trees. Shade that did a piss poor job of cooling the day. Then he turned to look at Cal. Cal was surprised the boy didn't put his fists on his hips and cock his lip up to one side.

"When was the last time you kissed Juss, huh?" The way Nathan stared at Cal, Cal knew he expected an answer. This was no rhetorical line of questioning. Cal grunted and lay back on the ground. How should he know when he'd last kissed Juss? "Look at me," Nathan said. When Cal didn't, Nathan came to stand over Cal. "How long, aye? How long since you kissed her?"

Cal didn't know, but for one infuriating moment, all he could think about was kissing her fucking brother. He rolled to his side, shielding his eyes from the tetchy boy.

"How long since you held her?" Nathan asked.

"Nathan, please . . . I can only nap for so long before I gotta get up. I got work to do." Cal expected Nathan's rebuttal at this mention of work, but Nathan stayed his course.

"Cal, your wife needs to feel you next to her. We came here because we believe in your idea, we believe in the well. But you spend most of your time hiding away from us. From her. From your kids."

"Lookit," Cal said, rolling to his back. Nathan knelt beside him. "It's been a tough few weeks, I'll grant yeh that. But the weather'll break soon. Then you'll see. Things'll look up."

"Cal," Nathan said, putting his palm on Cal's chest, "I ain't talkin' 'bout the weather. I'm talkin' 'bout you bein' a husband to my sister."

The wind gusted, and on it rode the sound of a scream. A woman's scream. Nathan was gone in a blink. Cal sat up, confused. Another scream came from the direction of camp.

"Gods confess it," Cal fussed, "what in bloody fucks is wrong now?"

He stumbled to his feet, stretched out his back—this inspired a deep yawn—and walked out into the blazing sunshine. When the third scream came, he stopped dead in his tracks. When the fourth came—and it wasn't his wife's voice, but her brother's—he ran.

What he found back at camp made no sense. Juss was straddling the lip of the well, her dress hoisted up to her breasts. Nathan gripped her around her stomach, trying with all his might to pull her away. On the far side of the well stood Helen, a blend of fear and curiosity on her face.

Juss was volatile. Cal got close enough to see scratches around her throat and along her jaw. All the way up her left cheek to her eye. Nathan's nose was bleeding, and his lip—his pretty lip, Cal could not help but think—was busted. *Not so pretty right now*, Cal mused. But why the commotion? He stepped closer and tried to take Juss's hand, but she swiped at him, hers more of a talon than a hand. Cal stepped back.

"What in bloody fucks—" Cal began, but then he saw a peculiar thing inside the well. Careful to stay clear of Juss's reach, he stepped closer.

The well was fashioned from chunks of rough-cut stone, with no care to the sharp edges they possessed. Cal could clearly see those edges jutting outward from the inner wall, some sort of gray matter smeared along them. The matter was accompanied by something that looked suspiciously like blood.

"What in bloody fucks is that?" he asked, suddenly very afraid of the answer.

"Juss, Juss, shhh . . . ," Nathan whispered in his sister's ear. "It's all right. It'll be all right," he said, but Cal noted a very obvious lack of conviction in the boy's tone. Regardless, Juss was not consoled. She continued to thrash against her brother, pleading and screaming inarticulate jumbles of panic-stricken words.

Cal looked around. He looked at Helen. He looked back inside the well.

"Where's Brok?" he asked. Juss continued screaming. Nathan lifted his eyes to Cal, and Cal understood. His knees went delicate, and his legs folded beneath him. "Where's Brok?" he asked again, not wanting to believe what his mind told him.

Helen walked to him, a blade of grass caught in her wild thicket of hair. She had a half smile on her face, and looked particularly cute. She put her small hands on both sides of his face and leaned in to whisper.

"He went explorin' the well, pooey," she said. She was so close, Cal smelled her breath. It stank like clabbered milk. "He said it were yer idea."

"What?" Cal asked, his vision blurring in and out of focus. "My idea?"

Helen smiled a pretty smile. "The gray man helped him."

The well was good and spoiled, after all. Or would be if they left Brok's body in it to rot. Juss had taken to bed. She hadn't spoken a word for the rest of the day, and well into the next. But she had blessedly stopped screaming, at least. Come morning, it was Cal and Nathan's task to clear the well. A grim and gruesome task it was. And complicated.

They tied a rope around the mule's yoke, the other end around Nathan's chest.

"I'm not so sure 'bout this," Nathan said. "Cal, you gotta keep that mule steady."

Cal didn't mean to reply. Of course he had to keep the mule steady: that was his role in this pitiful affair. But he did reply, though it had little to do with the mule. "Good thing you don't have breasts," he said.

"What?"

Cal shooed away Nathan's question, and Nathan started climbing down the well's throat. Cal *obediently* steadied the mule, backing her up one step at a time to give Nathan enough slack to find his way down with, but not enough to plunge to his death. Just when Cal began to seriously worry their rope would not be long enough, Nathan called out.

"Aye, I've reached bottom."

Cal soothed the mule by rubbing its flank, then cautiously stepped to peer into the dark. The light from Nathan's lantern glowed like a single malevolent eye. "What do yeh see?" Cal called. Nathan didn't answer, but the evil eye jiggled around. "Nathan, what do yeh see? Did yeh find—"

Brok, he'd almost said.

"It's dry," Nathan said, alarm and doubt shading his words. "Dry as a bone."

"What do yeh mean, dry?" Cal asked. The well was obviously not dry; they drew water from it daily.

"There's somethin' . . . ," Nathan called back, but the rest was incomprehensible.

"Somethin' what?"

"It's got the . . . but I can't find the end . . . ," Nathan yelled.

"The end of what? What are yeh sayin'?" Cal waited, but Nathan remained quiet. "Boy! Nathan?"

"It's the . . ." The evil eye jerked and jiggled. ". . . and goats."

"Goats?"

If Nathan responded, Cal didn't hear. He was focused on another noise, one that rattled in the grass. Cal stumbled backward in panicked fear, and as he did, he stepped on the prongs of a rake leaning beside the well. The handle sprang forward and struck the mule at precisely the same moment as the rattler struck the mule's belly. It must have been coiled

44

beneath a rock or in a burrow. How they had missed it, Cal could not say. But if he'd had to choose, he would have chosen the mule over himself to find the snake. The mule cried as it was attacked by both rake and snake—just like a female, Cal thought—and bounded forward.

The snake turned its attentions on Cal, who was scurrying to get away from it. It struck, just missing Cal's ankle. The rope sizzled as it was pulled across the stone lip of the well at a mule's gallop. The snake struck again, this time catching Cal's boot. He felt two razor points slide into the arch of his foot, and his scream came out jagged and raw.

The rope snapped. The mule trundled off into the distance before collapsing in a heap. The snake, desperate to retrieve its teeth from the leather of Cal's boot sole, thrashed. Cal had to get the boot off. He hoped the snake had spent its venom—or enough of it, at least—in the mule's belly, but he could not manage hope on that account. Not while the vicious thing still remained attached to him. With his other boot, Cal kicked at the heel of the snake trap. He felt liquid fire seeping into his foot and up his ankle. He pushed harder and felt the boot slip, but just a little. His foot was already beginning to swell. He had to get the boot off while he still could. He was bleeding, and this helped. With one final grunt, the boot slid free. His sockless, blood-slick foot looked mangled, the swelling already taking its shape.

But what to do with the angry snake? Throw it down the well? He had to. The scythe was in the house or on the wagon. He didn't remember which. He had no blade, and he didn't trust himself to kill the snake with only a rake. But he could use the rake handle to lift the boot off the ground, and with a little luck on his side, he could toss the boot—snake and all—right down the well. Except . . .

"Cal, help me," Nathan said.

Cal turned to look at the well. From its dirty mouth, an arm distended. It was bleeding, the skin ripped to ribbons: Nathan. Cal had forgotten Nathan was in the well. Another arm appeared, followed by a head. Nathan was no longer pretty, Cal saw. He smiled despite the burning liquid fire—it had reached his knee now—and wondered over his own sanity.

Nathan must have been scraped along the rough edge of the well when the mule took out. How he'd managed to catch himself when the rope broke seemed near a miracle, but Cal couldn't think on that just then. The rattler, in a remarkable feat of persistence, had freed itself from the boot. Apparently having had its fill of Cal, his boot, and the whole fuss, the snake slithered away in the brittle grass.

"Cal, get off yer fuckin' useless ass and help me!" Nathan screamed. His face was grotesque with blood and agony. It looked like his left ear had been ripped clean off, and most of that side of his face. He still had one pretty eye, though. It was wild and fevered, the hostility in it almost enough Cal could smell it.

Cal hobbled to the well. "I were bit by a rattler," he said, grabbing hold of Nathan's wrist. "It's bad, Nat. Real bad." Cal had never called Nathan Nat before. That was what Juss had called him when they were kids. It was so funny what a brain might conjure up during dire circumstances, Cal realized. But he couldn't take back the nickname now, and he doubted Nathan had heard, anyway. The boy was near senseless. And he was offering little help to Cal to lift his bulky body out of the well.

"Cal, please," Nathan cried, and now Cal saw the boy was crying. Pretty like a girl, cried like a girl. Of course he did. Annoyed, Cal grabbed both Nathan's wrists.

"Kick with yer feet," Cal said.

"My legs—" Nathan began, but screamed before he could finish.

Cal released Nathan's wrists. It was reflexive. He hadn't meant to, but what else could he do? The boy had screamed—he must have caught a wound on the rough stone of the well, Cal thought . . . but only after— and sent panic through Cal's spine like fire. Or like snake venom. Nathan disappeared down the throat of the well, his scream following after him. That alone would have been enough to turn Cal's blood cold, but the scream wasn't just a scream.

"Eat them all," Nathan screamed, all the way down. All the way until the darkness swallowed him whole.

Cal didn't move. He stared at the well, not believing. Not truly understanding. This couldn't be happening. There was too much, too many complications. Too many factors to weigh, too many desperate choices to be made. He had to get the poison out of his foot or he would lose the leg, maybe even his life. And that wouldn't do. Juss and Helen needed him. He couldn't leave them all alone out here, especially since the well was spoiled. Could Nathan have survived the fall? Cal didn't see how. At least paying back the loan was no longer an issue: it had been Nathan's loan, not Cal's. His grandmother used to always say, "Even a maggot can grow wings." That seemed more appropriate now than ever: Cal knew how to see the brighter side of things. Always had. It was his gift.

He pulled himself up using the well. The well that had called him out here, a well that might certainly be haunted now, Cal thought. Tentatively, he stood. He knew better than to put any of his weight on his bitten foot. He managed to grab the rake handle and used it as a makeshift crutch, meaning to work his way to the house and wake Juss—

That's when he smelled the smoke. The house, simple as it was, blazed. From inside it, Juss began screaming.

"Juss?" Cal called. "Baby, are you okay?" It was a ridiculous question, sure. But Cal didn't know the proper protocol for asking after your wife when she's caught in a burning building. But it didn't matter, he saw. For here she came, bursting her way through the front door, her head blossoming with fire like a fresh lit match. She ran straight for him. "Juss?" he cried, feeling that panic in his spine twist. "Honey, where are you goin'? What are you doin'?"

But he knew: she was running right at him, her dress floating around her, a halo of flames. Here ran his beautiful, curvy wife, and he saw one of her breasts had gotten free of her burning dress. It bounced like a sack full of water as she ran, and he honestly thought it might burst.

"Eat them all!" Juss screamed just before she ran straightaway into Cal, both of them falling to the dusty ground in a thump.

Cal felt heat inside his leg and groin and, now, burning on his hands as he tried to shove his wife off of him. Her eyes were crazed, and she smelled like bacon. Cal managed to kick at her, only at the last second remembering the snake bite. He kicked her square in the belly, and his swollen foot popped like an overripe watermelon. He screamed. His wife fell dead beside the well.

Cal continued screaming. His foot was a riot of pain. His whole body was. He had to . . . well, he didn't know what he had to do. Get help? There was no one else here.

Except the gray man, Cal thought.

Cal held his breath. A new villainous thought had occurred to him. "The gray man helped him," Helen had said. But where was Helen?

"Baby girl?" Cal called. "Helen, dear?"

The wind stirred the grass into whispers, and Cal felt a coolness spread over his hot face. He looked over his shoulder: a storm cloud approached. They would have rain. Lots of it, if the sky told the story well. Rain just then could be a blessing or a curse, and Cal did not know which. And he still did not know where his daughter was.

"Helen, honey?" he called.

More whispers rode the wind, and the air grew chilly. Not just cool. Then the whispers began to separate. Cal turned to look again at the well,

47

his smoldering wife lying beside it. The whispers were not the song of the wind and grass: they came from inside the well.

"Not all of them," Helen said, "not yet, leastways. Right, pooey?"

Cal turned. Here was Helen, right behind him. His beautiful daughter, except her pretty smile was smeared with ash. Her hands, too. A crazy thought crept into Cal's mind. Had Helen started the fire that burned the house? That couldn't be, could it? She held the scythe. It was far too big for her, but she tried bringing it to Cal. Or so he thought. But rather than handing it to him, she went past him and handed the instrument to her mother.

Cal screamed, but the scream had no sound. He had no mooring. His dead wife was standing, the scythe gripped between her hands.

"Good girl," Juss croaked. "Now kiss yer daddy."

Helen ran to Cal, her arms stretched for him to pick her up. He batted her away. The girl whimpered and then started crying. Cal looked at his crazed wife. Had she died? He wondered if the snake bite had toyed with his head.

"Juss," he started but got no further than her name.

"Shut yer fuckin' gob, Cal-En Ferret," Juss said. "It wants to eat us all, 'member?"

"Not all of us," Helen said through her tears.

"Not yet, sweetie," Juss said, "but soon enough."

She swung the scythe. Cal watched it fall in a wide arc, felt the wind of it slice right in front of him. For a truth, he had no idea how it hadn't sliced open his belly and spilled his guts on the dusty ground.

Except it had. He meant to look down but instead inverted somehow. He was floating. Beneath him was the viscera that had poured from his belly. His body fell onto its side, his face a rictus of pain and surprise. And above all this, he floated . . . disembodied.

What was happening? He must be dreaming.

"Here, darlin'," Juss said.

Helen skipped over to her mother, hugging her around the waist. Cal no longer smelled Juss, but he wondered how the girl could stand to clutch her mother's waist since fire still smoldered in the folds of her once pretty dress. But then again, anything is possible in dreams.

Then Juss used the scythe blade to cleanly remove Helen's head. Cal watched in horror as it fell to the ground and rolled against the stonework of the well. His daughter's glassy eyes stared up at him, unseeing.

"Now it can eat us all," Juss said. She stepped over to the mouth of the well and tipped herself down its dark throat.

For several spectral moments, Cal floated. Why wasn't he waking up?

"Because you aren't dreaming," the whispers said.

Then he saw a gray arm reach out from the well. It came and came, just an arm but impossibly long. Impossibly wrong. The hand at the end was gruesome: the fingertips had been sliced away, the bones protruding from them sharpened into points. The fingers dripped blood and gray goo. The hand grabbed Helen's hair and lifted the child's head, dropping it into the well. After, it found the girl's body and did the same.

From the far side of the well, another gray form skulked out from the darkness. Then another. These looked like folken, or a near approximation of folken. They were naked and slicked with a dark oily substance. Three more climbed out, and Cal had an idea the well was full of them. They took up Cal's fallen body, hoisting it on their rotten shoulders like a grain sack, their bone-pointed fingertips piercing his skin. He saw his ruptured foot, his charred hands, and his confused, pained face. The creatures dropped his body into the well, and he felt himself sucked into its vacuous cavity.

As he fell headlong into darkness, he was certain he heard one last whisper: "We always eat them all."

The wind stirred the sun-scorched grass just as the first drops of rain fell. Then the sky opened, and a flood came. A cleansing flood to reshape the face of the grassland, flooding it with life and filling the well with water so fresh and sweet.

It tasted of salvation.

Author's Note

I am fascinated by cause and effect. In one genuine sense, this series hinges on the concept of what is left behind when someone experiences life-altering trauma. We follow Eliot in part to see how he overcomes his dire challenges in *The Scarecrow Hunters* and *A Greedy Shadow*, but also how those challenges leave a permanent residue on his life and those he loves. Similar residual consequences may be true of places and objects. In *The Singing Bones*, we learn of the village of Thren and what became of it. Here, we look many years down the road, after the grasslands have reclaimed that lost village, re-assimilating it into the natural landscape . . . all save one market well.

This was a fun story to write because it is, essentially, a ghost story. And, oh, how I love ghost stories. They are perhaps the quintessential tales told to examine that residue left behind I mentioned earlier. And so I took great delight in telling this story, and particularly in letting it unfold as words formed on the page rather than having an ending in sight before I began. I also admit I enjoyed writing a character who is thoroughly detestable and yet wholly unaware of this. After all, our own truths can be the most difficult to sort.

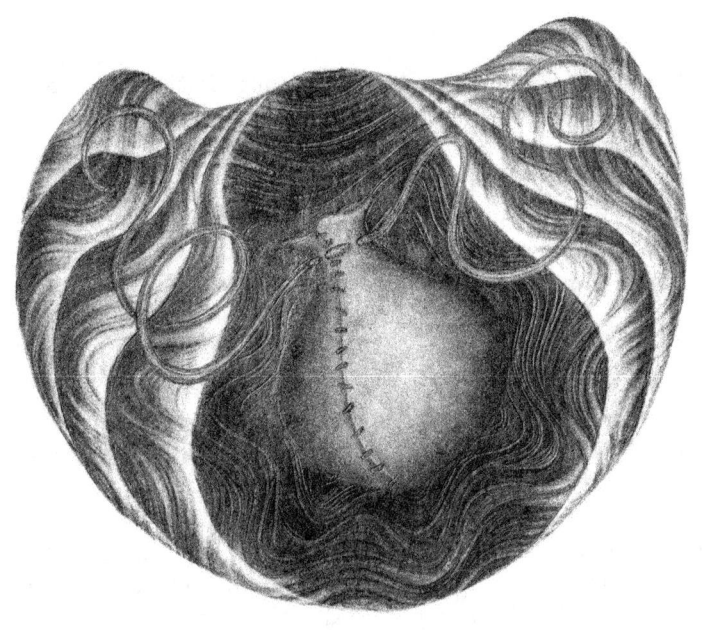

LEO AND THE MAGIC BEAN

Back and back, when the world was new, there lived a little boy named Leo. He was born in a small coastal village in a valley beneath the grand mountains. The valley cradled the tiny cottages built there and collected the breeze that blew in like kisses from the ocean. Leo loved the ocean. He spent most of his time dipping his toes into her salty crests, pretending he understood the gull songs. He delighted in picturing himself walking on the ocean's belly, teasing her fishes with stories from the mountains. He knew no story from dry land could be as thrilling as what must happen beneath the great blue fury's surface—her mysteries beguiled him—but he guessed fishes would be just as thrilled by stories from the dry world as he with theirs.

When Leo wasn't sitting endlessly on the sandy shore, he was wading waist-deep in the meadow. It was just like the sea, he reasoned. The wind moved the leafy waves around his little waist. He would hold his breath and plunge into the green bucolic brine, flailing his arms out in front like a boy-shaped sea turtle. Every day found him within the scent of saltwater. He loved it. This, to Leo, was paradise.

Not everyone shared Leo's joy. In fact, no one that he knew of did. Hard times had come to the little valley Leo called home. The hardest anyone could remember, and some of the village's folken must have been as old as the stars, Leo thought. Still, he was a boy, and what a boy he was. He played all day and sang and ran and dreamed. He wouldn't have noticed the hard times at all if it wasn't for his empty belly and his mother's tears.

At first, his hunger was just an inconvenience. Everyone was hungry now and then. Boys had to get hungry, Leo reasoned. How else would he know when to eat? But soon it grew painful. Through open windows, he heard babbies crying. The mothers holding the babbies cried as well. Fathers cried, too, as they walked from door to door asking for work or charity or crumbs. The weeping of children was to be expected, but the weeping of noomies and pooeys made little Leo's heart hurt.

The hard times began when the crops failed one autumn. Crops didn't always do so well, and everyone knew it would simply make for one hard winter. Winters are often hard. Come that spring, however, the ground was still frozen solid, and their seeds didn't take. The birds ate most of them up before they had a chance to root. What little did sprout withered away with the summer's fierce heat. It was hotter than anyone could remember, even the ones who were old as the stars. The crops had no chance.

Leo, like everyone, became very hungry.

In fact, Leo went so long without proper food, he forgot what a good meal was like. He had forgotten the taste and texture. The aroma. He and his parents mostly survived on roots his mother boiled in water. Leo knew little about the plants growing around their cottage, but his mother did. She knew the ones to select for their broth. Leaves from this one, twigs from that one. Leo would pretend the broth was a magic potion that transported him to anywhere in the whole wide world, even past the grand mountains . . . though he had never heard of anyone venturing that far. Sometimes he sipped his magic potion slowly, feeling it go down his throat just one swallow at a time. A single sip after another. He imagined this made his flight to other worlds slower so he might enjoy all the sights and smells and flavors. He wouldn't want to miss a thing, after all. But most times he guzzled the odd-tasting liquid down. Easier to get it over with in a few quick gulps. It tasted like the earth, after all.

That was before his father went away, leaving Leo and his mother to fend for themselves. His noomie said his pooey went away to find food, but Leo wasn't so sure. He thought mayhap she said this just to keep Leo from knowing the truth. He was a little boy, but he knew some truths hurt like sticky brambles. Worse, even. No matter why his father left, he must never have found what he was looking for. Or perhaps he did, and it was enough to keep him away, for Leo never saw his father again.

After his pooey left, Leo's mother still made the broth using twigs and roots, but she also began boiling her baskets. Before the famine, she had made a fair living drying the woody fibers from the bailey cane his father had grown, weaving them into sturdy baskets. No one ate bailey cane, though Leo supposed it could be eaten. Fresh chunks of stalks were often added to stews to make them thick and hearty, but no one ate these. The children often tussled over who got to remove the stalk when the stew was done. Doing so was good luck. That was, however, when the crops grew. That year, there were no bailey crops. His noomie had used up all her dried fibers to make baskets. No one was buying baskets, though, because no one had food to carry in them.

That's when his mother got the grand idea to eat the bailey cane stalks to provide her little boy with something more than hot grass broth to eat. Leo hadn't the heart to tell his noomie the baskets were too tough—the juices that made stews so delicious had all been baked out of the cane as they dried in the sun for basket weaving—but she knew. He knew she must, unless she did not eat the broth herself. So it became a game they played, one in which he pretended the soup was yummy, and she pretended to believe him.

Sometimes, the pain in Leo's belly was almost too much for him to bear. He bore it anyway. On many days, he secretly watched his mother holding her own tummy while fat, salty tears rolled down her cheeks. She always looked saddest when she didn't know Leo was watching. He knew it hurt her that he was hungry, so he never told her he was. He just smiled a big smile and rubbed his belly after forcing down the not-so-yummy broth. He would smack his lips together and exclaim that no other mother was so talented a cook that no boy's noomie ever made broth quite so good as his own.

Leo did not like for his mother to be sad.

So it went. Days were all the same for Leo. Despite the famine, Leo had fun. Boys will always find a way to enjoy themselves, even boys who must play alone. For all Leo's friends had gone away. This made Leo sad, but still he played and sang and ran and dreamed. That's what little boys are made to do, after all. He enjoyed the ocean surf and swam through the meadow grass. But one day, something odd happened. Something that changed everything for everyone forever.

Leo walked down a narrow little street in his little village, on his way to his favorite spot on his favorite beach, when he passed a dark alley that smelled of sally weed and earth. A shadow moved in the alley, grabbing hold of Leo's attention. He stopped, not quite sure why, then walked closer to the alley's dark mouth. He peered into the dimness like a hoot owl watching for mice in the night. As his eyes adjusted to the dark, he saw a man. The man was very old, so very wrinkled, and smelled like an attic filled with old dusty books. The old man's eyes were wild but not ferocious. His were a friendly wild. A good wild. The kind of wild Leo saw in a kitten gnawing on his knuckles. The kind of wild he imagined the birds wrote their songs to. That wild lived in the man's eyes, a glowing elixir glinting against the gloom of the alley. Leo was transfixed.

Should he have been afraid? Perhaps. Strange men in dark alleys should frighten little boys.

The old man laughed. It was the sound of a rusty wheel turning on a wagon. Or how Leo imagined the sun must sound extinguishing itself into the sea at bedtime. Or like bells, yes! Zyphlen bells in a vaulted forest. It was a warm laugh, and it made Leo smile. It had been a long time since he heard someone laugh. He had not before considered the power the sound of laughter holds, but then he understood. The sound was magical.

"Why are you so happy?" Leo asked the man, but the old man only pointed his crooked finger at Leo and laughed. This was very amusing to the boy, and since he didn't feel frightened of the man at all, he plopped down in front of the wrinkly, mirthful thing. He watched as though, at any moment, the man might pop open and little elves would come running out. Or, at least, he hoped to find out how the man could laugh so freely when there seemed so little about which to laugh.

Without warning, the dark alley fell silent. It wasn't that the sounds stopped. No, the awful racket of folken with nothing to do but moan and cry and bang noisy things about remained. For a truth, that was one reason Leo loved his spot on the beach so much. It was quiet and peaceful. And the surf sang away the noise of all the folken's troubles, or at least made it impossible for Leo to hear their lamentations. Not to mention, having sand between his little toes made little Leo feel awfully good inside.

But now Leo suddenly discovered a silence he'd never noticed before, and it was this he heard instead of the noise coming from the village.

The silence almost resonated in the small alley. It reminded Leo of a warm fire in the hearth on long winter evenings. Like tasting honeysuckle after he swam so hard he saw black spots and had to lay his body out to dry in the sun, panting from exertion. The old man smiled at Leo as he reached inside the dark folds of his cloak. Leo's eyes followed the old man's hand. When it reemerged from within the earthy cloth, the man's long sinewy fingers were wrapped around a small pouch. A very, very small pouch. A pouch just small enough to be the perfect size for a little boy, particularly a little boy named Leo.

Without thought, Leo reached out to take it. The aged fellow put a knotted finger against his lips. His eyes sparked with tiny jubilant flames. He paused for only a moment before he reached out his weathered fist and placed the pouch into Leo's awaiting palm. The old man then cradled Leo's hand with his own, the knobbed burlap of age pressed against the smooth satin of youth. Wisdom commingled with curiosity. Eternity kissed the moment, and the effervescent hommie threw back his head and cackled into the cool of the morning.

With one last wink and giggle, the old man left Leo alone in the alleyway, the simple pouch clutched in his dirty palm. Leo watched the man leave. For such an old man, he walked well. So well, in fact, Leo wondered that mayhap the old man did not walk at all. Rather, he appeared to float a finger's width above the dusty ground. At length, Leo looked again at the pouch he held. Then he heard a voice, one very much like a rusty wheel on an old wagon.

It said, "Leo, you hold great magic."

Leo looked again at the pouch in his hand, his body trembling with wonder. He needed to see what magic was inside the pouch, so he pulled its leather strapping away and peeked inside.

"Huh," he said, confounded. What he saw inside was so simple, all he could muster in response was to scratch his chin.

A bean. Black with white markings, sort of like webbing on a bee's wing. Simple. Elegant, even.

A revelation struck Leo: it must be a magic bean. The old man told him he held magic, after all. What else was he holding but the little pouch hiding a single black bean? Every little boy should have a magic bean, Leo thought. In his mind, he imagined preparing a great and fabulous feast

55

with his bean, enough that the whole valley could eat their fill. Surely, with a magic bean, his mother could cook up a world's worth.

Then his mind wondered . . . what if? What if magic beans weren't meant for eating? What if they had better uses? His smile made his eyes glow as he imagined a fierce battle where he, Leo the Mighty, stood alone before a broken dragon, slain by Leo and his magic bean. He could nearly hear the people heralding him as their hero. How he beamed at the thought.

But he also conspired in his little boy's mind that he might take this special bean and paint the whole world all new colors—he might paint the mountains and the sky, the oceans and the prairies, inspiring them all with the magic he held in his hand. What a dazzling sight that would be.

Then, quite enthusiastically, he had another idea. A better idea! He pictured himself playing the resonant strings of some ancient musical instrument, his magic bean a talisman for releasing enchanting melodies, creating tunes that rivaled that of the birds. He could all but feel the rough strings on his fingertips.

Oh, the things he might do with his magic bean.

Then again, he could take the bean home and throw it in a pot with some water and root, and make his mother the best bean broth she had ever sipped. It would be nice to prepare her a delicious meal for a change.

He toiled for several moments over this new dilemma. He had made his way out of town and was sitting at his favorite oceanside spot, contemplating the spellbinding bean in his fist. Should he use it to do wonderful, fantastical things, or should he cook it for his mother? Having a magic bean implied great responsibility. Not everyone had a magic bean, after all. It was his duty to use it for the greater good. He might cook it only once. Mayhap eating a magic bean was the worst thing to do with it.

Cooking a magic thing seemed tricksy, he reasoned. But he pictured his mother holding her empty belly, and he could not get free from the image. He would do anything for her—even cook his one and only magic bean. Just as he resolved to run home right away to do just that, he had an even better idea. It was like a bolt of lightning, it came to him so suddenly. He knew he was a smart boy to have thought of such a perfect plan. He would plant the bean—that is what you do with seeds. Why hadn't he thought of this sooner? he wondered. No doubt the bean would grow despite the drought. It was magic, after all. Then he would have lots of magic beans. He would be able to do anything he wanted with that many beans. Cook them, slay dragons, or paint the world. He could even give some away to his friends, if he had any friends. With a magic bean, he would soon enough. With such a special talisman, he would soon have too many friends to count! Besides, all of the villagers were hungry. Mayhap they could each one harvest and eat their fill. Mayhap hunger would never haunt their cottages again.

Perfect. Now all he had to do was find the perfect spot to plant his funny little bean. It wasn't long before he did. It was a quaint spot on the side of a tender hill, grassy and shaded just the right amount. The earth was soft, and a freshwater stream murmured quiet whispers nearby. But it was well within sight of the sea. He would never find a more suitable spot—he himself could grow here, he imagined. It stood to reason, then, his magic bean would love it also. Leo planted his bean in that perfect place and gathered himself in a ball a short distance away to watch and see what happened. It was a magic bean, so was it not possible it might grow at a magic speed? Leo thought of all the beans he would soon have. He wouldn't have to make broth—no, he would make bean soup. He licked his lips in anticipation, all the while his little eyes never left the small mound of brown earth.

There was nothing he could not accomplish with his magic bean, except . . .

Nothing happened. He waited as the sun stretched its way higher into the sky. He waited as the breeze tickled his nose with sea salt and honeysuckle. He waited as a caterpillar crawled up his leg and perched atop his knee, king of the mountain. He waited as clouds took shape. He waited as those same clouds became nothing more than cotton against a blue canvas. He waited as ant soldiers carried beads of food on their backs to their queen. He waited and waited and waited.

Leo was so intent on seeing what the bean might do that he did not notice the sun dip himself into the sea for a long, quiet nap. Neither did Leo see the moon rousing herself from behind the mountains, lifting from among the evergreen folds of the distant hills. It grew cool, but Leo didn't mind. He was sleepy, but the bean was important. He was hungry, but that wasn't new. So he watched.

Time slipped away. Nothing happened. Finally, Leo broke his focus on the mound of turned earth and the secret planted beneath it. He looked around. The place was dark except for the light coming from the moon. Ah, and here was a wonder. The moon was not where she should be. She hung strangely low, as if floating on the calm face of the ocean. Leo had never seen such a grand sight. He thought he could swim out and touch it . . . if he had been allowed to swim out. His mother had always told him to stay out of the water. Then he had an idea. A most excellent idea indeed! He ran down the hill to the edge of the forest, straight to one of the large old trees that grew there, and ripped from its side a great chunk of sturdy bark. It was thick and strong, and it was plenty big enough on which to float.

He did just that. He placed the bark in the water, smooth side up, and lay on it, belly down. He had taken off his clothes and laid them in the grass so that, in case he got wet, they would be dry and warm to put on when he returned. Then he pulled himself across the resting sea, paddling his feet and splashing his hands all the way to the edge of the moon. Yes, it was just like he thought it would be. The moon hung so low, its lower-most edge dipped into the sea. Leo floated right up to its cool face and carefully stood on his sturdy bark. On the side of the moon's surface was a round hole just big enough for a boy his size to squeeze through. So Leo did.

Inside the moon, he found a spacious, empty room. The walls were liquid velvet, cool and wet to the touch. Strange light danced across Leo's skin like sunlight reflected off water. It was violet-gray, and it made Leo laugh. How light could tickle, he did not know, but it did. He felt raw happiness there inside the moon. He spied lots of tunnels leading out from his spacious room, and Leo could hardly wait to try them all. But there was one hole, near the top of the velvet wall, that seemed to call to him. Leo believed in simple magic most of all. So if this tunnel called to him, this tunnel is where he should go. But what if he imagined it? Did he not plan to visit all the tunnels? Should he perhaps start with those closest? It was a difficult choice, but one for which Leo was ready. *Well*, he thought, *that one is as good as any. I can try them all in good time.* So he climbed up to the tunnel using the cavities and holes in the moon's walls as steps. Once he'd pushed himself through the tunnel opening, Leo climbed higher. The tunnel went way up and up toward the tip-top of the moon. In and out of twists and corners and crooks, Leo crawled and climbed through the velvet maze. On and on he went, bathed in purple light and filled with endless joy. For years it seemed he went, and so it must have been because his little boy body grew muscle and strength. Soon, Leo no longer looked like a little boy at all.

By the time he reached the end of the tunnel, he was a handsome fellow with several years more than when first he had clamored his way inside the moon. Now, Leo had the body of a strong young man. He marveled over his muscled arms and his beard-scruffy chin. Over how tall he'd become. He laughed and was thrilled over how deep his voice sounded. He climbed from the tunnel and stood atop the silky orb.

Leo was surrounded by a blanket of sleepy stars, each of which turned their faces to look at him. They knew who he was, he felt certain. They looked at him as someone would a long-lost friend. He did not know how this could be, but then he remembered how often he had talked to the stars from his open window at night. How he had told them stories of all the wonderful things he would do once he was old enough to do them. Now they talked back to Leo, but not with words. They winked and fluttered instead, and they explained he had always been old enough to do those things. He smiled at their twinkling message. These, he knew now, were his brothers and sisters, and they bore witness to the growing light inside him.

That's what they said: light grew inside him, but not normal light. This was the kind of light only little boys and girls could create, the kind of light that grew as they did. In both understanding and stature. In good character and kindness. In believing in good things and doing better things. A magical light, of course. And he had it. And it was growing. Leo smiled so big at this.

The moon purred beneath his feet as he stretched himself on her velour surface. He reclined on a narrow beam that trestled out from her top, over the ever-deepening vault of glittering darkness. There he lay, one celestial body atop another, dangling his bare feet in the cool firmament beneath him. A lazy comet shuffled past, its tail tickling Leo's toes. He meant to repose this way for several minutes, for climbing had made him tired.

Then, from way across the darkness, a light emerged. Leo realized almost at once it was the sun, and for a moment, he was oddly afraid. The sun soothed his fear, however, and the touch of the sun's rays warmed Leo's bare skin. The young man watched as, from the sun's surface, a flame kindled. This flame was alive with a vitality different from the giant star, and it began moving like an eel through the darkness, swimming its way toward Leo. Leo thought of running, but he was on the moon. Where might he go? Besides, part of him wanted the flame to reach him, and that is just what it did. It circled Leo like a playful puppy, moving around his body, under his arms, and through his legs . . . in and out, wrapping around his torso and waist. Circling him again and again.

Then it stopped in front of Leo's nose. It waited, and the two watched each other. The young man who used to be a little boy opened his mouth in wonder and anticipation, and the flame flew into his mouth and down into his lungs. The heat was so intense, Leo knew he would burn right up. He felt it moving throughout his entire body, a rampaging bull on fire, until every part of him was touched by its heat. He flung himself down on the cool surface of the moon, but she could offer little relief. The fire was much too hot. And then, just like that, the heat was gone.

Only then did Leo remember his magic bean. And his mother. And the whole of the world below him. Had he been on the moon for years? What had happened to his mother while he had been away? Had she worried about him? No doubt she had. What about his village? And what of his magic bean . . . had it grown?

Quickly, Leo made his way back down the winding tunnel and soon found himself in the moon's belly once again. He found the little hole he had climbed through so long ago. Though it had only barely allowed his little boy body to squeeze through the first time, now it seemed just the right size for his young man body. However, to his surprise and alarm, the moon had risen high in the sky. The sea and beach were far below him now. He could see his clothes resting on the beach so far away. To jump that far, he would need a running start. He made his way back across to the other side of the violet-gray room and ran toward the little opening at the bottom, hoping for the best. His strong feet kicked up velvety lilac moss as he ran. The moon tilted. Just as he jumped from the little hole, a cloud of blue diamond dust emptied into the night sky and enveloped Leo, carrying him to the sandy beach below. His entire body glistened with diamond dust then. When he breathed, it filled his lungs. When he swallowed, it fell into his belly. He was saturated by it, inside and out.

Back on land and exhausted from his travels, Leo lay himself down in a soft bed of flockie-moss. It was warm and soft and comforting, mayhap more so than his bed back home. There on the beach, the sun, which he had seen plainly from the top of the moon, remained hidden in some distant part of the sky. His bed was so soft and his body so weary, he soon drifted into sleep. There he slept through all that remained of night. Before he knew it, however, the sun kissed his skin the way friends may kiss each other's cheeks. Morning had returned. Leo stirred himself, washed his face in the cool spring, and wrapped his robe around his waist.

That's when he saw it.

Over to one side of the tiny stream, a large leafy bush grew, full of giant pods and delicate flowers. It was his bean, or it had been back and back. Now, there were hundreds of beans on the bush. Thousands, even.

Leo was mystified as he looked on the miracle of it. He took up his too-small clothes once again, tying knots in his sleeves and pant legs to create pouches. He picked as many beans as his clothes would hold, which was quite a few, and still the bush was full. He couldn't be sure, but he thought the more he picked, the more they grew. With his load, he made his way back toward his mother and home.

On his way, he told everyone he saw of the miracle beans growing on the seaside. It must have been an odd thing to see, a half-robed young man walking into town with bundles of beans, but no one seemed to mind at all. For his skin, tanned golden, had a gentle blue glow about it. This could be his ehwain, true, but not just. It was also the kiss of the moon. His eyes held the color of the sun, and when he spoke, invisible fire came from his lips and burned away the hopelessness and despair, the bitterness and rage from everyone who heard his voice. His words were healing and a comfort. All at once, those who heard him ran to the beach to gather in the bounty of a long tardy harvest. There was enough there for the whole valley to enjoy. No one ran in selfish haste. Instead, they had caught Leo's vitality. They did not fight or shove. Rather, they turned each one to this side and that, finding someone less able than themselves to help on their way. And that is the way their long fast was broken.

In a single season, the little valley became known throughout the countryside as the wealth of the land. It seemed no one would ever have to be hungry again. And indeed they would not. For on and on, into the time that came, the bush grew into a tree, and the tree into a grove, and the grove into a forest: a vaultine that dazzled the senses. And time sped on. The folken changed. They grew to believe themselves more intelligent. Some even came to think of the bean tree as just a quaint story: a children's tale not worthy of serious consideration. But there were always those who ate from its branches, and they were ever full. Not too much, just right. Even to this day, amid the hustle and haste of fussy folken who do not believe in the magical things around them, indeed in the magic of the world itself, the tree still stands. Tall and strong, it remains unscathed by the saw teeth of the skeptic's voice. Of the heavy doubt of the disbeliever's heart. Of the ugly baskets of selfish men who might take it all for themselves. The villages grew to cities, and the cities grew large around it, but the tree's shadow always found room to rest in the hearts of those who saw it.

But what of the boy, Leo? That day he returned home to his mother. Though he had aged a lifetime and eternity, he found her where he'd left her. She did not wonder at his new body, but only smiled as she saw him cross the threshold into their tiny cottage. He kissed her on her weary face. He smelled her fine golden hair. Then, he took down her largest pot from the rack above her tiny stove and cooked for his mother the best bean soup her weary lips had ever tasted.

Later, Leo went again to the seaside, for he still loved her so. And he had made new friends, besides. Along the way, he heard a familiar sound scuttling on the breeze. Like rusty wagon wheels or zyphlen bells. It was the sound of the old laughing man's voice. It called to him.

> "LEO, THE MAGIC WAS NOT IN THE BEAN
> FOR BEANS HAVE NO PARTICULAR GIFT.
> THE MAGIC LAY WITHIN YOU, MY CHILD,
> THE SECRET OF IT ALL IS THIS:
> NO WEALTH IS GAINED IN MAGIC WORDS,
> NOR GLORY IN FLIGHTY SCHEMES . . . .
> ONLY BY HOPE, LIKE THAT OF A CHILD,
> CAN REALITY SPIN FROM DREAMS."

With that, the voice and the old man who carried it were never heard from again. Not by Leo, leastways. He pondered the old man's words, studying them like jewels found in the bottom of a deep well. Suddenly, things became clear: it had been his dream, and his trust that dreams come true, that had conjured his little boy magic and made all the difference.

Dreaming, imagining that impossible and fantastic adventures linger around every tree and rock, is the most natural thing in the world for a child like Leo to do. And my, the dreams Leo dreamed. His wild heart would burst had they all surfaced at once, and it felt as though it might. Now he could see: the stars had been correct. They had always been correct. Dreams come true when you dare to believe in them strongly enough. When you work hard to catch them. When you see and make them true.

And Leo saw. He believed in the magic of faith, the risk of dreaming, and the glory of hope. All along this power had been locked away inside him as if in a tiny little-boy box. It very well may have stayed that way forever had not the old man's knotted fingers lay hold to the clasp and opened it. Now Leo's dreams, mixed with sun-fire and moon-dust, were free.

This was not so magical. Dreaming was quite normal for Leo. With a deep breath and a quiet smile, he was content.

Leo set about doing the things he'd always wanted to do. He was old enough to do them, certainly. The stars had said so. He tamed many dragons with his skillful hands, though he left them wild enough to be dangerous yet. It turned out, Leo enjoyed the company of dragons. He created beautiful melodies and sang them loud and clear. I am certain you have heard the birds singing at least one of them. It is true—the birds have always loved Leo's songs. And yes, Leo painted the world a tapestry. Such handsome colors had never before been seen. You've seen these, too. The sunsets were Leo's favorite. He painted them with all the passion of the sun and moon, colliding in a perfect dance hovering above the milky blue plane of the sea. How stunning they were to look upon.

Leo grew to be a good man, and everywhere he journeyed, the light, buried deep inside him, touched all the people he met. It was the fire of miracles. And though he grew old one day, he never lost that little boy inside his heart. And one other thing he never lost: a small leather-bound pouch he kept inside his coat pocket. Inside the pouch was a single bean. For no doubt, in time, a famine might return. And a hungry little boy or girl may wander into a dark alley, looking for hope.

Oh yes, and one more thing. Leo fulfilled the most dazzling and ambitious dream he ever dreamed, the thing he wished for above all else as a boy: he walked along the ocean floor telling the fishes tales of his travels. They were enchanted.

Certainly, by now, he must have told them all.

Author's Note

Leo's is a bedtime story. It is a fairytale any noomie or pooey might recite for their children in front of hearth fires on stormy winter evenings or beside the little ones' beds at bedtime. Perhaps more Hans Christian Andersen than the Brothers Grimm, the intent is to delight and teach children. This story would be told within the world of the Glint, whereas the previous stories concerned the experiences of characters inhabiting that world: in other words, "Kolinga" and "Noways Place" are "true" stories *about* that world and characters in it. I make the distinction not because it changes the experience of reading Leo's tale, but because reading fiction—as this story is—requires a different imagination from reading nonfiction. Particularly with a children's story, since things such as natural physics or even basic logic are often secondary to the greater lesson being presented.

Within the world of the Glint, Natty's and Cal's stories were not made up, but were rather believed to be true accounts of their experiences. They happened as told, or at least as the narrators telling the story remember—or want you to remember—the events. Leo's story is different. It is fiction, but often truths become mythologized in the zeitgeist of popular culture, so you may recognize a thread here and there that strikes you as familiar. If so, you may have stumbled upon a fictionalized version of someone or something "factual" from the world of the Glint.

I originally wrote this children's story for a boy named Daniel, who came to the youth home where I worked for many years. I enjoyed writing stories for family and friends for birthdays, Christmas, or other special occasions. In the story I wrote for Daniel, who was in his teens, I wanted to include elements of things he himself enjoyed. He loved painting graffiti, surfing, and learning to play the piano. There are hints at these hobbies in Leo's story. Even Leo's bean is a reference to Daniel's surname.

I think the thing I loved most about Daniel, right beside the fact that Daniel loved to learn more than anyone else I've known, is that he embodied the raw wonder of boyhood—he was, after all, the template from which Leo sprang. Yes, he was by most measurements an adult, but so long as I knew him, he never lost his childlike love of adventure.

I changed Daniel's name in the story to Leo. Mostly, however, the story remains close to what it was: a fairytale written to inspire children to be good, and to love big, and to never lose that sense of childlike wonder and the magic it holds.

I am sad Daniel and I grew apart after he graduated from our program. We remained close for a few years after, but time and life have a way of shuffling us off in our unique directions. But I tell true: he remains one of my favorites. So, Daniel, if you are reading this, I hope you still dream, because I still believe in your magic.

MAD MISCHIEF

"Yer jest bein' a babbie. Do yeh wanna be a babbie?" Yuli sniffled. He was trying to muster the same obstinate courage he'd seen in his father. The same defiant refusal to fear. Yuli wanted to be like his father, to make his father proud. That is why he wanted to be ready for today. That is why, on this morning of all mornings, he hated his tears.

"The way is the way," his father had often said. "The way things have been, the way things are, the way things will always remain . . . ." This was sacred scrip among their people, and it had been branded on Yuli's bones. Today, he would take his first steps in the way.

He pulled on his breeches and fastened his belt. Then he pulled on his boots. Any other year, today would involve pastries and a gift. But this year was different. This year he turned seven. Still, his mother had sneaked him a sweet divet the night before when she came to say their nightly thanks. She'd kissed his forehead and assured him he would do well next day. Then she'd handed him the divet—goat cheese, strawberry, and honey . . . Yuli's favorite—and wished him sweet dreams. His dreams had not been sweet, but the pastry had. Now, as he finished lacing his second boot, he felt it twist in his stomach as if jeering at him.

"Jest don't be a babbie," he reminded himself.

Yuli remembered a time when he was excited for his seventh birthday. Now that it had arrived, he dreaded it. He could not help it: he was afraid. He did not want to be, but fear swelled in him like an infection. That would not stop him, of course. Afraid or not, Yuli would do his duty. He would meet the woodsmen and begin his quest. He would make his father and mother proud. And when he returned to Gal-Braith, he would be a man full-grown. He would be strong and fearless, just like his father.

Yuli took one final deep breath to reinforce his legs for walking, opened his bedroom door, and stepped into the living room.

"And what do yeh make of it?" his mother was asking his father. "Should we go through with it? Should we wait to see what—"

Yuli's father had placed a large hand on his wife's shoulder as Yuli stepped into the room.

"Here he is, then," his father said, standing to face Yuli. He grabbed Yuli's shoulders and gave them a comforting squeeze. The weight and heat from his father's hands fortified him. "Do yeh know what today is?"

Yuli nodded, realized he needed to use words for this part, and prayed his voice didn't warble as he said, "Aye. Today begins my kohlas."

His father smiled. Yuli felt that smile saturate him. And for a wonder, his voice had been full and strong when he spoke, just like he hoped to be on his quest.

It was no secret that every boy in the valley began his kohlas the morning of his seventh birthday. Yuli's father had talked more with his son about the quest than perhaps other fathers would. Yuli suspected this by his father's hushed tones, as if his words were being sanctified by quiet. And his mother had told him so, also. That his father had always regretted not understanding more about his own father's kohlas. How he wanted things to be different for his own son. And now, due in large part to his father's instruction, Yuli felt ready. He felt his fear taking a step back to allow pride to step forward. Pride in himself for what he was about to begin, but also for his father.

The kohlas was designed to frighten. No one had told Yuli this, but it seemed obvious. It was designed to frighten the childishness right out of the boys of Gal-Braith, and it had always been very effective at its work. His father was proof of that. And so in the days and weeks leading up to his kohlas, Yuli had braced himself by looking toward the wood as often as he could. He could not see the Dark Wood from his farm, but he felt it like a great shadow over every moment of his young life. He pictured himself stepping beneath its dark canopy and taking hold of the woodsmen's hands. Of becoming a scarecrow hunter. In this way, he had hoped to prepare himself. Now that the morning of his kohlas had arrived, he felt ready, frightened or not, but he did not feel prepared.

The door opened to the world beyond their small cottage, Yuli's father holding the knob in one hand and Yuli's shoulder with the other. The two stepped together into the yard. Yuli's mother stepped up behind him, sweeping him into a tight hug and assailing his face with a barrage of kisses. Yuli allowed this, but his eyes drifted across the yard to the path that would lead him and his father to the wood.

"Aye, let's go then," his father said.

They walked across the yard, thick with spring grass, and took the path that would lead them to the Dark Wood. As they walked, the sun shone cheerfully, its warmth a comfort on Yuli's neck. His father had told him he would likely have to say goodbye to the sun once his quest began—days seemed perpetually dark beneath the canopy of the wood—so Yuli was happy for this last farewell. It was not a long walk, a half hour at most, and the time passed quickly as Yuli's thoughts were distracted.

"Is somethin' wrong?" he asked finally.

His father looked over at him but didn't speak. His eyes asked the question instead.

"I heard ma' talkin'," Yuli explained, "sounded like somethin' were wrong."

His father looked ahead again, their pace slow but steady. His face pulled, demonstrating confusion, perhaps. Or worry. After a few moments, he spoke. "It's nothin', Yuli. Just a strange feelin's all."

"What do yeh mean?" Yuli asked. "Is it about my kohlas?" Yuli heard his voice tremble, but his father did not seem to. Or if he did, he made no comment. For several moments, neither spoke.

His father sighed. "Yeh know that feelin' how the house'll sway in the wind durin' a storm?" Yuli nodded. He hated the feeling. It frightened him. "Aye, well imagine the storm kept goin', but that feelin' left. Can yeh understand that, boy?"

"I think so," Yuli said, but he knew he didn't.

His father went on. "I felt like the wind stopped, but the storm kept goin'. Not a proper storm, but somethin' in here." He tapped his chest. Then he reached his palm out toward the valley surrounding them. "Somethin' here," he said. "Somethin' with the Dark Wood . . . ."

Yuli now understood even less, but his fear multiplied, fresh as spring rain and bitter as coffee. They continued on in silence. When they topped the final hill and the Dark Wood came into view, his father stopped mid-stride. His mouth fell open as if he sensed a wrongness he had not expected.

To Yuli's eyes, the Dark Wood appeared as it ever had. He had not often seen it, not being allowed to venture close to it unless it was truly necessary, and then only at his father's side. But even he felt a difference he could not name. This must be what his father had meant.

"It's dead," his father said.

"Da'?" Yuli asked, confused.

As if the wood had heard his father's comment, it suddenly sprang to life with a deafening roar of rattles and scrapes. The trees—their ancient limbs hanging heavily with moss and fern—thrashed. Dust kicked up from the darkened ground beneath like vaporized poison. A groan began deep within the wood, and it rushed toward Yuli and his father. The boy felt ice take hold of his toes as his breeches filled with warmth. His father had not mentioned anything like this happening. He needed nothing further to understand something was horribly wrong.

The groan grew louder—closer—until it became a scream. It was not human. It was not animal. Yuli, even at seven years, understood this sound came from the forest itself. The trees bent and released, a violence so unexpected and volatile it did not seem real. Then the scream reached the perimeter of the Dark Wood, the trees closest to where Yuli stood with his father exploding in a cloud of dust and splinters. Yuli was grateful they remained at a safe distance. Then the ground split.

"Run . . . ," Yuli's father said, but Yuli did not register the command. For just then, from within the crack in the ground, a thick heavy vine emerged. It fractured at the end into several smaller vines, and each of these reached for Yuli and his father.

"Run!" his father screamed, but before Yuli could move, his father's arm had swooped around him, and the two were off. Hanging over his father's shoulder, Yuli saw what his father could not. He saw more hideous vines come from the crack in the ground and begin pulverizing everything within their reach, the first one having quit its pursuit of Yuli to join the others. Trees and stones and earth were beaten into sticks and pebbles, enormous gashes left behind in the wake of the violence.

Yuli's eyes must have been deceived in those brief moments, for the boy thought he saw a mouth open within the darkness of the wood, rows of razor-sharp stakes gilding it like teeth. But just before his father reached the crest of the hill and dipped below the other side, the Dark Wood fell preternaturally still once again, its long arms rescinding back into the earth. The gaping mouth—whether real or not—fastened shut with a final clap. But for a long time after, Yuli's heart would beat the fevered cadence of the wood, bruising his chest with fear.

Only later would Yuli understand, some of the matter, at least. It was that evening, and they had just finished their supper. Neither he nor his father had eaten much, though both had given it their best effort.

"It don't make no sense," the man said. "No one can make sense of it . . . ." Yuli's father had visited other farms in the valley, hoping to find an explanation. He found none, which seemed to devastate him nearly as much as what he'd seen at the wood.

Yuli's mother wore her concern as if it were painted on her face.

"It's broke," his father said. "The pact. It's broke, and no one can say why. I felt it even before we left the house . . . ."

He trailed off after that. Neither Yuli nor his mother responded. He could not speak for his mother, but Yuli knew with absolute certainty that if he opened his mouth just then, he would do more than cry. He would wail. The pact could not break. The pact was the salvation of his people, an ages old covenant between Gal-Braith and the Dark Wood, the most sacred of all their venerated truths. Back and back for unknown ages, the pact had stood as a beacon between the valley folken and the wood, a safeguard against terrors too hideous to name.

Should the pact fall, would not evil have full reign in the valley? And it was not simply for the sake of protection against evil: the pact was holy. It made sacred the people and their sons, making men of these last. Making fathers of them. The kohlas was the great honor of his people, and it was tethered to the pact.

"What does this mean, lover?" his mother asked.

His father looked at his mother, and Yuli held his breath. This was the question he'd wanted to ask: what did this mean? Were they in danger? Besides that, if they could not approach the Dark Wood, was there a kohlas? And if there wasn't a kohlas, how would he become a man? His father's eyes left his wife and fell to stare through their kitchen table.

"I don't know. I suppose we will see."

Yuli grew to manhood without a kohlas. Ten years had passed since the Dark Wood had tried to eat him and his father—and Yuli felt certain that had been the goal: consumption. He had escaped more than his kohlas that day. He had escaped death.

He would never have admitted as much to his father or mother, but secretly he felt relief. Even at the age of seventeen years, he was glad he had not stepped within the shade of that low place even for a sacred act. Could he not become a man without the kohlas? Even before his seventh birthday he'd worked, and not just at his chores. He'd helped his father shoe their horses and sheer their sheep. He'd helped butcher several cows and pigs and dressed more deer than he could count. He reasoned these were the acts of men, not boys.

Considering himself now, he believed his body and mind had proved he could become a man. He had, after all.

He knew the idea was blasphemy, yet here he was: a man grown. He understood there was more to the kohlas than his learning to be a man. He understood the livelihood of his people depended on their faith in the kohlas, and faith that can be easily explained is not real faith. Even so, Yuli felt relief at having missed his kohlas. And after so many years, he could not account for the need of such a quest. He had become a man, after all. He was strong and clever. He'd learned endurance from his father and patience from his mother. He had learned love from both. He'd gained skills to work the farm and double the farm's yield.

Yet each and every day was lived in constant dread of the Dark Wood. The pact had been broken, and no one could explain why. Each year, the folken of Gal-Braith had gathered during the days leading up to Sauingrey to hold council, to try and make amends. They provided sacrifices to the Dark Wood of cattle and ox, and on several cases, the lives of men and women who ventured too close to its borders. Though mostly quiet, the wood remained a fevered thing: a silent predator waiting for its prey.

Death seemed always to hang just above the treetops, waiting for an opportunity to strike. Whether reality or superstition, the people of Gal-Braith believed their livelihood had been poisoned, that the crumbling pact had measured out their demise in steady doses in the prevailing years. Storms had ravaged the valley in Yuli's eighth and tenth years, alternating with a severe drought in between. Many believed these were the fruit of the broken pact. The earth shook a few years later, and again it was thought an omen of their faithlessness. In fact, any calamity, whether personal or spanning the breadth of the valley, was considered the rotten fruit of a spoiled covenant. A spooked mule once kicked a toddler, spraying his brains on his two siblings. *That must be the broken pact,* the folken judged. A band of reavers torched an inn, having murdered the innkeeper and trapped three other residents in the cellar as it burned on top of them. *It's the curse,* the folken reasoned.

Two years back, during Yuli's fifteenth year, a raiding band of Skree had decimated Gal-Braith. Yuli's farm was one of the few left intact, and that only because it lay on the farthest western side of the valley. Even that attack was considered the fruit of the broken pact, and of the very few folken who survived the attack, all hoped it was the end of the curse.

No one could explain the wood's sudden aggression after so many ages of peace. The valley folken remained befuddled and afraid. There seemed to be no reparations they could make, because no apparent offense had been named. What does a people do when their gods turn on them? How can they survive such betrayal?

It made no sense, and the nightmare was not ended. For one night, Yuli was snatched from sleep at the sounds of a violent storm. But there was no rain. Still, the calamity drew Yuli outside his family's cottage to stand barefoot and bare-chested in the dim light of the moon to watch a firestorm above the Dark Wood. He watched lightning bolts shatter the darkness of night. Thunder, sharp like whip cracks, rattled their cottage, but that was not all. He heard rumbling, as if the earth was sick and belching. And the wind moaned. All of this Yuli might have dismissed as nightmares, a fever dream and nothing more. But he was awake. This was no dream.

The worst part was the other sounds. These he recognized, for they had been the anthem of his would-be death on his seventh birthday. These were the screams of the Dark Wood. These were the rattling chaos of a hungry and malevolent low thing, only now it was fueled by more than anger. Yuli heard hatred in the cacophony, and fear.

The eastern horizon burned alternating shades of gold and orange, the ground trembling beneath his feet. His father came out of the house to stand beside Yuli. Both stared into the glittering darkness, but they waited for daybreak before venturing forth to investigate.

Forbidding clouds had always threatened the sky above the Dark Wood, as if the wood itself was allergic to sunlight. But on the morning after that menacing storm, the clouds were different. They churned, billowing from the earth beyond the treetops. These clouds looked like smoke. Yuli did not know what to make of this. Never—not even on the morning of his would-be kohlas, when the Dark Wood had tried to devour him—had he seen a sky so turbulent. The smell came then. It smelled as if a campfire had turned rancid. Did this come from the Dark Wood as well? Was the forest burning?

The path to the wood had become considerably overgrown in the years since his seventh birthday. Though he and his father made a yearly pilgrimage to stand at a safe, reasonable distance from the forest—and this only to pay honor to the pact that was and to leave sacrifices—they never went at other times. There was no reason to return to that place except out of their sacred duty. Any place within the valley could be reached by other paths.

Yuli had often wondered what good their sacrifices might do. Furthermore, he questioned why anyone in the valley, Yuli included, should work so hard to honor a religion that had failed them.

The way was the way until it wasn't. No amount of sacrifices or sacred pilgrimages had revived the covenant. Nothing had satiated the wood's hunger . . . but now a new mystery came to light. As they topped the final hill, sunlight beamed through the filtered sky. Yuli's mouth dropped open as the wood came into view. Or should have come into view . . . .

The Dark Wood was gone. It was charred to dust, the heavy roots of the trees—all that remained of the once mighty wood—scorched like ashy bones. Even the fence that had separated the Dark Wood from the rest of Gal-Braith was gone, consumed by fire.

"Da'?" Yuli said, his voice sounding small. It had been years since he had addressed his father this way, but just now the little boy inside him seemed to be the only part of him capable of speech.

His father did not answer but walked toward the wood. Yuli followed, cautious. No sound came from the low place. Except that wasn't exactly true. There were sounds—wind, for example, and the final sputtering of pockets of fire and embers—and that was perhaps what made Yuli wish for silence. He had only heard sound issue from within the Dark Wood twice—on the day it had nearly killed him, and in the wild of the storm the night before. Otherwise, the forest had always seemed to tamp out sound, silencing it with dread. These new sounds were far too normal to belong in the wood. This unnerved Yuli. He watched as his father knelt to run his fingers through the soot. Yuli approached, careful not to disrespect his father's reverie. He found tears on his father's face. He had wondered before what a people do when their gods turn on them, but now a new and more troubling question came: what does one do when their god is dead?

"Da'?" he said again. His father turned to face him.

"I don't know . . . ," he began. Then he breathed deep and stood.

Movement drew their attention deeper inside the ash. Something wriggled beneath the surface. Unbidden, images of those devilish vines came back to Yuli's mind. He tried to push these aside, certain they were unhelpful just then. He and his father approached the movement, his father reaching out a boot to trouble the soot. From beneath the ash spilled a small snake. It was gray and scaly, more than half its body charred black, but Yuli thought it was harmless.

"Tree snake?" he asked.

"Aye," his father replied, kneeling.

He picked up a twig and pressed it against the snake's body. Lethargic, the creature wriggled but did not try to escape. Perhaps insensate, or perhaps nearly dead, Yuli thought it too weak to escape. His father reached his hand toward the snake, his fingers trembling slightly.

"Don't, Father," Yuli said, but his father had already grabbed the snake and lifted it into the air for study.

"Aye, it's a tree snake, is all," his father said, the creature hanging mostly limp in his father's loose grasp. "You can see the markin's here . . . ."

And Yuli saw. As his eyes adjusted to the uniform grays of the defunct wood, he realized he saw movement scattered throughout. Mounds of ash squirmed as far as he could see. From some of these, he made out the telltale forms of other snakes, but there were also rodents. Rats and the like, and gods only knew what besides.

"Look," he said, pointing.

"Aye," his father said. "The lot of them seem scorched near to death. Scores of 'em, no tellin' how many—"

A cry cut off his father's words. He'd dropped the snake, the languid creature making no effort to escape. But Yuli's father's hand—the free hand that had not held the snake—blossomed red on its heel from a snake bite.

"At least it's not an asp," his father said, "but it burns like damnation."

He stood, pulling a rag from his pocket and tying it around his hand. The two men stood staring out over the devastation of what had been the keystone of the Gal-Braithians' faith. It stretched out before them like a giant corpse, smoke and ash guttering into the sky, a brilliant sun profaning the deathbed with its light.

Life went on despite the catastrophe. Yuli was unnerved by what he'd seen, but he knew the sight had devastated his father. The man seemed slow to recover. He seemed vacant, preoccupied perhaps by the memory of his faith charred to cinders. With each passing day, his face grew more gaunt, his dark skin paling to the color of ash. All Yuli's life, or at least since his seventh birthday, he had questioned the beliefs of his people. Whether the loss of his faith at such a young age was a blessing or an affliction, Yuli could not say, but he saw this new development taxed his father to a crippling extent. He could only hope the damage was not permanent.

They continued with daily tasks, the farm in constant need of tending. But Yuli's father's mind seemed almost always to wander. At first, his distractions were mild. Once he forgot to lock the gate and several cows ventured into the broader pasture during the night. Yuli easily recaptured these the next day. But on another morning, his father left a lantern burning on the floor of the barn, and the heat had nearly caught the hay alight. Yuli had prevented this, but his father had never been so careless, not in any way Yuli could remember.

And he became plagued with nightmares. He would not speak of these, but Yuli heard his father's cries during the night. Yuli saw his father's bruised eyes on the following days and his mother's clear concern.

One afternoon about a week after the Dark Wood had burned, Yuli made a choice to broach the subject neither he nor his father had seemed quick to discuss. Yuli was uncertain what he would say, only that he must say something. He found his father outside the barn, repairing a portion of the rabbit hutch—a leather strap had broken, allowing the door to fall askew.

"Father," he began, "can we talk?"

"Aye," his father grunted, not taking his eyes from his work.

"It's about the wood." Yuli hesitated a moment before saying, "The pact."

His father's hand went still. Then his shoulders sagged. A few moments passed before his father stood straight, wiping his hands on a cloth and turning to look at his son. He was nodding.

"Aye, let's talk."

Yuli waited, wondering if his father might begin the conversation. When he did not, Yuli did. "I know nobody knows what all this means, not in the proper sense, but I want to know what it means to you."

"What it means to me?" his father repeated, lines crisscrossing his forehead. "Speak plain, Yuli."

Yuli cleared his throat. "I know it hurts yeh. I hear yeh at night when yer dreamin'." His father's jaw tensed at this, but he did not deny his nightmares. Yuli went on. "Yeh've been distant . . . ."

Even now, Yuli saw his father's attention threaten to wander. He was absently massaging his palm, his eyes gone soft. Yuli waited to see if his father would respond, or if he might lose focus altogether. He was just about to speak again, certain his father would not, when his father's eyes cleared.

"Son," he said, "it is hard to not take this personal. I don't know if I can explain it to yeh or not, but ever'thin' I am is because of the pact. Ever'thin' we are is due to that pact. I don't know who we are now that it's gone. I don't know what . . ." He trailed off, his words growing thin. He swallowed, the knot in his throat bobbing like a large black stone. Then he finished, ". . . any of this means."

Yuli was shaking his head. "No, Father. I don't believe that." His father put his hand on Yuli's shoulder, but Yuli did not stop. "You are who you are 'cause yeh made yerself. I am who I am because I make myself. The pact has been gone most of my life, Father. And we've been fine without it."

His father's hand now clamped down on Yuli's shoulder. There was pain, but only a little.

"Don't speak that," his father said, his voice a forced whisper. "Never say that again, Yuli. Promise me."

Again, Yuli shook his head. "But why, Father?"

"Because the way is the way," his father said.

Yuli felt anger flush his face, but not at his father. Frustrated, Yuli said, "Is that even true?"

He did not want his father to feel disrespected by his words or tone. Yuli loved his father, and he needed to help him find peace after the Dark Wood's decimation. "The way is broken," he said, his voice as gentle as he could muster it. "Yeh said it yerself the mornin' of my kohlas. Yeh've seen it all these years since."

"Boy," his father began, but Yuli went on.

"I mean no disrespect, Father, I promise yeh that. But we don't need the Dark Wood."

"Yuli—"

"We don't need the kohlas to become men. I didn't need it. I'm proof. Look at me—"

"Yuli, please—"

"We are fine, Da'. And we will remain so. Even without the pact, we are—"

Fire sliced the phrase in two, and it fell dead in Yuli's mouth. His father's bare palm, the one he'd been massaging—the one the charred snake had bitten, Yuli realized—had scorched Yuli's face with a slap. Regret and tears filled his father's eyes.

"Yuli," his father said, "my boy . . . I'm sorry."

"I'm fine, Father," Yuli said, swallowing spit and anger. "I know it's hard for you. The pact is all yeh've known, but I lived most of my life with the pact like a filthy stain streaking all our happy moments. Before, we lived in fear that we might not live up to the pact. And since my seventh birthday, we lived in fear that the pact would never mend. But you tell me, Father, why should we care? I don't see how any of it did us any good."

His father's hand clenched into a fist, released, and clenched again. A struggle raged within him, Yuli saw this clearly. He had not meant to blaspheme their faith so completely, but once he began, the words came blazing out of his mouth, almost as if without his consent. His faithlessness would, without doubt, warrant fierce repercussions, and Yuli was not certain his father would withhold punishment. But Yuli's conviction in his words was steadfast.

"Father," he said, trying to take his father's hand into his own to calm him. "Listen to me. If I'm wrong, I'm wrong. I'll admit it freely. But, please, all I'm askin' is that we look at this without our faith gettin' in the way. Without what we believe tellin' us what we see before we even have a chance to see it. Can we do that?" He waited. The tension had not left his father. "Can you do that with me, Father? Will you try?"

His father's eyes squeezed shut. When they opened again, they were red-rimmed and tear-filled. His dark skin twitched on his face. He looked at his son.

"I want to," he said.

Yuli exhaled, relief taking the place of the breath he'd been holding. Before he could say anything, however, the rabbit hutch devolved into chaos. The rabbits—there were seven—began pounding their hind legs against the wooden floor, frenzied. Then one began to scream, its body convulsing.

Yuli looked at his father, who stood, mouth agape, as if in a trance. Turning back to the hutch, Yuli snatched open the gate and yanked out the crate to get to the panic-stricken creature. The other rabbits rushed to the gate, two toppling out before Yuli's father apparently came to his senses and grabbed up these two while holding the others inside. Yuli took hold of the mad rabbit, lifting it gently to see what ailed the creature. One hind paw seemed caught on something. Yuli reached to the leg, brushing the fur out of the way to better see. Heat drained from Yuli's face, settling like embers in his gut. Wide slits had been left between the hutch's floorboards to allow the rabbit pellets to drop onto the ground below, fodder for the chickens. From the space between those boards, two tiny, clawed paws held fast to the rabbit's leg, pulling the foot through the slats, where sharp teeth gnawed on it. A rat.

Yuli pulled the rabbit. The rabbit screamed louder. The rat refused to relent.

"Father!" Yuli cried, but his father only stood next to him, two rabbits in his arm and four more pinned just inside the gate. "Father, help!" he cried, snatching the rabbit away from the rat.

The rabbit flailed in Yuli's arms, smearing blood all over his skin and clothes. Its claws opened bleeding ribbons on Yuli's arms and stomach. Panic once again roused the other rabbits, all but two escaping his father's grip. The hutch shook with the violence of their escape, the offending rat scurrying to the top of the hutch.

Yuli gasped. The rat was large and unafraid, and it was clearly mad. Its fur alternated between raw patches of burned flesh and gory tufts of dried filth. Yuli knew this creature had once lived within the Dark Wood, had survived its burning. He could only guess at what had driven the rat to madness: the fire and smoke or the wood itself. The rat stood on its hind legs, its jaws and claws glistening with rabbit blood, and reached for the rabbit in Yuli's arms. Again, Yuli looked to his father, but his

77

father only stared at the rat. Yuli reached for the knife at his belt. The rat hissed, its body shaking with hunger and anger. Yuli's knife came down, stabbing through the rat's back and driving deep into the wood of the hutch.

"Yuli," his father said, but Yuli was studying the rabbit's foot. "Yuli," his father said again.

"What?" Yuli asked without looking at his father. "Get the rabbits, Da'."

"Yuli!" his father said a third time, this time taking hold of Yuli's arm.

The boy looked at his father, but his father's eyes were turned away. Yuli followed the gaze to find two more rats perched atop the wood pile. They watched Yuli, hissing. A sound drew Yuli's attention to the right. Another rat clawed its way out from underneath an overturned barrel. Yuli took a step backward, his heart thrashing in his chest with the ferocity of a frightened rabbit's hind legs.

Then Yuli's mutt, Torch—named for the bright orange tip of his tail— came running around the barn, his jaws frothing with passion, his hackles raised into spikes along the ridge of his back. The rats took this as a cue to flee, Torch running back and forth between the barrel, the wood pile, and the hutch, sniffing as if he, too, was under a fever.

The rest of that day was spent reinforcing the rabbit hutch. Yuli's mother tended to the wounded rabbit's foot while he and his father added more slats to the bottom and walls of the hutch. The attack lingered in Yuli's chest until long after the sun had set, sleep refusing to come for quite some time. The racket of the rabbit's cries sounded again and again in Yuli's mind. It was perhaps the most horrific sound Yuli had ever heard. It had pealed like a screaming child. The violence done to the rabbit was enough to make Yuli feel sick, and he could not get rid of the image of the rabbit's foot being chewed by the rat. But what made Yuli's stomach yawn wide into a void of fear was the look in the rat's eyes as it perched atop the hutch and demanded Yuli return its prize.

The rat's eyes had been wild, but they had also been aware. For when it had looked at Yuli, Yuli felt the rat's intention. The rat had threatened him, he had no doubt.

Sleep did come in time, though his dreams were red. With sunrise, Yuli was out of bed and heading to the barn with a bucket of slop in one hand—the pigs would have a good meal—and a mug of coffee in the other. He stopped by the rabbit hutch to see how the rabbit's wounds were faring, and he almost dropped his slop bucket. The hutch had been disassembled, wood littering the ground in chunks and splinters. Blood and grimy tufts of rabbit fur covered the floor of the hutch and what remained of its walls. The rabbits were gone.

Sick sprang up and out of Yuli's throat. He stumbled, falling hard against the side of the barn, his mug of coffee slipping from his grip. The tang of blood curdled the morning air, and Yuli knew he would become sick again if he didn't move. A sound drew his attention from the hutch. Dazed, he stumbled around the barn toward the pigsty, but again what he found stopped him where he stood. His palms wept, making the handle of the bucket difficult to grip, and his knees shuddered as if they might buckle beneath him.

Lying belly up in the muddy heart of the sty was their sow. She had been pregnant and could have delivered any day, but now her body was splayed open. Her blood coated the mud beneath her with a glossy sheen. Then Yuli saw the rats. They came out from the shadows beneath the slop trough, climbing on top of the gutted pig's body. They did not move aggressively. Rather, they moved with mild lethargy, slated as they were on pig and rabbit flesh. There were nine that Yuli could see, which meant there were far more he could not see.

"Torch!" Yuli shouted. Leaving the house, he'd stepped over the dog as it slept on the porch, and he needed the dog's volatile energy to scare away the rats just now. "Torch, come, boy!"

He heard the clatter of the dog's claws scraping for purchase on the porch boards. The rats heard, too, and they turned to leave. They did not run. Rather, they sauntered. Only two remained in the bright morning sunshine when Torch came into the sty. Both rats stood on hind legs and turned to face the dog. Torch froze, sniffing the air. Finding his suspicions confirmed, the dog retreated several steps, a soft whine escaping his throat. The rats lowered to all fours and calmly slid into darkness beneath the trough.

Yuli put down the slop bucket. Now that the excitement seemed to have passed, the remaining pigs came out to inspect the bucket, immediately knocking it to its side and feasting on its contents. Yuli stepped to the sow's carcass, nudging it with his boot. A wet gasp ripped through the pig's throat, causing Yuli to cry out. He had assumed the pig dead. By all indications, it should be. Could he dress the beast and salvage the meat, or had the rats poisoned it somehow? Yuli did not know if fevered rats might pass on their sickness to other animals, but his father would.

Except his father provided no insight. Yuli brought his father from the breakfast table, but he only stood, staring as if he'd never seen a pig before. "Father," Yuli said, "should we kill it? Can we eat it?" His father did not answer. The man's eyes looked scorched. His hands trembled. Yuli shook his head. "Help me," he said.

Together, Yuli and his father tried to turn the pig to better study its wounds. The beast's breaths were shallow and ragged. As Yuli pulled the upper half of the animal's body onto its side, the pig spasmed. Its body first became rigid with what Yuli assumed was fright, then it convulsed. Its hind legs kicked into Yuli's father's chest, sending the man onto his back in the mud. Yuli released the pig's body. After several moments, the pig became still once again, even its breath falling so quiet as to be almost undetectable. Yuli looked at his father scrambling to right himself in the mud and then back to the pig. He realized he had to act, that his father would have no sound advice.

Once again, Yuli removed his knife from its sheath. Once again, he used the tool as an instrument of death, but this time, as he sliced the pig's throat, he hoped it was also an instrument of peace.

Yuli helped his father back to the house, the man's chest bleeding slightly from the pig's hooves, and helped him into bed. His own breathing sounded labored, and Yuli hoped the man would recover quickly. From whatever damage may have been caused by the kicking pig, but also of the reverie that seemed to have saturated his father's limbs and mind. Yuli's mother brought his father a cup of hot tea as Yuli went back outside to finish his chores. By the haggard look on his father's face and his jagged breathing, Yuli understood he would have to manage all the day's work himself.

Yuli focused his attention on his tasks. He hoped it might serve as a fair distraction from the problem with the rats and his father's deteriorating wellness, but it didn't. In his head, Yuli believed the mad rats were the result of a life spent within the Dark Wood, being poisoned by its shadows until firelight boiled the poison into madness. This seemed obvious. But in Yuli's gut, he felt a calm certainty that the problem was more than crazed animals forced from the protection of their home, even a dark home like the wood. As much as he wanted to scoff at the notion that the broken pact continued to punish the people in the valley, one phrase blared over and over in his mind: *this must be the broken pact.* The idea stuck to his thoughts like tree sap.

The way had always been the way. He could not argue the people of Gal-Braith had flourished, not even before his seventh birthday, but they had at least lived in a state of relative peace. Having a purpose provided that to people, he thought, at least to an extent. People needed to feel like they had a reason for existing, for waking up each morning and setting their hands to whatever work lay before them. In fact, Yuli feared his people had so longed for such a sense of purpose that perhaps their need had blinded them to an obvious yet somehow obscured truth: the pact had always taken more from them than it gave.

His father had told him when he was six that not all boys returned from their kohlas. This perhaps frightened young Yuli above all as he'd prepared for his quest. However, his father had assured him he would return, that he was a strong and clever boy. Now as a young man, he fretted over how strong and clever he actually was. He felt a bright spark of panic swiftly turning to a flame of conviction in his gut. The Dark Wood, his people's fallen god, had perhaps never been a benevolent god. The way was the way . . . it was, it always had been, and for his entire life, Yuli had been told it would always remain. Even after the wood became violent toward his people and the woodsmen stopped coming for the sons of Gal-Braith, the village folken had clung to the hope that the wood and pact would mend themselves. They had to for the way to remain.

But Yuli feared the way perhaps had never been for them. It seemed possible—probable, even—the way was only meant to subdue them. To somehow hold his people to a flimsy hope of becoming transcendent. And just now, Yuli felt certain the broken pact was not quit of his people. As if they owed an undisclosed debt, one they likely could not afford to pay.

It would do no good to conjecture, but Yuli could not stop his thoughts from wandering over the oft-tread path of speculation. What if he had been able to begin his kohlas as intended on his seventh birthday? Had his birthday been one day sooner, he would have been eaten by the Dark Wood on the following day when the pact had apparently broken. But overlooking this reality, he could not help but play out the things he knew would have—or should have—happened.

Yuli would have spent another seven years or more on his quest, sitting at the feet of the woodsmen for training and counsel. He would have hunted the fabled scarecrow. And after his kohlas was completed, he would have returned home to his family's farm. His father would have been gone by then, though he had never been able to explain where he would have gone or why. His father believed the final act of a man's kohlas took place on the day his son completed his quest. His father would once again have communed within the shadows of the Dark Wood, perhaps in the heart of the place. A sacred spot with a bleeding stone, his father had called the place a dun-twille. Whatever this final act might be, the sons who returned to the valley returned to empty homes. They would mend the farm, find a wife, father a son, and perpetuate the cycle. Had Yuli completed his kohlas, he would have eventually taken his own seven-year-old son to the fence surrounding the forest, entrusting the boy to the care and tutelage of the woodsmen. And by the time his son's quest was completed, Yuli would have gone the way of all fathers before him.

And what did his people glean from this arrangement? Each new generation of sons came home to cottages bereft of family and committed their lives to bringing the next generation of sons into the valley. The pact was not just difficult, it was pointless. So far as Yuli could see, it robbed his people of so much.

And where were the woodsmen now? If his father's stories were to be believed, the same woodsmen had served the valley for so many generations back and back as to suggest they had always been a part of the way. They must be immortal then, or else fayelee besides. So where were they now? Had they died? Had they abandoned the people of Gal-Braith because of some unknown slight the valley folken had committed against the way?

Shaking his head of these thoughts, Yuli put away his tools, his body aching all over, and went inside the house, Torch bounding at his heels. He looked in on his father. The man slept fitfully, buried beneath a mound of blankets. A fire burned in the kitchen hearth even though the weather outside was mild. The inside of the house was stagnant with heat, and Yuli had to step outside to breathe.

He drew well water into a pail and used a ladle to drink from it. His eyes scanned the falling darkness for rats. He'd seen no sign of them since that morning in the pigsty, but he knew they must be around. He could not shake the suspicion that the rats had a plan. The way the first one had looked at him. The way the others had seemed unafraid. No, Yuli knew he had not seen the last of the rats, but perhaps they would bide their time. Perhaps Yuli would sleep that night. He was desperate for rest. He returned the pail and ladle to their hooks next to the pump and turned back for the house. Torch, who had been licking himself on the porch, stood, waiting for Yuli to open the door so they could step inside.

The mule's bray cut through the night like a warm knife through fresh bread, sending Yuli's skin into fields of gooseflesh. Torch let out toward the sound before Yuli could stop him. He stepped inside the house, grabbing his hatchet and a lantern, then went after his dog. Yuli knew the mule would be dead before he reached it.

On that last count, however, Yuli was wrong. When he came within sight of the mule, the animal was fighting to stay upright. Its braying rose in a sharp crescendo as a shadow engulfed the beast. Yuli did not understand, not at first. Not until Torch, who had been circling the struggling beast, leapt at the darkness. That's when Yuli watched part of the darkness break away, falling apart into individual bodies of sleek, seething rats. They were on Torch before the dog could change course. The dog's growls turned to yips and then howls of pain.

Yuli threw his hatchet, overcome with revulsion and concern for his dog. Just as Torch disappeared in the writhing mass and the mule succumbed to the hoard of rats, Yuli saw a broken rat body fly, carried forth by the momentum of his hatchet. The rat mass suddenly went still. Even in the near darkness, Yuli felt an infinity of black orbs staring at him from within the mad rats' fevered skulls. For several moments, the only sound was Yuli's breathing.

Then the mass shifted. It spread from a seething mound of rats into a swift wave of them, and it sped toward Yuli. He lifted the lantern overhead and threw it. It hit the hard earth just in front of the horde, the glass shattering and the oil scattering flame in a wide spray. In the flare of firelight, Yuli saw the rats' faces. Their collective hissing raised into the night sky, and just like when Yuli had seen the Dark Wood come alive on his seventh birthday, once again he filled his breeches with warmth. But the flames slowed the advancing rat army, and this provided Yuli with a chance of reaching the cottage door before them.

He ran to save his life. Whether it was imagination or truth, Yuli felt certain he heard the rats behind him, their countless clawed feet making the sound of heavy rain as they came at him. He reached the porch, knowing the rats would take him soon. His fingers found the knob, and he pulled just as teeth bit into the flesh of his ankle. Yuli cried out as he fell across the threshold. A rat clamped onto his ankle, and two more clawed at his pant legs. He scrambled inside and slammed the door shut as the seething mass beyond it moved like a flood to engulf the house. Yuli bolted the door, kicking at the rat on his ankle.

A second rat, one of the two that made it inside before he could shut the door, scampered up his pant leg to sink its teeth into Yuli's thigh. He grabbed the rat by the head and pulled. With both hands, he gripped the creature, squeezing and twisting it the way he might a wet, dirty towel. The body broke and tore in his grip, gore spilling over his fingers and falling to the floor. He dropped the carcass and stomped the rat at his ankle. He felt the creature's teeth rip his flesh as they pulled free, but he also felt the rat's body crunch beneath the force of his foot. He kept stomping until the rat was little more than a furry blood stain on the floor.

Yuli took in the room. His mother stood in the open doorway of his parents' bedroom, her hands to her mouth and panic in her eyes. Yuli looked at the door he'd just shut. It appeared to be holding against the onslaught of rats outside it, but he did not know how long it might. Countless claws scraped at the wood. They would make it through in time. His frantic mind threw a nonsensical question up: what was a collective of rats this size called? He shook away the ridiculous thought and looked to the hearth and the fire burning within it. He looked at the other door, the front door on the far side of the house. He went and bolted it. He studied the shadows beneath the table and chairs, the hatch to the root cellar, the bread pantry . . . . Besides the sound of the rats outside the door and the cheerful pops and cracks of the fire, the house was still. Lanterns filled the space with warm light, but they also cast shadows deep enough to provide cover. This troubled Yuli, for he felt certain three rats had made it inside the house. He had killed only two. Where was the third?

He scanned the room again.

"Yuli," his mother began, but he shushed her quiet. He needed to think.

The room was empty, but the world outside was not. He saw rats outside the windows scurrying along the sills, their tiny claws seeking to dislodge the panes. He heard them on the roof just then, and his attention turned to the hearth. He had to close the flue. He ran to the fire, reaching his arm inside the hearth. The stonework was hot and burned his skin, but he tried to ignore this. His fingers at last found the mechanism, and he pulled it, the heavy metal grate falling into place inside the chimney, shutting off the flue from the outside. He pulled his arm free, his skin blistering already along his forearm and palm.

The third rat found Yuli then, falling on his shoulders from the rafters above. Its teeth bit into Yuli's neck, and his mother began screaming. She came at Yuli with a broom, swinging it at the rat biting and clawing at his neck. The wooden handle struck Yuli's head and neck and, finally, the rat. It fell to the ground and flew out of sight. Crying out, her words incoherent, Yuli's mother came to him, her fingers probing his bleeding neck.

The cottage rattled as if a bull had rammed it from the outside. Yuli turned to the door. The cottage shook again, and this time he saw the bolt shake loose. The house shook again, and the bolt slid. The house shook yet again, and the bolt fell free of the door. Yuli leapt for the door, falling upon it and sliding down to the ground, his body trembling against the onslaught from outside as he held it shut. He felt the door threatening to open, felt the hoard of rodents on the other side of it pressing to get in.

"Mother," he cried. "The bolt! Replace the bolt!"

She came to him, her eyes wild, and lifted the bolt to replace it, but the rat leapt from the table then, landing on his mother's chest. He saw with horror as it bit into his mother's breast. The woman screamed, slapping at the rat and swinging the bolt wildly through the air. The wood caught Yuli on his head, and for a moment, he feared the blackness at his peripheral vision would fill his sight and he would fall unconscious. He shook his head while his mother fought against the rat, blood pouring down the front of her nightgown. She ran, screaming and slapping at the rat, the heavy wooden bolt falling to the floor. Yuli wanted to go to her, tried to reach the bolt with his foot, felt the door shuttering behind him. If he went for the bolt, the rats outside would certainly come through the door. If he did not, his mother would continue to be ravaged by the rat inside. Then he remembered how the rats had stopped at the explosion of fire from the lantern.

"The hearth!" he screamed. "Ma! Use the fire!"

Whether his mom understood, he could not say, but she ran for the fireplace. The rat was now chewing at her neck. She took only a handful of steps before her shin caught a chair and her body went sprawling. She fell, her head cracking against the stone of the hearth with a sickening pop. He watched in horror as her body fell limp to the floor, her head and shoulders landing in the hearth. She did not move as flames turned her hair and gown into a glowing halo of fire.

Yuli wanted to scream, but he couldn't. The rat that had attacked his mother now gnawed on her heel, but it kept wary eyes trained on the fire festooning the fallen woman's upper body. Tears burned Yuli's eyes. He was going to die. His mother was dead already, or he hoped she was. And his father—Yuli had forgotten about his father. Was the man still asleep after all that had happened? Could he have slept through the screams?

"Da'!" Yuli called, and then again.

The door to his parents' bedroom remained open, a lantern burning just beyond it. He saw the bed, but he did not see the mound of blankets where his father's body should be. That's when the man shuffled into view from the bedroom. He made no sign that he saw or understood the calamity that had befallen his wife and son. His eyes were set in hollow sockets, his cheeks deflated and sagging as if melting from his face. How had he gotten so bad so quickly? Yuli could not say, and he did not have time to ponder it further, for just then he realized what his father meant to do.

"Father, don't!" Yuli screamed, but the man went to the other door and removed the bolt. "No!" Yuli cried.

He watched his father grip the doorknob and pull the door open. He watched his father step through the door into the full dark of night outside it. He watched as nothing happened. For several agonizing moments, Yuli waited for the hoard to come in. Fire had licked more than halfway down his mother's body, the rat still chewing away on the bottom of her foot, but the light did not illuminate the darkness in which his father stood.

Carefully, Yuli slid to his feet, keeping the door at his back pressed firmly shut. But even the door had seemed to still, the fighting rats beyond it having calmed. Yuli needed to see his father. He needed to understand what was happening. He still could not reach the bolt, but he could reach a chair. He jammed the chair beneath the doorknob and took a lantern from the kitchen table. Firelight now made the walls of the cottage shift and jump as if coming alive, but Yuli needed the light to illuminate the porch at the front of the house. He needed to see his father.

He stepped closer to the front door, one step, then another. It was dark outside, but he could make out the silhouette of his father's form. He was a hulking man just beyond the reach of the lantern light. Yuli took another step closer. His father stepped back through the door, and Yuli screamed. The silhouette had had the shape of his father, but now Yuli realized it wasn't just the darkness of night that had covered his father's form: it was rats. They covered the man like a hooded robe, crawling and quivering, their pink, charred tails whipping about him like thirsty tongues.

Then the mass collapsed, the body within it separating in bloody chunks as if some magic thread had been pulled, all of its pieces now falling apart. Yuli threw the lantern at the floor in front of what had been his father. The oil scattered along the floorboards and the wall on either side of the open door, fire spreading in a violent crescent. Again, the house shook. Yuli looked at the door he'd held against the maddened mischief beyond it, and the house shook again. The chair faltered. Yuli ran for his parents' bedroom, reaching the doorway just as the chair fell and the back door swung open.

Yuli took up the final lantern from inside his parents' room and held it aloft. Rats filled the house, but none approached him. The smell of burning hair and meat scorched Yuli's eyes and nostrils. A strange sound squeezed its way from his chest, up his throat and out of his mouth. He was laughing, he realized. Maniacal, he screamed laughter. The rats only watched as Yuli threw the lantern on the floor in front of him, the burning oil spraying out in a fan of flame. Yuli backed into his parents' room, his laughter ripping his throat into shreds even as smoke scalded his lungs. He shut the door.

As smoke poured beneath the door to his parents' bedroom, Yuli continued laughing. He had the strangest thought as he slid to the ground, his laughter turning to choking in his constricted throat: perhaps he had been arrogant to assume he'd grown to manhood well enough, for no man would laugh as his mother's body burned to cinders in the next room, as his father's bones were picked clean, as his home fell down around his own head. But laughter was all Yuli could manage just then. As flames burned their way around the closed door, he laughed.

He laughed until smoke sealed his lungs shut.

Then he died.

Author's Note

On the surface, this story answers a very simple question: what happened to Gal-Braith in the aftermath of Eliot's story? For clarification, Yuli's seventh birthday coincided with the culmination of Eliot's kohlas at the end of *Scarecrow*. Again we see the threads of cause and effect at play here. The breakdown of the pact would have had a potentially devastating impact on the community of Gal-Braith. I was curious to travel back to the valley and see what had changed.

Beyond this premise, the story is a contemplative look at how communities—whether a small village like Gal-Braith or groups that span entire worlds, ours included—can be inextricably shaped by their faith. Religious beliefs can inform a group with a code of ethics that lead them to strive toward transcendent excellence, or their unchallenged convictions can lead to aggression, exclusivity, and entitled judgment, ultimately undoing the principles on which the religion was built. In my experience, these beliefs are often based on the culture into which a person is born rather than deep speculation or introspection, more often a matter of chance rather than educated choice. Yet many fervent believers *know* without doubt that their beliefs are the most correct out of all the others in their world. The same is often true with patriotism or political leanings—anything to which people may cling with blind passion. The identifying factors within those deeply held convictions become lenses through which adherents view the world around them, so what happens when those lenses are violently shattered? How does one cope when such a major part of their identity has been stripped away without explanation? That premise is what this story explores.

PARSIMONIOUS

Being goodhearted don't make a man wise. Know you this? A man's intent reveals the color of his heart, but good intentions do not guarantee wholesome yields. Mark that truth and hold it close, for it is the bitter reality of Red's tale.

Babbies were often left at the front gate of the orphanage. Folken have endless reasons why they might do such a thing . . . abandon a child. Sometimes poor mountain folken couldn't afford to feed another body. In those cases, the babbies were better off without a family rather than starving to death. Sometimes the mother died during childbirth and the father was too bereft—or too lazy—to care for the child on his own. Sometimes the babbie were sickly, and the parents hoped the khamun could heal it, or, leastways, handle it. But you and I know sometimes the child simply was not wanted. Do we have place to judge? No, but we do anyway, don't we? Aye, we judge right well. Red did not know why he was left at the gate of the orphanage, only that he was left.

The orphanage was a simple place, though not in a simple location, nestled as it was in an ancient wood in the rolling foothills of the broader mountains. It was isolated from the surrounding world, though there was a village near enough for supplies and news. The khamun who tended those lost children communed with the forest, trusting it for protection and guidance. These holy men taught the children about all things. About the Hidain and moon cycles. About cooking and cleaning. About gardening. Practical skills needed to grow up and be strong menfolken and womenfolken, loving spouses, and good parents. They loved the children in their care. Truly.

Our boy, like so many of the orphans, did not know who his true parents were. However, Red was not like the other children in appearance or nature. For one thing, his hair was a shocking shade of red, a trait uncommon in the region: that is why the other children called him Red. Perhaps his parents came from another land and were trekking to some distant place: a babbie would be most unwelcome under such circumstances. Perhaps they'd traveled far and settled near the village of Traigen, only the move had taken their wealth, and they couldn't afford a newborn just then. Red could only speculate.

His hair color made him stand out from the others, and this distinction, as is normal with children, made him an object of scorn. No doubt you know how cruel children can be. Despising people who look or sound different is an instinct, wouldn't you agree? At best, the other children saw Red as someone who was not like them. At worst, someone to be ridiculed. That is how Red became fascinated with firesprites.

Of all the khamun in the orphanage, one man took particular interest in our boy. Red did not know his true name, but the children called him Pepper. Pepper was a fat man who hadn't fit in as a chubby child. His nose had always been a bit too big and far too round. His feet had been heavy and clumsy. And his belly had always gone before him into any room. When he began to sprout hairs under his arms and between his legs, his face blossomed into oily fields of seeping pustules. It had been littered with bleeding pimples he'd scratched and popped until they left him scarred. Yes, he had been scorned for all of his young life. Weren't we all? Mayhap. But Pepper refused to let this malfeasance turn him bitter. Pepper instead followed higher pursuits, dedicating his life to service. Thus, he came to the orphanage as a khamun.

"Think of the firesprites," he would say whenever Red's tears came. Pepper saw much of himself in the red-haired boy, I think. "Think of the firesprites and remember who you are. You are lovely and brave, and what marks you as different also marks you as special."

At his core, he was a curious child. Even more so than most. The child asked endless questions about the sprites. Do they eat? Do they sleep? Do they have names? Ever patient, Pepper answered these questions as best he could. Yes, they eat. Yes, they sleep. No, they do not have proper names. Instead, they have an essence—an ehwain, mayhap—that is unique and special. The sprites know one another by these.

Red would listen, rapt. It came into the child's mind he should find a firesprite. If he and the faye were so very alike, their meeting seemed necessary and inevitable. The hoary forest surrounding the orphanage, the khamun had assured him, was full of the enchanting little creatures. But any time the boy talked of finding one, the fat man only laughed. It was a laugh that suggested one day, when the child was all grown up, they would no longer believe in such silly, childish things. Is this true? Mayhap. But how many stupid, childish adults do you know? Grown folken have a knack for being self-centered. Is that not the most childish thing of all? Even the selfless khamun of the orphanage—including our favorite, Pepper—were selfish adults. Did Pepper not choose a life of servitude to compensate for his inadequacies and rejection growing up? Was his service to Red and the other children not a desperate attempt to feel better about himself?

I know. I am jaded. You would be too if you knew what I know, and soon you will. But make no mistake here: Pepper was a good man. Through and through, he was decent and kind. A better man would be hard to find, but, mind you, don't forget: being good don't make a man wise.

In any case, Pepper and Red spoke at length on the firesprites. And Red, being a greedy boy, wanted one for himself. And why not? He wanted to love and cherish it. Much like the khamun's service, Red wanted to serve the little faye creature. What child wouldn't? Having a firesprite all to himself would make him privileged beyond his imagination. And so important! The sprites were keepers of the natural world, and if he was a keeper of a keeper, would that not make him transcendent? That's how Red saw things. Did it matter that Red's motivation was a selfish one so long as he meant no harm? Is doing a good thing for the wrong reason the wrong thing to do?

"Aye," Pepper would say to Red when the boy insisted he must have a firesprite for himself. "If any child could see a firesprite, it would be you."

"Have you ever seen one, hommie?" the child asked the man, for that is what the children called the ascetic khamun.

"No," Pepper said. But with a smile that seemed mischievous for a holy man, he added, "Not 'sides you, leastways."

Oh, how Red loved this. To see himself as a creature of the forest, and not only, but also a faye, made him very happy. It was nonsense, of course: he was just a boy. Sure, he had a touch of otherness about him, and not just in his appearance. There was a sterling quality in his ehwain, a webwork of magic . . . or leastways, the possibility of it. But Red did not know this. Nor did Pepper.

Pepper was a smart man even if his heart was too big and sometimes made him stupid. But he warned Red against seeking out the firesprites. Mayhap that's not quite true. He warned Red that seeing a firesprite would be nearly impossible. It takes years to learn how to see the faye creatures who live in the world with us, even if you are born with the gift of sight. Without the gift, you might spend a lifetime dedicating yourself to spiritual things and never attain the capacity to see. Most of the khamun at the orphanage were this latter way. They believed in spirit things, but they saw little evidence of them. Their faith, however, was proof enough for their ilk. And though this is not an entirely dubious trait, I think you can spy what makes such faith problematic.

Furthermore, Pepper explained to Red the sprites were wild things. And wild things are unpredictable at best. They aren't meant to be kept as pets, and they need no folken protection. Anywhat, Pepper tried to explain to Red just how unlikely it was the boy would ever see a sprite. And worse, even if he did, he could not possibly catch one. Pepper believed this. Had he not, mayhap he could have better served our boy. Because Red was a greedy child. And even a greedy boy who is also good may yet prove risky. What Pepper did not think to do was warn Red that firesprites could be very dangerous. Something you cannot see—much less touch—can do little harm, after all.

My point is, Pepper taught Red all about the creatures . . . he just didn't teach him about the risks. He saw no need. Ever vigilant, Red explored the surrounding woods to spot a firesprite. Red knew the spores of firesprites were birthed en masse in the spring. He knew they would float for a couple of weeks and then crystalize to form chrysalises. He knew that one year later, these would hatch. What he could not comprehend at the time was that firesprites, being wild creatures, were at best unsuited for cohabitation with a boyfolken. At worst, the beautiful, enchanting beings could be quite deadly. To call firesprites good would be to misunderstand them entirely. They are neither good nor bad. Like children, they obey instinct, and if their instinct tells them someone is a threat, they will not be good at all.

But why would the boy with red hair—so very much like a firesprite himself—ever appear threatening to the glowing faye?

When spring arrived that year, the boy spent all his free time, and a good portion of his chore time, surveying the surrounding forest. On one cloudy morning, when all the children had been released from their chores to celebrate Lunauinbroc, Red began his explorations. At the orphanage, the khamun celebrated the Hidain after the old fashion. As such, the celebration of Lunauinbroc began weeks before the day and culminated with the festival itself. Not only did the break proffer the boy an opportunity to explore the old forest, but it also increased his chances of seeing a firesprite.

What the boy did not know was that the season was a tweeny time. The forest itself, old and knowing, was a tweeny place. The boy's curiosity and faith had made him, after a fashion, a tweeny himself. Even had the boy understood these things, he would not have known the overcast sky would grow into a storm and the day would venture into dusk before his adventure was spent. That both storms and dusk—the shedding of day and donning of night—were tweeny times. Transitions . . . the space between spaces. The time between times.

As each tweeny layer met, the scrim between worlds grew thinner and thinner—until the veil was little more than breath.

A leetide.

Functioning similar to pitfalls in a forest, or holes washed in sea stone, a leetide is an opening that can be stepped into. Fallen through. Or worse. Like a rip but unfixed. A folken can slide between worlds without even knowing it, though only those with a touch of tweeny themselves.

In short, the little boy with fire-red hair, who believed himself kindred to the firesprites of the forest, did not know that he was stumbling into a leetide. Had he known this and understood its full meaning, perhaps many things that came to be would not have, and our little boy would have found happiness. As it happened, and as you must have already guessed, things turned out differently.

The fire-headed boy left the orphanage grounds, eager to begin anew his search for a firesprite. He had looked before, but something felt different this day. Truth be told, every adventure felt special to the boy, as they do to all little boys. But today was very special indeed. He climbed into the trees to search. He crawled across boulders, through burrows and scrapes. He explored along the river's edge. The river was fat from the melting snows of winter, so the boy was even more cautious than usual when he tried to cross. Yes, he only tried. Red did not succeed.

A thick mossy trunk lay across the river, a rawboned remnant of the mighty tree it once had been. The boy crawled the length of the trunk on his hands and knees. It was wide enough to walk across, but the boy was afraid of high places, and the tree trunk was at least a tall man's height above the river. Red's caution was not enough, however. The bark beneath him went loose. A chunk dislodged, and the boy fell. He was a good swimmer, but the current was strong. It pulled him along for what seemed an age before Red was able to crawl up on the bank.

There, in a pool of unfiltered sunshine, he stretched himself on the ground to rest and dry. That is how he came to sleep in a new part of the forest, one he'd never before visited. And that is why he didn't take note of the coming storm or the ebbing day. Ah, the reckless wonder of boyhood. When every moment is fringed with adventure, every shadow a secret to explore. If that wonder had a name, it would be Red.

We can all reckon that by the time the boy awoke, it was a tweeny time. And not just, but a stacking of tweeny times. The coming storm. The ancient forest. The coming dusk. The changing season and the approaching Hidain. And not the least of factors, the boy's own wonder and expectation.

When first he opened his eyes, just a crack, Red thought he was dreaming. The surrounding forest was alight with fireflies. Huge ones. Hundreds of them. Thousands, even. The boy sat up, rubbing his eyes with his palms. Sleep still hung over his thoughts like webbing. No, he realized, this was not his imagination. The fireflies were everywhere, and they were huge. They were bigger than his fist. Bigger than fireflies. And fireflies blink. These did not.

He jumped to his feet and looked closer. Could it be? Yes. Red was surrounded by the glowing orbs of firesprite spores. Distantly, through the canopy of tree limbs above him, he saw other lights. He knew these must be firesprites, fully formed. Unlike the floating spores, the firesprites kept their distance from the boy, but that was okay.

Red reached out his hand, now sweaty with excitement and anticipation, and cupped one of the spores. That quickly, and with no fanfare other than his own beating heart, he had hold of a talismanic treasure. He closed his fist and tucked the glowing, magical thing into a pocket in the folds of his robe. Having accomplished far more than he had hoped when first he entered the wizened forest—for his hope had been no bigger than to glimpse a single firesprite, not to swim through a sea of them, not to hold one in his warm little palm—he lost interest in the wonder around him and instead turned his thoughts to home. The storm, which had silently crept in while he slept, now fussed and growled. It was ready to release an angry deluge, and he was far from the orphanage. Light was fading, and even the bravest little boy is afraid of being lost in the dark.

As he fled in search of a way back, he patted the hidden pocket where the magic thing waited. As Red walked, he woke more fully into consciousness. At times he wondered if he had witnessed the spores in the forest at all, or the wary sprites keeping their distance in the trees. Perhaps he had dreamed them. His hand never left the pocket where he hid the glowing orb, but he wondered over it.

He followed the river up and up, higher into the foothills, until he came to a spot he recognized. Had it been any darker, he may have missed it. He had returned to the log he'd failed to cross. Thankfully, he had pulled himself out of the thrashing river on the correct side. He headed for home, where a rain-wet and anxious party was searching for him.

Having been found, our boy was lightly reprimanded. Mostly, he was hugged and patted on the back. The fat old khamun gave him a warm, dry blanket, a large bowl of hot broth, and a huge chunk of the day's bread, considerably more than his normal portion. Pepper favored the boy, it's true. And with those things, Red was encouraged to go straight to his bed, to eat his supper, and to go to sleep. He needed rest.

But the boy would have none of that. And you knew that already, didn't you?

Red had to know. He had to see for himself if it had been a dream. He went to the room he shared with several other boys roughly his own age, but he didn't go inside. His room was the first at the top of the stairs. Right next to this door was a door that led to the attic. He opened the attic door and began the short flight into the dusty space beneath the rafters, but he did not climb to the top. Two-thirds of the way up was another door, one very small. A hatch, really. But it was large enough for a boy his size to climb through. He opened this little door, placed his supper inside it, and then pulled himself up and in. This was his most favorite, most secret place. His magical mezzanine.

He crawled down a short corridor till he came to his private space, a hidden alcove above the attic stairs. There, he lit a candle. The walls, covered by his fanciful drawings, became visible in the orange light. Also now visible was his collection of toadstools and magpie feathers, a small smooth stone with veins of gold crisscrossing it, and even a divining rod made of aspen—one he believed he would wield someday to grand effect. There were snake skins and locust husks. He even had a dried up gindy wasp, kept in a jar just to be safe. Sauingrey fricks hung in the corners, adorned with dust and cobwebs like grave clothes. Hidain lamps stolen from the attic were scattered among his things, a few with candles. Red lit these, too. He even had an embers pot—one the khamun had searched for during Feilebroc past, scratching their heads over the mystery of where it might have disappeared to. Remember I said Red was a greedy boy? All boys are. In short, all of his favorite possessions were on display in his private room, a little boy's trove of secret treasures. In one corner, he had arranged a small bed of straw covered with a threadbare blanket. Beside it was a little wooden chest, its heart filled with shiny, secret things. Things that made Red smile when he held them in his palms. He pulled himself onto the bed and drew the hood of his robe up over his head. Cautiously—reverently, even—he reached inside the inner pocket. From there, he pulled out a small glowing orb, and his heart filled to bursting.

He hadn't imagined it.

Within a week, the spore began spooling itself with silver webbing, tucking itself away in a protective cocoon inside Red's cloak. Our fire-haired boy visited the crystal chrysalis every day after that, taking it from its hidey hole and stroking it with the affections of a lover. He'd kiss it and whisper to it. Then he'd tuck it away again. As the sprite pupated, it did what firesprites do: it took on the vitality of the thing to which it was most connected . . . our boy. But Red was going through changes of his own. He'd reached his change—the slow process when his own body began losing its boyhood and taking on manhood—years sooner than many of the other boys and girls his own age. A changeling himself, the boy was becoming more and more open to the world around him. More and more open, though he didn't know it yet, to the gifts that had waited patiently since his birth for his quickening. For the child was no mere child. As I mentioned, he had the touch of magic.

As time passed, the firesprite fed on this magic. It became confused. Disoriented, as it were. It was, after all, stolen from its natural world—and not Red's world, mind you, but an adjacent world—and thrust into another.

What Red could not know was that he had fallen farther than from the log to the river that tweeny night. He had slipped through a thinned veil into another layer of the world—one with slightly different rules from his own. The firesprites he spied in the forest were not quite the same as those he might have seen in the lofty trees outside his bedroom window. This firesprite did not belong with our boy. It did not belong in the attic. It did not belong in this realm.

A full year passed. On festival day, Red removed the firesprite from the attic for the first time. It was a glorious thing that looked hot enough to scald away our boy's skin, yet cool to touch, and refreshingly so. Lunauinbroc was here. There was a malkein moon besides. And the boy himself was a tweeny, a khamun just coming into his potency. This was another stacking . . . a stronger leetide than even the year before. But our boy did not know. No one knew.

The orphans sang songs celebrating the season. Small fires had been built in a circle around a larger bonfire. The children and khamun danced around these smaller flames, many holding aloft Hidain lamps burning with incense and spiced wax. Others held sticks fitted with brightly colored ribbons that whipped and danced behind them in long colorful trails.

Red raced into the throng of children, cupping the bulge in his coat pocket where the firesprite curled. Jubilant cries and laughter lifted into the tree branches above where sconces with sputtering candles hung. A group of khamun plucked at stringed instruments. Smoke from stone ovens filled the yard with the delectable scents of roasting meats and vegetables. The fire-haired boy felt elated. He felt electricity ringing his fingers. He felt transcendent, after all. Perhaps that is why he didn't see the other two boys. The three collided and fell in a heap, squeals of laughter peeling from their open mouths. Our boy stood again, helping the other two to their feet. At first, Red did not see what had changed. He could not tell the firesprite had left his pocket. In fact, he was so taken by the celebration that he'd forgotten about the creature secreted away in his coat. Just for a moment, mind you. Then he remembered and panicked. He felt for it, his hands frantically checking his body, but the firesprite was gone. Eyes wild, our boy searched the ground where he'd fallen, but he could not find it. Not at first.

Then he saw something not quite right in the frenetic celebration around him. One of the boys he'd fallen with had stopped playing—stopped moving altogether—his back to Red. Our boy walked around to ask the other child if he'd seen anything, but there was no need for questions.

Here was the firesprite, flitting in front of the boy's face. The boy's jaw was slack, drool slipping from one corner of his mouth. Red reached, but just before his fingers took hold of the sprite, the burning little creature slipped in through the other boy's eye and disappeared inside his head.

Red froze. What should he do? No one knew he had a firesprite. Had he not wanted to keep the faye creature all to himself, he would still have been unlikely to share its secret. For one, no one would believe him. Instead, they would laugh at him. Except, perhaps, Pepper. For two, something in his gut told him he shouldn't keep a wild creature locked away in the attic. Somehow, he understood that was not good for the sprite, but greedy boys excel at justifying bad behavior. Still, Red was also a good and loving boy. He meant no harm, and he believed himself truly kindred to the firesprites of the forest. They were keepers and protectors. Mayhap he, too, was the same. But now he'd watched as his little friend burrowed its way into another boy's skull through his eye socket. Red peed his pants right then and there. And for shame, his immediate concern was that the other children would see and laugh. Except the children would not laugh for long.

A flash caught our boy's attention, and he saw the sprite zip out of the boy's head to find the other boy involved in their tussle. But all around them, children were racing. Confused, the firesprite threaded its way in and out of the children's heads, one by one. In through an eyeball here, out through a nostril there. An ear. A mouth. Each child went stupid as the sprite scrambled their brains. They did not scream or panic, rather seeming unharmed on the outside. They became simple, their eyes dulled and their mouths gaped. Alarmed, our fire-haired boy went straightaway to Pepper. It was time he must tell secret truths. Pepper had been more like a father to him than all the other khamun. But how could Red explain what was happening? How would Pepper receive the news? It made no matter, for Pepper would know what to do. Or leastways, one among the khamun must. That was their job, after all.

A scream stopped Red. He turned to see the first boy standing on the lip of the well, peering down into its murky depths. Then the boy fell into the well without making a sound. But others—those apparently unaffected by the sprite—had seen and screamed. Still others had climbed their way to the tip-top of the temple and threw themselves from its highest wall to soar into the valley beyond. Red understood these children were dead—or would be soon enough, yet he could not help finding the sight of them soaring above the trees a lovely thing. Others had dropped their fire sticks to sizzle in the grass and began moving, as if in a dream, for the forest. The khamun, now alert and alarmed, joined hands in small circles throughout the yard, calling for assistance from the forest and its keepers. But our boy somehow understood this wasn't the answer. And he understood that even the khamun, with their faith and sight, could not see what he saw. For out from the forest came a host of flames: fist-sized torches with arms, legs, and faces rigid with purpose, each one intent to answer the call. Each one ready to defend and protect: an army of firesprites . . . . And here they found one of their own, already about the work of protecting their home. The forest. The trees and grass. The water in well and river.

They moved swiftly, flooding the open yard with warm light only Red could see. They each found a child or khamun, sliding in through the eyes, ears, noses, and mouths to commingle with the minds behind them. And each person—child and khamun alike—fell dumb.

Listen to me, I beg you. Listen and believe I mean you no harm in telling this tale. And I know you will be tempted to assume it is a babbie's tale, and nothing more. That it is folkenlore. A regional legend to explain a natural phenomenon or an abandoned orphanage hidden in the mountain folds above Traigen. For all abandoned buildings are filled with ghosts, aye? Except, sometimes they are. I cannot say the orphanage—or what little remains of it—is haunted, but I can tell you our boy was. Red was haunted by what he saw that day. Yes, he lived. And that was the worst part.

Our fire-haired boy took in the yard. So many firesprites had issued from the forest, there seemed a bushel took up residence in each and every skull . . . save for Red's. Remember, his firesprite had spent a year absorbing Red's ehwain into itself. This is the way: if a spore alights upon a tree, it absorbs the tree's energy. Those who pupate beneath the water absorb the current and flow of the river. Those who spend a year among mossy stones will feel most kindred to the moss and stones of the forest. And Red's firesprite felt kindred to Red. The other sprites followed its lead. So Red was never in danger. But the others—the children and their guardians— died, each one to the last. Not for malice, but misunderstanding. For the firesprites were not malevolent. They simply did not understand the spectacle. They knew nothing of folken or the games of children.

Pepper was perhaps the most difficult for Red to watch. The fat man shuffled through the yard toward the chapel, whose tower made the perfect launching point into the valley below, only he shuffled his way through one of the fires burning in a low pit. His trouser legs caught, but this did not stop him. As he entered the chapel and climbed the staircase to the towerhead, the flames spread. By the time he leapt—ironically, very much like a firesprite himself, gilded as he was by flame—the chapel surged with smoke and fire. Only the stonework would remain standing after.

I know you do not blame Red. I do. I blame him, but I believe his restitution was equal to his offense, or as close as it might get. Because he lived. And even after he stopped living, he could not rid himself of his guilt. It plagued him through his life and beyond it. As if his broken heart and his grief wrapped him in a dark approximation of a firesprite's chrysalis. Except his was a death shroud, but even death did not save him. Rather, it released him . . . dumping him into some in-between. A melancholy shade haunted by his truths. No matter if abandoned places are haunted for true in our world, they are in his.

Author's Note

The inspiration for this story came as I was writing the first draft of *The Singing Bones.* My friend Logan—before he became my illustrator—had drawn a floating man with what appeared to be flaming hair. I loved the imagery, and I felt there must be a fascinating backstory. I'd gotten Grey and her friends very near to the village of Traigen in *The Singing Bones.* They met a stranger in the mountains outside the village who told them about creatures inspired by Logan's illustration. Grey, Fenn, and Pedorah's excursion off-path inside Sol's hut became one of my favorite scenes in *Bones.*

II

PART TWO: SCENES

The following chapters provide deeper insight into the primary books' main characters and could perhaps fit as scenes within those novels. However, they are meant to be enjoyed regardless of whether you have read the novels in the series. To help you understand where these scenes take place regarding the main books, I have included time references in the author's note following each scene.

THE WAY IS THE WAY

Asha woke to a band of sunlight beaming between the curtains. He pulled on his breeches, his boots, and a shirt, worn but clean. In the kitchen, he put coffee to percolate on the stove and ripped a hunk of stale bread off the last loaf in the trunk pantry. He ate his breakfast in silence: bread and goat cheese, sliced tomatoes and black coffee. A small cup of warm cream to wash it all down.

Fastening his belt around his waist, one he used for tools—the only tool it bore now was a small knife—he walked out into the spring day, the sun shining and the birds festive. He ducked into the barn, then the chicken coup. All was well. Merle, the old man one farm over, would be by in a day or two, three at the most. Likely with one of his old wife's loaves in hand. Merle could tend to the animals. They had water, hay, and feed, plenty for the time being.

Asha walked back into the sunlight, the day already warm. It would be hot by midday. No need to linger. He checked again the door of the cottage. Old habits were hard to quit. It was fastened shut. It had no lock, but the catch would hold against an early summer storm. That would do. Then he turned toward the hill and the derelict fence at its feet.

His legs soughed through the grass. It grabbed at his knees and ankles with thirsty lust as he walked down the hill. He slapped at a yellow fly buzzing around his neck. He scratched at an itch beneath his arm. It smelled like rain, but the sky was blue and untroubled by clouds.

When he reached the fence, he stopped before it. Almost to the day eight years before, he had stood in this very spot and said goodbye. Asha ran his palm along the topmost rail. It was rough. A splinter stabbed into the fleshy heel of his palm. He jerked his hand away and studied the wound. The wood tip showed just beyond his puckering flesh, and he pulled the splinter free. It was wet and red and fat. Long, too. The length of his thumbnail, at least. He almost placed the splinter in his hair, tussling it to lose it there. He still remembered his father telling him as a child, "Asha, if yeh put the splinter in yer hair, like this, and yeh rough it up, like this, yeh'll not feel another bit'o sting."

Instead, Asha dropped the sliver of wood and wiped his palm clean, then he climbed over the fence. As he walked closer to the Dark Wood, nostalgia flooded him. He could still remember the fear and excitement commingling in his gut on his seventh birthday when his father walked him down to the fence. It had made little sense to him then, and less now. Still, pride flooded him when he remembered that day. He'd gone with the woodsmen and performed his kohlas to the best of his ability. When he first returned home, he'd felt like a failure. He hadn't caught the scarecrow, after all. Part of him felt actual relief his father was dead then: he would not have to face the man's shame over his son's inefficacy. That relief shamed him further to this day.

As he got older, Asha understood: capturing the scarecrow, or even killing it, had never been the object of the kohlas, only the kohlas itself. It was the very act that transformed him from a boy to a man. The woodsmen were stern and vacant, but they had taught him well. Like a blade against flint, he'd grown sharp against their coarse dispositions. He'd learned to accept his role as a man, a husband, a father. Had he not had their tutelage, he would have been soft. Pliable. He would have been weak. He remembered himself before his kohlas, the disappointment he saw radiating in his father's eyes whenever he looked at his son.

But the kohlas had hardened Asha. Yes, it tolled a heavy price, but it had proven worth it. Like this act now would prove itself, his kohlas had been worthwhile. He'd returned home, took a wife, and became a father himself. And he'd strove never to cause his own son to feel inferior to him, only to see him as a standard. To encourage reasonable ambition for an attainable goal. Eliot had been a strong boy. Yes, he had been childish, and his mother'd loved to coddle him. But Asha had seen the boy's strength often, despite those things. When he remembered coming to this forest on his own seventh birthday, he did so with pride. When he remembered bringing Eliot here on his seventh, however, it was not pride that haunted his heart.

Eliot had wept that day. Still, he had shown his strength despite those tears. Eliot was a smart boy. Asha often saw deep understanding in the child's eyes, a knowing no six-year-old boy should possess. Yet Eliot had. Perhaps it had been the degree to which he understood things that broke the boy's heart that day, causing it to spill as tears from his eyes. But Eliot did what must be done, and Asha was proud of him for it. Asha, too, had done what was necessary, as he would now. His pride in his boy paled in the shadow of his own regret. He had understood even then it was the last time he would see his son. He'd lost the boy's mother, and now he was giving up his son. It was for the boy's own good. That truth made the sacrifice palatable, but the taste remained stale in his mouth. On some days, particularly spring days, the taste grew rancid.

The way is the way. But was it? Could he not be as good a teacher to his son as the woodsmen? He'd thought these thoughts often for more than a year after Eliot left for his kohlas, second-guessing the whole business in a vicious spiral of self-doubt and self-loathing, but he knew there was no good in this. Questions like those were dark, meaningless things. Blasphemies. And he knew his son would return home one day, a man himself. Strong. Wise. Capable. And that made it all worth it. Asha's only regret was that he would not be here to welcome Eliot home. That was not the way.

The way is the way, Asha thought again, *but why?* For back and back, time out of time, this had been the way of things in the valley. The way things were, the way things are, the way things would always remain. And the bitterness of that truth reeked. Still, questioning the pact was questioning everything, and that heresy was not the way. This was Asha's sacred duty, his debt to be paid to the pact . . . or what was left of it. It was every son's sacred duty to begin their kohlas and to perform it to the best of their ability. It was every father's duty to finish what he'd began as a son.

What came next was a mystery. He knew well enough what would come of Eliot: Asha had, after all, completed his own kohlas. But what of the fathers? He did not know. He knew enough, however. This act, too, made the way for Eliot to return home. To be a man, full grown. Inside the forest, Asha would use his knife, but after that, he could only guess. There were whispers—rumors no sane man would believe—that the fathers moved on to another part of the forest, perhaps. Or beyond it. That Asha would soon be reunited with his own father, and one day with Eliot, when Eliot's own son completed his quest, and Eliot walked into the wood and offered his blood. This felt foolish to Asha, and he knew better to hope for such nonsense. But couldn't it explain so much? Wouldn't it justify all the sacrifices made, at least to a point? Perhaps, but it would never make up for the lost lifetime his son would live without him.

Asha stood before the Dark Wood and took in a deep breath. The dry scent of the forest saturated it, bringing back so many memories. Feelings, mostly. He remembered little from the years of his kohlas other than how he'd felt. In the days leading up to when he brought Eliot to meet the woodsmen, more had come back to him. But like a frightened rat, the memories scurried away again. Something about the smell of the Dark Wood, when it would ride a gust of wind on cloudless days, always triggered an emotional recollection in Asha. Over time, the details blinked out of his memory one by one, and Asha understood this was a good thing. Forgetting was perhaps the one mercy that kept him sane. What memories he had kept from his kohlas were few but potent.

He remembered the wise witch and the honor he had felt when she declared his kohlas completed. He remembered embarking on his return journey to home, all the hope in the world taking root within him. Even then he was deciding on the father he would become. Even then he celebrated that his son would enjoy this same sense of accomplishment after completing his own kohlas one day. He remembered the talking woodsman returning with him to the dun-twille, the skulls and bones clicking in the trees. How he had used blood from Asha's palm to mark the cyth and prepare for a son not yet conceived, much less born.

He fidgeted with the knife's grip on his belt. It had been a gift from his father on the day of his kohlas, a parting gift. Another regret: Asha had meant to get Eliot a knife like this of his own. But he hadn't. Part of him had hated the idea of sending his son away so much, he'd acted as though it would never happen. Laila had almost convinced him to leave, to forsake the faith of his people. To protect their boy, she'd said. She had not understood. Eliot did not need protecting from the kohlas. The kohlas was his protection. That reality, however, did not make bringing him to the woodsmen easy. Getting Eliot a knife for his quest would have only made the inevitable more stark inside Asha. The temptation he had felt to flee with Eliot, to run like a coward from the boy's honor, still resonated as shame within Asha. But he hadn't fled. He had remained strong for his boy. And this day, he would prove strong once again. Eliot made this worth it.

More than once in the months after Eliot had left, Asha gathered hunting supplies. Camping gear. Food and provisions. He meant to go after Eliot. He meant to find his boy, kohlas be damned. But he always realized the folly in this notion: it was his own greed that motivated this thinking. Asha wanted to satisfy his own desire. Having his son by his side was more important to him than what he knew was best for Eliot. Asha had never thought himself a selfish man, but here was the proof, and that proof shamed him. Even at his best, he could fail his son. In the end, he let the way run its course. He allowed Eliot the chance to meet and conquer his kohlas, without the interference of a selfish father. But what if Asha hadn't? What if he had succumbed to his weakness?

Asha shook his head. He wanted to see his boy again, to watch him grow to manhood. He mourned that loss even as he celebrated his son's own accomplishment on his quest. Not all boys returned home from the kohlas, but Eliot would. Asha had no doubt. He'd witnessed Eliot's strength of character. His heart. His energy. Eliot had been a rambunctious child. He'd always needed to understand why things were, not just that they were. Asha smiled. He loved his boy. He was proud of Eliot. More than any other thing in life, Asha loved his boy. He hoped Eliot knew that. His smile faded. He removed his knife.

Asha would have given Eliot the world had he possessed the power. What he had been able to give his son, he'd given. A stable home with food, warmth, and shelter. A disciplined lifestyle. And when the time came, his own kohlas and a chance at greatness. And now, Asha would give more. He would give drops of his own blood. Deep in his gut, he feared he would give more than that. He feared he would forfeit any last chance of a future with his son. But the way is the way.

Eliot had always been a boy. He'd explored like boys explore. He'd lived as boys live. But Asha had taught him responsibility. Even at six years, Eliot had understood carrying his own weight. And most importantly, Asha had allowed Eliot to be curious. To ask his questions.

To seek his truths. As a boy, Asha had asked the same sort of questions. His raw curiosity had always seemed to pit him against his father, who found Asha's questions disrespectful. He would whip the questions out of Asha's head with a switch on his behind, and Asha had hated his father for it. That's why he had not discouraged Eliot's questions. Like his mother, Eliot had always wanted to know more. To understand more. This, Asha believed, would make Eliot more.

Asha had provided his son with the one thing all fathers in the valley bequeathed their sons: the privilege and honor of proving their sacred mettle, of earning their stance, of solidifying their person by taking up the challenge of the kohlas, and thus finding themselves in its glory. When Asha brought his son to this wood, he had initiated Eliot into an ages old covenant, one which had protected his people for as long as they had lived in the valley.

"The way is the way," Asha muttered. He was surprised at the emotion he felt. He saw again the look on Eliot's face when they'd stood before the fence, a look that haunted Asha still. Even as Asha understood the necessity of his boy's quest, the desperate fear in Eliot's eyes and the look of being betrayed pained the man. Remembering these hurt Asha, but not so much as what had come after, when Eliot's eyes went dead in the woodsman's grip. Asha knew, in that moment, he'd ceased to exist in Eliot's mind. That bit was worse than the boy's tears. Worse than Eliot's pain over the betrayal he had felt from his father. His son's dead eyes haunted Asha . . . .

"It is the way of things," Asha said, as though he needed a reminder. "The way things have been, the way things are, the way things . . ." He stopped.

He was not a man capable of tears, but had he been, they would have come now. Laila once called him dead inside. This was not true. He could not show her his true feelings; he'd tried. She had not understood the ways of the valley. She had considered the kohlas ruthless and unnecessary. Barbaric, even. If she had been right, if even by a thread, Asha would have conceded. He would have agreed with her: he almost had. They would have taken their boy and left the valley.

Asha had wanted Laila to be right. Not trusting his boy with the kohlas was a painful memory. Still, he was a selfish man and could not help but imagine what a life with his son and wife may have been without his son's quest. Laila had left him, and that wound was still tender even after eight years. Why she'd left their son alone in the woods, to find his way home by nothing more than moonlight, Asha still did not understand. But neither could he hate her for it. Laila was his life. Before Eliot, she had been everything. Perhaps her leaving was the best way she knew to honor the way of Asha's people. To honor Asha and Eliot. But there remained too many sharp points on his memory of Laila's leaving for him to dwell on it. If his thoughts lingered there too long, he would bleed from it. He would bleed regardless, but not on his memory of his beloved Laila.

Perhaps this day was as much for her as it was for their son. He'd not known what he would do when he went to bed the previous night, only that he must do something. The details came to him upon waking. Truth to tell, he'd expected to find the woodsman here. The one who spoke rather than his creepier companion. But now that he was here, Asha was not surprised to be alone. And he was not surprised to find disappointment lodged between his ribs over the woodsman's absence. To see his kind face one last time would have been a balm. Just a single good word about Eliot would have been a miracle.

He thought again of his boy and wondered where he might be. Asha did not know if every boy's kohlas ended the same as his, or if it was specific to each boy. Part of him liked to believe Eliot followed in his own footsteps. The Snake River ravine. The Moon Cave. Perhaps even now he had reached the shack on the Crag, had met the drinker and the wise witch. Perhaps he was on his way home this very moment. Something deep inside Asha told him this was true. That even then, Eliot was finishing his quest, learning from the witch, settling debts with the scarecrow—found or unfound. It had come to Asha not as a suggestion the night before but as an imperative: this morning would require Asha's final act of his kohlas, bringing his role in the covenant to a close. The call could only mean his son's quest was ending. Though the ways of the kohlas remained a mystery to Asha, the way was the way . . . and his trust in it held firm. Even his own cowardice could not prevail against this faith. The thought of his boy completing his quest made Asha lament his incapacity for tears. They felt appropriate.

He sighed, squaring his shoulders and clearing his throat. Had his father stood in this place years ago while Asha himself completed his own kohlas? Perhaps. But Asha saw this as an act of love, a gift from Asha to Eliot and not just another cog in the wheel of tradition of a long-held pact. He would like to think it so, though something told him this gift was a requirement of all kohlas fathers. Still, for Eliot and Laila, Asha gave it. And that made it personal, unique to him and those he loved. What came after would come, and that would be enough. And if the whispers were true? When next he saw his boy—his grown son—Asha would take Eliot into his arms and weep against his neck. He would tell him how very much he had always loved him. How very proud he was of his son.

With his left hand, Asha pulled the sharp blade of his small knife across the palm of his right, blood pouring from the gash. Then with his right, slick with blood and weak from pain, he pressed the tip into the flesh of his left hand and pulled. Asha returned the bloody knife to his belt and held his arms out before him, palms facing down. Blood dripped in a steady flow.

The Dark Wood came alive. It rattled, shuddering with hunger, knocking and beating against itself.

The wind kicked up. It was dry and dusty. Asha's eyes watered against it, stinging. The cacophony within the Dark Wood rose, the volatile chaos of sound swirling in an arcade, an audible roof concealing Asha from the sky above. He felt his heart beating its rhythm in the wounds in his hands. He heard the raw noise of the forest coalescing into a rhythmic pattern, a stoic beating in time with his own heart.

"Eliot," Asha said in little more than a whisper. "This is for you, my son." And he thought, too, of his wife, Laila. Surprised, Asha felt an actual tear escape his lid and slide down his cheek, fighting against the dusty wind for purchase. He smiled. It may be the fruit of a heavy wind in his eye, but it was still a tear. His smile widened, and Asha walked into the shadows of the forest. Only then did he see the truth.

Author's Note

Any good character should be too complicated to be all good or all bad. Asha demonstrates this very well for me. While reflecting on this scene, please forgive me for growing glassy-eyed as I swim into the depths of philosophical ideologies, but it is difficult for me to frame my thoughts without doing so.

This scene devastates me. It would be easy to see Eliot's father as a villain, but I find easy is rarely the path to truth. Asha and all the fathers in Gal-Braith are victims like their sons. The thing I most love about sharing Asha's last moments is that I get to show you he was not simply a monster. He loved his son the best he could. He loved his wife the best he could. Their loss was enormous, but he was a man of duty because he had been crafted to be. It is difficult to fight against a religion you are born into. It can be nearly impossible to see its violences for what they are, causing a believer to be blind to how they perpetuate those offenses. And although religion does not always incite violence in the heart of its believers, it often does. This is certainly true for Asha. If judged only on the merit of his intention, Asha is an honorable man. The fact that his actions—which he believes are sacrosanct—are vile and devastating to those he most loves is the greatest tragedy.

I have mentioned before that Eliot's story came to me in a dream. The dream felt inspired, and I mean that literally. Coming from a holiness tradition of Christianity, by college I had a deep sensitivity to spiritual matters, soon following what I would consider the path of a Christian mystic. I very much believed the dream was divinely inspired. It was one of two motivating factors that led me to upend my plans for a career and begin work instead at a youth home for troubled teenaged boys who would otherwise be incarcerated.

The dream shaped me in a way I cannot overstate. It is perhaps due, in part, to this and my own background that so much of Eliot's story hinges on the fundamentalist beliefs of his people, which, for the record, are perhaps an oblique reference to my past but not a true mirror reflection. It tells of Eliot's journey of discovering himself independent from the collective beliefs of the community he was born into. My own path of self-discovery against the backdrop of religious belief was very important to me. A mantra of mine in my twenties when I dreamed the dream was, "God, I want to see you without my mind telling me what you look like." For many years, this attitude framed my existence, and it helped me lay the brick on the path of discovery that was mine alone rather than the product of a faith I inherited. Weighed by my fundamentalist past, the prayer would have been met with skepticism, as though I sought an excuse to invent a god in my own image. The opposite was true, however: I sought unmolested truth with total sincerity. As I saw it then, and still see it today, if God is God, they are big enough and smart enough and love well enough to answer honest seekers with truth. They are not fragile or thin-skinned, and they will not break beneath my scrutiny. Furthermore, I believe if all people approached their brand of faith with genuine open-mindedness, perhaps we would be a far less divided people, recognizing just how similar the cores of our unique faiths are. How spiritually related we are, after all.

This philosophical approach to faith now reaches into my overall worldview. Daily, I look around myself and ask, "Now, what am I missing?

Where am I wrong?" A variation of this mentality has been with me since as early as six years old. You see mirrors of this in Eliot when he asks "why" rather than accepting that "the way is the way." You see hints of a similar struggle in Asha when he states that his wife almost convinced him to leave Gal-Braith and abandon his religion. Unfortunately, the straps of his inherited faith were too tightly fit for him to struggle free.

This scene takes place during the final chapters of *The Scarecrow Hunters* after Eliot reaches the Moon Cave. At one point, this scene opened book two, but now we see a good bit of this at the end of *Shadow,* only from Eliot's perspective.

A BOY IN THE CHAPEL OF SPRING

It wasn't that Cora had expected anything from the whelp of a boy. She had long ago learned to expect little from menfolken—all save her father, of course. He was the exception. And yet, she had allowed herself to become vulnerable with the boy. She had been weak. Perhaps, too, she had been foolish.

She plucked a petal from the flower she held, looking at it. "He needs me," she whispered, dropping the petal. She plucked another. "He needs me not." Cora sighed, flicking the petal into the shadows beneath the trees.

His name was Jory, and he lived on a neighboring farm. He'd come the previous autumn to assist his uncle, who had broken his leg falling from a rowdy horse. Cora had liked Jory. He had a strong work ethic and was terminally polite, a thing over which Cora teased him relentlessly. Politeness had never been a weakness she shared.

Although she had never learned the full truth of Jory's circumstance, she had come to understand—primarily through her mother's conversations with Jory's aunt—that they had brought the boy as much to get him away from a difficult situation back home as to help with his uncle's farm work.

Cora shook her head, remembering Jory. More specifically, she remembered how they'd first met. There had been nothing special about that encounter. For that matter, there had seemed little special about the boy. He was unremarkable to look at. He could blend into any crowd of boys from Throm. There was nothing interesting whatsoever to mark him as unique.

Well, that was not entirely true. He had one thing that made him special: his smile. In an instant, his face sprang from unremarkable to glorious when he smiled. That was when she'd first taken notice of him.

"He needs . . . ," she began, a petal pinned between her thumb and forefinger. She knew she was an odd girl. A child's game of deciphering a boy's feelings was just that—a game. It could not accurately determine matters of the heart. And, in any case, she had not loved Jory. She had felt deep affection for him, but not love. She had not wanted him to love her in return. That would have been ridiculous! But she had liked him very much as a friend, and she had believed she could help him. "He needed me," she finished after a moment, dropping the petal. She plucked another. "He was a selfish boy who thought he didn't need me and will get what's coming to him . . ." A crooked smile formed on Cora's lips. ". . . a painful rash in his nethers, mayhap," she said, snorting a small laugh. She dropped the petal and began humming.

She didn't want bad things to happen to Jory, not really. Not even an inconvenient rash. She was not so base as all that. And she really didn't blame him for leaving. He'd had the decency of saying goodbye, at least. He'd shared his plans of joining a merchant's ship in Gal-Galleen. In that regard, he was a boy to the bone: living for swashbuckling adventure, for wealth and honor. As if there was any honor more worthy than being a good and decent man. Greater wealth than becoming a husband and a father. Not that he would ever have become *her* husband. No, but they could have become lifelong friends. Unfortunately, silly boys had silly notions of what made boys into men.

Cora continued toying with the flower in her hand, her song now replacing the recitation of a girl's childhood game, before tossing the stem to the ground. Jory had not broken her heart. This was a simple fact. He had undervalued her friendship. He had failed to listen to her advice—sound advice at that. He could have made a good living near Throm, and he hadn't needed to work his uncle's land to do it. A ways place, Throm bustled with exciting people—Jory could have found employment there without having to leave behind all the people who cared for him. Not her so much, of course, but his aunt and uncle, surely. It made little difference at this point, however. Cora had enjoyed Jory's company. She had come to look forward to their meetings almost as much as getting lost in one of her books. But she had known long before Jory shuffled into—and subsequently out of—her life that boys were rarely worth the effort. Yes, her father would insist Cora had a fondness for strays, as he called them. And yes, her mother would agree, accusing her of having a vagrant heart that chased after any set of sad eyes that crossed her path. A *fixer*, she'd once called Cora. As if her mother was any different.

Her parents did not understand her. She did not *need* to help people. She chose to. She enjoyed the effort, enjoyed watching the results. But she did not need it. And she would not call her inclination for helping wayward young men fondness for them.

Cora shook her head, the melody slipping from her throat in warm vibrations. "The singing bird will come," she sang with a smile. This was her favorite song, and it matched her mood so very well just then. It always made her melancholy, and that seemed right.

In truth, she wished Jory the best on his journeys. Perhaps he would come back one day and tell her all the ways and places he'd lived. Perhaps he might even thank her for her part in helping him realize his true self. Though it truly did not matter if he recognized this fact. Cora did not need recognition . . . still, she did enjoy it. But such thoughts were silly regardless. Jory probably had forgotten her within the first day of leaving his uncle's farm, and if not, he certainly would the moment he stepped aboard a ship.

"I have a green bough in my heart," she sang. "It takes one to make a garden, and it smells like—"

Cora froze, fear skittering across her back and belly, as she spied a haggard man stumbling into the shade of the trees next to the ruined chapel. He must have heard her song and came exploring. Her hand went to the knife in her belt. He did not stand like a man. Rather, he had the wild stance of something feral. The more she watched him, the more wary she felt.

His body tense and ready for flight, he took a single step inside the chapel, turning this way and that. Searching.

As his face came into full view, Cora realized she had been wrong. This was no man.

"Hello, boy," she said.

The boy cowered like a startled animal, his feral eyes widening at the sound of her voice. Cora wanted to laugh at the way the dirty boy moved when she spoke, like a young goat or newborn foal. Animalistic and wild, yet somehow adolescent. But she didn't want to laugh. The wildness she saw in his eyes ran deeper, she sensed. He may teeter now like a clumsy fawn, but a moment before he'd been a stealthy fox. The boy could yet prove dangerous. He was scarecrow thin, his skin was dark and ashen, and his hair was a mad tangle. His eyes, large ovals in his brown face, studied her with what she perceived was disciplined attention.

Cora sat on a chunk of stone in the far corner of the ruin, runic carvings adorning its cut surface. Part of an altar, she believed. And if it hadn't been, it was now. It was her altar. Honeysuckle and jasmine covered the fallen stones and crawled up two of the remaining three walls. There were dragonferns and gilly weed, their red and purple spores filling the air like fireflies in the sunlight. There was a host of flowers and sweet weeds. This was a very good place. Summer was only days away, but right now this was the chapel of spring. The air was alive with the full fragrance of it. This was a sacred place for her. No one bothered her here, not even her father.

She would have felt this intrusion insulting had she not found the lost boy so fascinating.

Cora rolled her eyes, laughing after all. She'd thought of him as a lost boy. No doubt her mother and father would accuse her already of making plans to scrub the whelp clean and teach him to be a proper man. That was ridiculous. She was far more likely to jab her knife into his thigh.

"She's beautiful," he said, his words carried on a breath as thin as his shirt.

Cora laughed again, the sound surprising her almost as much as the boy's words. Or his voice, for that matter. He'd spoken as if he'd come into the chapel for worship. She had to respond, didn't she? "Is she now?" she asked, bemused. Her cheeks burned a little, but the boy's face burned brighter despite his dark skin. He had not meant to speak aloud, she realized. Boys were such funny things, she'd learned. This one was fifteen or sixteen years, she guessed, a year or two younger than her, and like most boys their age, he appeared dumbstruck by her beauty.

He cleared his throat. It was a clumsy gesture, somehow inauthentic, she thought. "Heigh, kin," he said, and regret filled his face a moment after at the misuse of the phrase. It was not a Hidain, after all. Cora suppressed a smile. She did not believe he was a bumbling idiot, even if he played the part well. Perhaps this boy remained a stealthy fox and his ungainliness a ploy.

Cora made a show of straightening her blouse and adjusting the belt at her waist. Again, she marked with satisfaction her hunting knife sheathed at her back—should she need it. She stood, and the boy backed into the brush, pinned by its foliage. He wanted to bolt. She saw that as plain as the ruin of his clothing. She smiled to set him at ease, to show she harbored no fear of him and meant no harm. Funny: she pitied him.

"Heigh, kin," she said and looked around them. No matter the boy's intentions, she would play her own part well and discover if he was friend or foe. "I think this place makes every day a high day."

Relief passed over his features.

"Tell me, boy," she said, her smile widening. Her hand again found the hilt of her knife, just in case. "What makes her so beautiful?"

The wary boy watched as she approached. His body tensed, a deer at the twang of a bowstring. His eyes darted back and forth between her and escape. His chest heaved. She wondered what had happened to him. Maybe the Skree had captured him. There had been terrible tales of the barbarous group of late, but she knew Skree slaves didn't often live to tell about it. Still, he must have experienced an awful ordeal. There was no other explanation for his behavior, nor for his appearance. She knew it was foolish, but she felt empathy for this pathetic creature.

She stopped a few steps from him. No reason to frighten him off just yet. He was not an ugly boy, though it was hard to see that. His clothes were rags and ill-fitting. He seemed mostly clean, but his hair was a tangled brown mess of oily tufts. Even from this distance, she smelled him. It was the scent of boy musk. He was a wild thing. He looked almost dead, his body wraithlike. She could see the bones of his shoulders through his shirt, the blades at his collar sharp enough to sheer wool from a sheep. Trial had retracted his face, his cheeks concave. His jaw was tight and gray. Though dark-complected, he had little color to his skin except for bruising around his eyes and scars not quite hidden by his threadbare shirt. And his blush, of course. But his eyes were glittering things, exhilarated with sparkling life. She felt pity take a turn for admiration. Something she saw in the wild boy's eyes told her he was a survivor. Cora liked him.

"Can't yeh talk, boy?" Cora asked. "I would hear more about this beautiful girl."

"I beg yer pardon, lady," the boy said, his voice thin and shaky. "I did not mean to offend yeh."

"Offend me? Oh, aye." She laughed. "But why, pray tell, should I be offended? I believe yeh called me beautiful, unless there be another girl hereabouts." She stepped closer. "I'd like to know to who yeh said this, aye? Who were yeh talkin' to?"

"I have been travelin'," the boy said. He shook his head and tried again. *As he should,* Cora thought. His answer had not fit her question. "I haven't spoken to no one for a long time is what I'm sayin'." His words were more clumsy than his body. He was as much at home in this conversation as a bird in a seabed. And she could tell he knew it, too. It was clear as day.

His manners and words intrigued Cora. She watched him. Studied him, more like. They were close now. Could he be hiding something? Of course he was. Everyone was hiding something. More to the point, were his secrets dangerous? She was not afraid, no matter his intentions. She may be a girl, but her father and mother had not raised a dainty thing. Nor a stupid one. Her knife was there, but she didn't believe she would need it if it came to that. He was near starved. Unhealthy and used up. She saw him fighting the urge to back away. Or run. Or fall before her in worship. No, he was no threat. Not to her.

"So yeh traveled alone?" A new thought came to her. What if there were others? What if this boy was a distraction? Reaver attacks were uncommon this close to Throm, but not unheard of. And using a child or weak thing for bait was a common reaver tactic. She stepped back, a new awareness tightening her muscles, hoping the gesture appeared natural. Nonchalant. She scanned the surrounding area, the brush and path through it. If there were others, they remained well concealed.

"Aye," the boy said, drawing her attention back. "I traveled alone." She looked at him. He looked sincere, but also like the full truth was much more complicated.

"For how long?"

"Years."

More curious. "Years? Why would a boy travel alone for years? You are young."

"I am sixteen. I think."

Cora smiled. His tone was defensive. A year younger than her and already imagining himself a grown man. Fair enough. By all accounts, she was a woman, and he a man. But she could not let the last bit of his statement pass without inquiry. "Yeh don't know how old yeh are?"

The boy fretted inside his own head for a moment, his fingers fussing at the hem of his shirt. "Not right at it, I suppose."

"Well then, do yeh know when your birthday is?" The boy seemed perplexed by the question. Cora liked this wild boy. "Leastways, do yeh know what moon yeh were born under?" she added.

The boy thought another moment. "It were springtime, I know that. At the Coyote Moon."

"Coyote Moon at springtide . . . ," Cora calculated in her head. "Aye. That'd make yeh sixteen." She took his hand. She saw his exposed skin rise in gooseflesh and his face burn deep crimson. She saw the calamity of urges inside him: flee or stay. His wiry frame vibrated with raw energy, but whatever instinct may have told him to run, he seized it. She smiled.

Cora made a point of considering all he'd said. "Born in springtime. Coyote Moon. Yeh think sixteen . . . yet yeh can't recall yer birthday. Are yeh havin' me on, boy?"

"No, lady. It's that I just don't know how long exactly I were travelin'."

She chuckled and realized after how condescending it must sound. "Oh, aye. Well, now yeh know. Coyote Moon were sixteen years back." She squinted. "Lady, is it? And you . . . a mystery, boy."

They stood looking at each other, the boy's palm sweating in Cora's hand. She watched him with her most penetrating gaze, sizing his mettle against her own. She waited, but the boy did not speak for a long while. Just as the silence became too much, he finally did.

"What is yer name?" he asked. This surprised her. It was a practical question, and he had been anything but practical so far.

"You first," she said.

"Eliot." No hesitation. Cora smiled. There was no hesitation there either.

"Eliot." She considered the name. She said it again, slower, as if trying it out. "Eliot . . . . We should say today is yer birthday, Eliot." She held his gaze for a moment, then added, "Happy birthday."

His face flushed again. Empathy tugged at Cora; his vulnerability pulled at her. She softened her expression, feeling guilty for provoking him. She wanted to hug this strange boy, to tell him all would be well. That she would help him find his way. But she could say none of that, and if she hugged him, she would appear mad. What would her mother do? Leah would swat Cora's hunting breeches if she knew she was talking to a wild boy alone in a derelict holy place. But if Leah were here, she'd show this stray boy kindness, and she'd know just how to do it. She would act without hesitation. Not overthinking, Cora did the only natural thing that came to mind. She leaned in and presented a birthday kiss on the dirty boy's cheek.

Panic infused Eliot's body with nervous energy, and Cora immediately regretted the kiss. She hadn't meant for it to be romantic, but how else would a boy take it? If a hug was a bad idea, a kiss was far worse. He seemed near to swooning, only just remaining on his feet. Cora let go of his clammy hand and started back to her stone inside the chapel. Why had she kissed him? It was a simple peck and no more. Yet it was also a mistake. Foolish. Leave it to her to find the stupidest thing to do and then to do it. She needed space between them. She only realized he'd followed her when she stopped walking and he fell to keep from running her over.

She turned on him, her blade out and ready. The boy looked at the knife but showed no fear. That figured, but his eyes were on hers again, their vitality warm with something. Was it hope? *Cora*, she thought, *don't be a fool.*

Knife still out in front of her, Cora looked him over. The hope in Eliot's eyes vanished under her scrutiny. "So, Eliot, yer a sixteen-year-old boy. A little thin, mayhap. And wearin' yer grandfather's clothes, no less."

Eliot's face again burned as he must have realized how he looked. Cora felt wicked. She had not meant to embarrass the boy, only to put him at ease. She was as gentle as an ox sipping tea. That quality she got from her father. Eliot was emaciated. He looked ill, near to death. He had to understand he did not look well. He seemed far too self-aware, looking down at himself, crossing his arms over his gaunt chest. But when he looked back at her, he was smiling. It was timid but genuine and bright.

Her mouth slipped sideways into a smile as something occurred to her then: she had forgotten about Jory.

Cora shook herself. Eliot might be a nice distraction, but she had to make a choice. Would she attempt to help this boy? If ever a boy needed help, it was this one. She knew her father would not hear of it, would say her fondness of taking in strays clouded her judgment. He might even say the same of her mother, Leah. But Cora could convince him to allow the feral thing a bed of straw in their barn. For a time, at least. Eliot would not be the first young man to make a bed of it, and Cora was confident in her power to bend her father to her will. Her mother was another matter. Lucky for Cora, Leah shared a tender heart for lost boys. Eliot seemed in dire need of repair, yet she also felt a deep strength coursing through him, something, she had to admit, called to her. Yes, there was danger inside him as well, but few things were more beautiful than wild creatures—and the wild were always a little dangerous. She knew what her father would say. She knew what her mother would say.

She also knew that something in Eliot felt true. Truer than anything she'd seen or felt in a long time. Cora put the blade away. Her father may hate that she took in so many strays, but maybe just one more wouldn't hurt.

"Aye, yeh look road weary, but yeh have a good smile," Cora said and held out her hand.

Author's Note

This scene begins in the final moments of Eliot's story at the end of *The Scarecrow Hunters*. A variation of this interaction, only from Eliot's perspective and in truncated form, opens *Shadow.*

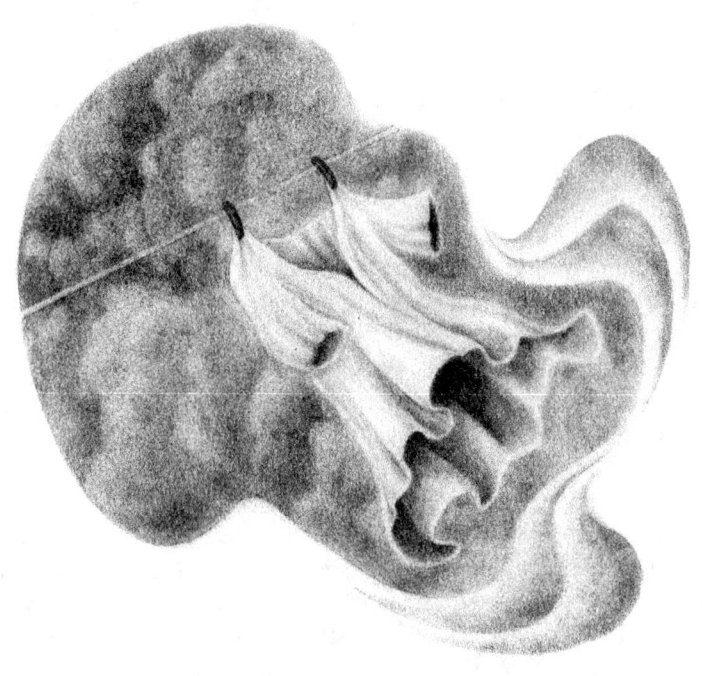

MORE MAGIC THAN DARK MAGIC

The first drops of rain streaked the window panes as the gentle patter from the roof filled the small cottage with its song. Leah loved the rain, especially on cold autumn days.

"Lollie," her grandmother Hazel said, "grab me the honey."

Leah hopped down from the stool she'd been perched on and retrieved the honey. Once her grandmother had spooned a dollop of it into a simmering pot of cream, she handed the honey back to Leah and took down a small jar from a shelf high on the wall. From the jar, she plucked two dry leaves and ground them between her fingertips before dropping them in the cream.

Leah's mouth watered. Her grandmother knew how much she loved honeyed cream. Perhaps all little girls did, but Leah liked to think she loved it more. It was a special treat she and her grandmother always shared. Leah took two cups from the cabinet and placed these on the counter next to the simmering pot, reaching for the ladle.

"No, Lollie," her grandmother said. "That ain't yers. Here . . . ." The woman reached to another pot farther back on the stove and brought it forward. "Honey this one," she said, placing the pot on the counter next to the cups.

Leah spooned honey into the second pot and used the ladle to stir it. Her grandmother handed her a jar of ground cinnamon, which Leah sprinkled into the pot as her grandmother dropped a twig of lavender in.

"Keep stirrin'," she said. Leah did.

The kitchen filled with wonderful scents. Leah knew she must wait for her grandmother's consent before ladling out their cream, but waiting was cumbersome. Her grandmother huffed. Leah looked and found the woman smiling as she watched Leah's expression.

"Aye," the woman said, "go ahead."

Leah filled two cups with steaming honeyed cream, barely able to wait before taking her first sip. It was happiness on her tongue. Her grandmother likewise took a sip and giggled. Leah looked back at the first pot, which her grandmother had lidded, taken off the stove, and placed on the counter. Curiosity flared in the girl, but she knew better than to ask what the pot was for. Watching her grandmother to see what would happen next was a game she liked to play. Her grandmother always surprised and delighted Leah.

"Grab me the big mug," the lady said, "the one for Big Geb." Big Geb was a young man Leah's father had hired several years earlier. Geb had been kicked in the head by a horse when he was thirteen. Ever since, making words had been difficult for him. Sometimes it took him longer than others to find simple solutions to everyday problems. But he had a strong back and a big heart, or so Leah's father always said, and Geb had worked on their farm for more than half of Leah's life. He belonged there, a part of their family.

Leah retrieved the mug. Into this, her grandmother ladled cream from the first pot. "A bit of honeyed cream, with just a touch of conjure," she said, placing the steaming mug on the counter.

Heavy footfalls sounded on the porch outside, followed by scraping. Signs that someone was coming in but wanted to leave the fields outside rather than track them into Hazel's kitchen. Leah didn't have to wait for the door to open to know who was coming.

"Yer mug's there," Hazel said as Big Geb came inside. "Drink it while it's warm."

Leah watched her grandmother continue to stoke the stove fire while Geb obediently took up his mug and sipped. His smile wiped the trenches from his brow.

"Good," he said, slow and heavy.

"I know," Hazel replied. "Now get on with yeh. There's no room for an ox in my kitchen on bread day."

Big Geb chuckled—he loved when Hazel called him an ox—and left the kitchen, steaming mug in hand.

Leah twisted the hem of her dress between her fingers, waiting to see if her grandmother would answer Leah's question without Leah asking it. After a few moments, Hazel stilled at her work, turned to face Leah, and winked. "Aye, girl," she said. "There's more magic than dark magic . . . ."

Leah smiled. A lesson was forthcoming. And just like the lesson, rain came then, turning from a gentle patter to a committed sigh on the roof. The window had grayed beneath the sky, its diffused light making the kitchen's bright orange lantern flames seem to burst with life. Hazel took down a large stone bowl and a heavy pestle. Into the bowl, she dumped a cup of grain, recently threshed. She rolled up her sleeves and began crushing those wheat berries.

"Lollie," she began, "you must always see the world through what is possible in it, not through what is wrong with it." Her eyes never left her work, but such an exchange was a practiced thing between Hazel and her granddaughter, so Leah knew it was her turn to speak.

"Because there is more magic than dark magic?"

"Aye, smart girl. Aye." Hazel sniffed, pausing in her work to push her face into her sleeve. She coughed. This was also common, though it hadn't always been. But lately, Leah had noticed how grinding the wheat berries always made her grandmother cough, as did other things besides. With her throat cleared, Hazel went on. "You are wonderin' 'bout Big Geb's cream. Aye, I knowed yeh would. How come I to know he wanted honeyed cream, is that yer question?"

Leah's head bobbed vigorously as she swallowed another sip of her own cream. She smacked her lips, unable to keep from it, and said, "And when . . . . Can yeh see the future? Is that the magic yeh mean?"

Hazel cackled. The cackle devolved into a fit of coughing, tears filling her eyes, her smile filling her face. "Ah, girl. Ever'one can tell the future if they want to. No magic in it."

Leah's nose wrinkled. That didn't seem true.

Hazel scooped another cup of wheat berries into her bowl and began grinding them.

"Eyes are magic things," the old woman said. "If yeh pay attention, yeh see things other folken don't see. Yeh learn things other folken never learnt. And if yeh do it right and proper for long enough, yeh come to see things before they happen. Or leastways, the possibility of things."

"But yeh knew right when Big Geb would come in the house. How could yeh know that from watchin' yer stove?"

Hazel slowed but did not stop her work. She turned to see her granddaughter. "The rain told me."

Leah gasped. She hadn't meant to, but she loved the rain. She had not known it could speak whispers, however. "How?" she asked, nearly breathless.

Hazel, her attention back on her bowl and yet another cup of wheat berries, explained. "'Member what yer pooey said over breakfast? That the wagon wheel, the one what got broke last week durin' the storm, should be mended first thing today. That was Geb's job this mornin', 'member?" Leah nodded. As if hearing the girl's nod, Hazel went on. "When the rain came, I knowed Geb would take shelter, first comin' to the house. That's his way." She paused, looking at Leah. "Are yeh seein' it yet?"

Leah nodded, but slowly. "I think so."

"That's a smart girl." Hazel returned to her bowl. "I know rain makes Geb sad. I know hard tasks like replacin' a wagon wheel frustrates his head. And I know that 'cause I've watched him for goin' on six, seven years now. So I made him a warm treat to chase away the rain clouds in his head. And I put just a bit of conjure in it, too. For good measure. Just enough to lift his spirits." She looked again at Leah and winked. Leah giggled. "Grab me a pail and water."

Leah stepped onto the porch, pulling her shawl tight around her shoulders and neck. Yes, she loved the rain, especially on cold autumn days—but only from inside the house. Autumn and winter rain was sharper than that of summer or spring. It fell harder on the roof and pulled deeper in her chest. That was lovely, but it also stung more fiercely on her nose and cheeks. She trotted the few steps to the well, her pail in hand, and crouched beneath the old oak tree. She knew to only fill the pail a third of the way, which didn't take long. Then she scampered back inside the kitchen with its warmth and cups of honeyed cream and the wizened old woman she loved with her full heart. Hazel took the pail and set it on the stove to heat. She continued grinding her wheat while saying, "Grab me the oil."

Leah did as she was asked before sitting on her stool next to the counter. Making bread was a weekly affair. It was not so bad in the autumn and winter months, but baking turned the entire kitchen into an oven during summer. Just now, Leah welcomed the heat, her fingers still stinging with cold from the rain. She lifted her cup and sipped. Hazel reached out her hand, took the cup when offered by Leah, and refilled it. She handed it back.

Hazel dipped a finger into the pot of heating water. "Almost," she said. From the same shelf she had retrieved a bit of conjure for Geb's cream earlier, she now took down a small jar of yeast and a bowl of salt. "If yeh'll see the world through the possibility in it, yeh have to keep yer eyes and mind wide. Both have to stay open. The two are sisters, aye. A girl's eyes are the source of her magic, do yeh reckon it?"

"I think so," Leah said. But if she had to swear on it, she did not think she quite understood.

"There's a bit of magic in all things, I says," her grandmother said. "It's magic what makes seeds grow into grain and causes the grain to yield berries. It's magic what turns the berries to flour and the flower to bread. Do yeh see it?"

Leah shook her head. "No, hommie. That's just farmin'. It's just cookin', isn't it?"

Hazel shook her head, once again testing the water. Finding it the right temperature, she sprinkled her yeast over the top and set the pail aside. She draped a cloth over this and began clearing her counter for her task. "Lollie, folken tend to look at magic like a part of the other, when it isn't. It's part of all things."

"The other?" Leah asked.

"Anythin' folken don't know how to explain is what I call the other. And yer right enough. Aye, it's the sun and rain that makes the wheat grow, but what makes the sun shine? What makes the rain fall?"

"The Mother?" Leah asked, fairly certain she had the correct answer.

"Aye, some say it so," her grandmother said. "But who is the Mother? Where does she come from? Where does she live?" The old woman now poured the warm water and yeast into the bowl of flour—sprinkling in a bit of salt as well—using her fingers to work the mixture into a dough. "Well?" she asked, stopping to look at Leah. "Do yeh know?" Leah shook her head. "No, 'course yeh don't know. No one does, not really. Oh, some folken think they have more answers than can be had, but don't yeh see it yet, that's the magic in it. Or part of it, leastways. The not knowin' . . . .

"Folken talk of gods and spirits, of the sacred and the profane, and they talk as though such things can be explained. But how can a mere man or woman—or even a beautiful, smart girl like you—understand a thing like a god? Wouldn't our understandin' reduce her to somethin' less than divine? If we could understand her, we'd make her more like us just in the understandin', don't yeh reckon?"

Hazel stopped suddenly, leaning forward over her bowl. She took several deep, slow breaths before motioning for Leah to bring her a stool. Once she had sat, she pushed the bowl of dough closer to Leah's own stool.

"Knead the dough," she said. "Yer hommie needs to roll a smoke."

Leah did as instructed while Hazel pulled a satchel of tobacco and rolling papers from her apron. She began assembling a cigarette, but continued her lesson.

"Seein' other folken—really seein', mind yeh, not just watchin'—makes for understandin'. It makes for empathy. And empathy makes for kindness. A body should always be kind. Kindness is among the highest of magics.

"Lollie, do yeh know what happens when we hide the dough away beneath a cloth?"

"It rises," Leah said, her hands and forearms tired already from her work.

"Aye, but why do it rise?" Hazel waited, but only a moment. Leah didn't know why, and she knew her grandmother understood this. The question had not meant to be answered but heard. "It's the yeast. It does a thing and makes the dough swell. Yeh can see somethin' similar in the hearts of folken, in the minds of folken. That swellin' can be for good or ill, but I reckon you can see that much at least, aye?"

"Aye," Leah said.

"Let me see," Hazel said, and Leah slid her the bowl. "A little more'll do it." Leah continued her work. "Kindness is like a bit of yeast. It can make a heart swell and overflow with kindness of its own. It catches like a yawn, only sweeter. With even a little taste, a body knows it needs kindness to live. It needs to take it, and it needs to give it.

"Thing is, we are all puttin' a bit of somethin' into the folken we run into day to day. Frustration and anger, mayhap. Love and comfort, mayhap. And whatever we put in is most often what comes back out. Do yeh see it, Lollie?"

"Aye, hommie," and she did. "It's like a seed. What is planted is what grows."

"That's right," Hazel said, her laugh vibrant. "You are a smart one, aye. No one plants a watermelon seed and harvests a stinky rutabaga."

Leah giggled and slid the bowl over once again. Hazel stabbed it with her finger and nodded approval. "Grab me the towel," she said. When Leah did, Hazel covered the bowl. "Now let's go outside."

They left the kitchen but walked under the eave of the house to avoid the rain. While the dough rose, Leah knew they would step over to the garden so her grandmother could see what there was to see—for seeing always seemed a part of the old woman's conjure—and so she might smoke her cigarette. It would not do to smoke in the kitchen, she'd often said, because it would taint the taste of the bread. When they reached the corner of the house, Hazel reached her bare palm out into the rain to test it. Finding it acceptable, she stepped out into the slowing pour, opened the gate, and stepped inside the garden. Leah watched from beneath the eave.

"And hello there," Hazel said, bending over to brush the greens with her fingertips. "How are my lovelies today? And hello to you, also," she said, cupping a large acorn squash with her palm. "It's not just about seein' other people neither," she said, not bothering to look at Leah. Leah knew to whom she was speaking now. But the woman continued her circuit through the small garden, her fingers and palms playing among its residents. "A girl should pay attention to all livin' things. A girl should always see what she can see. In time, a girl can learn to see magic ever'where she looks."

"Do yeh mean real magic?" Leah asked.

Hazel stood up straight, her attention now fully on her granddaughter. "Love, there's only real magic." Then she continued her ministrations to the garden, finally coming to a trellis with sorry-looking roses woven through it. There were no petals, and most of the leaves had fallen as well. But Hazel took hold of the vine, careful not to avoid the thorns but rather the thorn points, and sang. There were no words to her song, only sounds and syllables. Leah smiled, then laughed. Hazel, her song finished, looked again at Leah.

"When a girl sees, a girl knows." Then they left the garden, closing the gate behind them.

Hazel reached into her apron and removed her cigarette and a match. She struck the match on the side of the house and began smoking. For several long moments, neither spoke. They didn't have to. The rain spoke for them. Not with words, as Leah would have been delighted to hear, but with song. The rain was slowing—more seemed to be dripping from the brittle leaves of the trees than from the clouds—and so its song was softer now.

The minutes passed as the two women—one very old, one only a child—waited in the stillness of the morning, perhaps seeing what there was to see. Leah watched a squirrel working to stow away treasures against the coming winter. She listened to the baying mule somewhere on the far side of the barn and guessed it was ready to be let out into the broader pasture to graze. The chickens clucked an endless pattern of complaints as they scoured the yard for bugs and mites, but Leah knew their grumbling was a sign of contentment. She wondered where Big Geb had gotten off to, certain he had found new work for his hands until the rain let up. He wasn't one to remain idle while there was daylight left, rain clouds or no. She wondered where her mother and father were just then. They'd left before sunrise, heading for Throm. It took most of the day to arrive there, so they wouldn't have made it yet. They would gather needed supplies and stay the night in a local inn, returning home sometime next day. This would be their last trip before Lunauinbroc, and on that trip, the whole family—including Geb—would go into Throm together. But that was yet some time away.

Finished with her cigarette, Hazel motioned for Leah to head back inside. The warm kitchen welcomed and revived Leah. Hazel went to her stool and sat again. She took several of those long, deep breaths that she seemed to need more frequently these days. She was an old woman, after all. Then she looked at Leah.

"Lollie, one day you will be a mother. Aye, a grandmother too, mayhap. And by then, yeh'll understand more than yeh think possible just now. But no matter what yeh learn, no matter what powerful revelations yeh believe yerself to have had, never, never forget to see. Never, never forget to be kind. The world is full of possibility, both good and bad. Take it, and make it good."

Again, Leah smiled, but something in her grandmother's words made her sad. It wasn't the words so much as the weariness behind them, though Leah could not articulate as much.

"Hommie?" she asked, her voice sounding so very small inside her grandmother's kitchen.

"Aye, girl. Go on."

"How will I know the difference 'tween good magic and dark magic?"

Hazel once again laughed, and her laugh once again rolled into a fit of coughs. After, she spit into a bucket sitting on the floor. "Look at me, girl," she said, her eyes holding Leah's own. She said nothing for several moments, and Leah wanted to look away, but she knew she shouldn't. She should let her grandmother see. After a time, Hazel smiled. "Aye, yeh'll know the difference. Yeh already do, love."

Leah wanted to ask how, to understand, but she knew what her grandmother might say. Knowing comes with time, she might say. Or, the *how* isn't the important part. Still, Leah could not help her curiosity.

"Will yeh teach me more conjure?" she asked after a time.

"Ah," her grandmother said, "that I will. And long after I'm gone, too. For an old woman's magic is not just in the words she speaks, but the ones she writes."

Hazel's eyes never left Leah's, but Leah's turned to study the shelf above the stove. A tightly bound leather journal lay there, bursting with loose pages and scraps of fabric as though these grew wild between the covers. This was Hazel's book of conjure, one from which she had shared many lessons with Leah over the years. These lessons Leah loved more than all the others. More than reading or prayers, even, and she loved those also. Conjure wasn't proper magic, or not as she understood it. But rather, it was the joining of natural things to magical things. The journal wasn't a spell book as much as a cookbook, and that seemed fitting. For even without her grandmother's lessons, Leah always believed there was a bit of magic in cooking.

And then she saw it . . . how magic could exist in all things. It wasn't the magic of hexes performed in witches' huts or oaths carved into silver objects, but it was magic all the same: true and proper. Life itself was magic. Growing food, crying babbies, falling rain, and baking bread. All these things and so much more. Seeing was magic, as were love and kindness. Leah smiled. Her grandmother smiled as well.

"Now, how 'bout a bit more cream?" her grandmother asked, standing. She took Leah's cup and filled it one last time. She filled her own as well. Both sipped their honeyed cream. "Now, tell me what yeh learned today, girl."

Leah bounced on her stool, happy to recite the valuables gleaned from their lesson. Hazel stood and began oiling her counter.

"There's more magic than dark magic," Leah said. "Life is magic, and everythin' I can see is filled with life."

"Aye, go on," her grandmother said, plopping a now swollen dough ball onto the counter. She punched her fist into the dough. "How is there more magic than dark magic?"

"How?" Leah asked, uncertain how to answer. Then it came to her. "The how don't matter. Seein' matters. Seein' and bein' kind."

"Good girl," Hazel said, beaming. "Very good. Always be kind. Always see the world around. Always feel it while you see it. Always feel its possibilities. And as yeh do that, the magic'll make itself plain to yeh. It's okay to wait for it. It's proper."

She pulled four loaf pans from beneath the counter and oiled them. Then she rolled the dough into a thick log, dividing it into four equal parts and shaping each portion into the pans. Leah opened the door of the oven and watched as her grandmother placed the pans inside. The old woman left her hand just inside the oven to gauge the heat, then nodded. Leah shut the door.

"Magic comes in the way we see each other, in the way we love each other," Hazel said, wiping the counter clean with a damp cloth.

Leah went to help her, removing the various pots and utensils to the wash pot next to the door. The rain had almost stopped, and it would be Leah's job to scrub everything clean after, to oil the pots and spoons and return everything to their proper places. It would be cold work outside, but it shouldn't take long, and Leah didn't mind.

"Hommie," she said, "do yeh think I'll ever know the magic as well as you do?"

"Lollie," her grandmother said, smiling, "do yeh know yourself? Aye, yeh do. And yeh'll know magic, too. 'Cause yer made of it, love."

The counter now clean and the dirty pots and utensils stowed in the wash pot, Hazel turned to face her granddaughter.

"Sometimes a body learns without knowin' it's learnin', do yeh reckon it?" Hazel asked, and Leah nodded. "Sometimes a body knows it's not enough to pay attention to other folken, or to the livin' things ever'where. Sometimes a body has to pay attention to itself. Yeh'll learn this too."

Hazel reached her hand to take Leah's.

"And sometimes a body knows when its work is done. Mine is pert near done, and I want you to remember: always be kind. For there's more magic in this world, girl, than dark magic. Chief among these is love and kindness."

Her hand, so bent and beautiful, stroked the girl's cheek. Then Hazel bent and kissed Leah on the tip of her nose. Leah smelled the tobacco on her breath.

"Now help an old woman to her bed, Lollie. I feel it's time for a long rest."

"It's very good," he said. "Thank you, lady."

His voice dragged Leah back from her memory. She could still smell her grandmother's kitchen and the bread baking in it. She shook the memory away, with all the melancholy and sweetness it conjured, and looked at this boy. He too had a strong back and a big heart. He too had been wounded, but much deeper than Big Geb. He too had found a home with Leah—now a woman grown—and her family, though he did not see that just yet. "You are welcome, Eliot. Would you like some more? I always like a little honey in my cream."

Eliot smiled despite the dark cloud simmering behind his eyes. He handed Leah the cup, and she turned to leave the barn, head back to her own kitchen, and refill his cup. Before she left, she stopped. Turning back to Eliot, she said, "I don't know where yeh've been or what yeh've seen, but Eliot, yer welcome here." He nodded, but she could see he did not believe her. "Yer safe here," she said. At this, he looked away.

Leah placed the cup down and walked to him. Kneeling, she took his hand into hers, and as if by magic, this act drew his face to look at her.

"There's more magic than dark magic," she said, feeling in her bones they were the words he needed to hear. Then she stood and left.

Thoughts of her grandmother Hazel came to her often. Every time she applied a bit of magic to her day—conjure, the old woman would have said. Every time she remembered to see. Kindness and love above all, her grandmother had taught her, and Leah had never forgotten.

That had been their last bread day together. By week's end, Hazel had taken to her bed and hadn't risen from it again.

"Now shush those tears," she'd said to the girl Leah, crying beside her bed during those final days. "I'm old, aye. And I'm happy. I been happy my whole life. Now you go do the same."

Leah had tried to do just that, and mostly she had succeeded. But even love and kindness can be difficult taskmasters, she'd learned. But always they were worth it, and she would never forget.

She refilled Eliot's cup with cream and added a dollop of honey, then she walked out of the kitchen, heading for the barn to see what she could see.

Author's Note

So much of Eliot's story in the first two *Glint & Shade* books revolves around fathers and mothers. This isn't an accident, though I didn't write it that way intentionally. Because I experienced this story originally as a dream myself, as I wrote, I tried to understand what caused those moments in my dream rather than invent them. Thus, a great deal of Eliot's struggle and growth involved his need for and reluctance to accept love because of his deep sense of being abandoned and damaged.

In a perfect world, I think we all would assume a starving boy presented with morsels of bread would eat them without hesitation. That perhaps works with food, not with love. A boy starved for acceptance and love can be incredibly resistant when they are offered. The end of this scene, the interaction between Leah and Eliot, is both beautiful and tragic to me, but mostly beautiful. Originally, these few lines were a complete chapter. But here, rather than showing you that interaction in full, I've pulled back the curtain to show what helped shape Leah into a woman Eliot might learn to trust.

The moments shared between Leah and Eliot take place shortly after "A Boy In The Chapel of Spring," later the same day that Eliot met Cora, Roland, and Leah in *A Greedy Shadow*. This was Leah's first interaction with Eliot and thus belongs early in that book. The memory of Leah baking bread with her grandmother happened when Leah was a young girl.

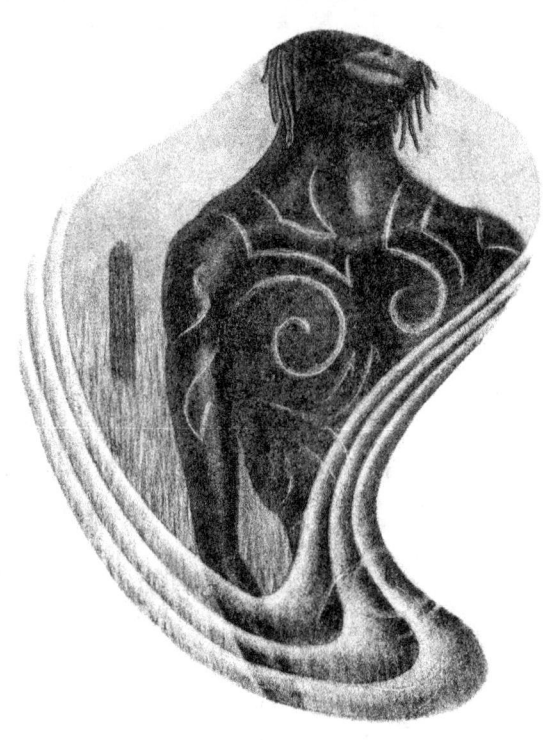

THIRSTY CURSE

"Only once the dust has settled and the blood dried can a man's mettle be measured . . . ."

Roland's mind had wandered all day. The boy was trouble, Roland did not doubt. And even if he didn't mean to be trouble, he brought it with him. Roland knew the look. Once he'd been a boy like Eliot, after all.

Again he heard that phrase echoing through his mind: *only once the dust has settled and the blood dried . . . .*

He sat on a stump of wood on the porch, a gentle rain blanketing the night in calm. It was a good evening for contemplation, and he tried to relax, taking another draw on his pipe. It was out. *But only once the dust has settled and the blood dried,* he thought again. But by then, so much damage could be done. He reached for his matches to relight his pipe when the barn door opened.

He didn't recognize the sound at first, even though some deeper instinct made Roland's chest tighten. It was an odd sound for such a time of night. No one would be going in or coming out of the barn under normal circumstances, not so late. Leah and their daughter, Cora, slept. But the boy was in the barn, or had been. When Eliot came into view, Roland was not ready for what he saw.

Eliot was naked. Roland could see as much, even by the meager light coming through the clouds. He was sleepwalking, that was obvious. He moved as if guided by an unseen influence.

They were close enough now Roland could hear Eliot's shallow breathing. Pale moonlight, diffused through rain clouds, pooled blue on Eliot's skin. Roland listened. The house was quiet. He breathed a prayer neither Leah nor Cora would wake up now and see this. He was uncertain who that discovery would damage more: his girls or the boy. He would not like to find out.

Roland had felt a quiet unsettling ever since he'd met Eliot. That had been nearly two months earlier. He did not worry overmuch about what the boy might do. He was a thin, gangly thing. It seemed a miracle he could command his frail body to walk most times, much less harm anyone. Still, harm would come. Roland felt it in his bones. He had once been very familiar with the low things found in the hearts of men, and as such had a deep-seated understanding of darkness. That was long ago, before Leah came into his life. Even so, Roland knew low things when he saw them, and this boy was fitted tight with vexing shadows.

He watched Eliot stop in the yard, his arms dangling lifeless at his sides. It hurt to look at him. Eliot might as well have been a corpse in the thin light. Roland watched, embarrassed for the boy, but nothing changed. If the boy made one move toward the house, sleepwalking or not, Roland would stop him. Perhaps he should do something regardless.

"Great stinking goat shit," Roland mumbled under his breath. He stood, thought better of it, and sat again. He wondered that a naked boy could make him so nervous.

He thought of the first time he'd seen Eliot's scars. He had been so skinny. He remained so, even after two months of Leah's cooking. But the scars made Eliot appear less than human. Roland now watched as the rain, little more than a shower, slid down Eliot's chest and stomach. Over his scars . . . . Still, Eliot did not move. From the scant distance, Roland could see how the boy's skin creeped into gooseflesh against the chill, his nipples hard little jewels on his dark chest. His chin chattering. His body trembling.

The wind was cool, and steam rose from Eliot's shoulders. Being naked and wet, Roland knew the boy must be freezing. Just as he decided to fetch him a blanket, Eliot's eyes shot open. They were blank. He still did not see the world around him, lost in whatever dream stirred him.

With slow dawning, Eliot came awake and realized he was naked and out in the open. Quick as a bolt, the boy went from standing tall and straight to being little more than a dark clump in the yard, crouched low. Roland couldn't bear to imagine what was going through his head. Eliot was disturbed: there was no question about that. And he may be dangerous, and not just to himself. But Roland felt grave pity for the boy. He did not like this. Aside from his wife and daughter, Roland preferred simple measures. He did not often entertain others who presented complications, not well at any rate. Yet here was a boy as complicated as any Roland had seen.

Like a rat, but slowly so as not to be seen, Eliot crawled back to the barn. When Roland heard the barn door close again, he exhaled, realizing he had been holding his breath. Again Roland's mind was transported to that other time.

"When the dust settles," he murmured. Simple measures rarely found footing in the real world, Roland knew. People were complicated. Emotions and logic were complicated. Even truth seemed more flexible than most people were willing to grant, and that often complicated things. Here was trouble living in Roland's barn, but that wasn't all Eliot was. There were better things in the boy, things that ran deeper than his trauma. "Only when the blood has dried," Roland mused. But how much blood might there be?

Roland sighed. He did not know what to do with this boy, or his troubles. He knew what Cora would say, and he knew what his wife would say. On the surface, Roland knew the right thing to do: get rid of the boy. Protect his family. Protect himself. But below this was another truth, one that begged for Roland's attention. Once Roland had been a rake, a boy who not only carried trouble with him but who had a knack for finding new trouble wherever he went. And unlike Eliot, Roland had meant to find trouble. He'd relished it.

Despite that, Leah had seen Roland through the haze of calamity that followed him and opened for him a door of opportunity. He had been changed as a result. Eliot did not seem to be willfully malevolent. Rather, Eliot seemed haunted. What might a kind hand opening a metaphorical door accomplish in Eliot's life? And was that Roland's responsibility?

His mind spun, and that phrase came back to him once again . . . .

"Only once the dust has settled and the blood dried," Roland said, "can a man's mettle be measured . . . ."

"Aye, that's the way of it. And we'll learn theirs soon enough." His friend spat into the grass before adding, "And ours."

Roland didn't respond. Rather, he continued peering through the glass.

"Tell me what yeh see, Rat?"

Roland thought for a moment. He considered what he saw, not just with his eyes but also with his gut. He'd learned his gut often saw far better than any other part of him.

"The pokes are close . . . ." He paused, seeing. "They suspect nothin'."

Roland bound his looking glass in a leather cloth and stowed it. He turned to look at Tig. Tig nodded.

"Then we go. Time is short."

They came into Throm about a week after Janith. The pokes, arriving from Gal-Cully on the western coast of Carde, were expected to arrive a few days after. So long as Janith had done his part, they would be ready.

They found the inn easily enough. All they had to do was follow the stench. Janith wasn't known for his tastes but rather for his savage cunning and merciless appetites. Janith had never been Roland's favorite, but Roland wasn't in the game to make friends. Reavers weren't known for being friendly.

Up a single flight of stairs and at the end of a long, dark corridor, the men found Janith surrounded by prostitutes. The six ladies and two men ranged in age and appearance to better satiate a plethora of interests, and their selection had not been random. Janith had researched the tastes of the pokes hired by what stood as the regentry of the tiny coastal village of Cully. No doubt he'd also sampled the goods. For good measure, he might say.

"This is it, then?" Tig asked once the door was closed behind him and Roland.

Janith nodded, presenting each whore in turn, providing a succinct yet detailed overview of the skills and reprobations of each, along with a reference for which poke each had been selected. The details did not matter to Roland, only that it seemed Janith had done his research. It was enough to convince Roland that the man had done more than fuck a bevy of whores in the week since he'd arrived in Throm. He had, no doubt, fucked them all, and likely more than once, but just now, Roland was satisfied to find Janith's work had been thorough, as was usually the case.

Perhaps Roland and Tig might also get a turn with each: their services had been bought for the duration of the job, after all.

Tig nodded when Janith had finished. "Aye, good, Jani," he said, clapping Janith on the back. Then he turned to the prostitutes, pointing toward the door. "Go to your rooms and wait there until called for."

Each flesh worker slinked out, more than one hand caressing Roland's broad chest or ferreting about his belt as they passed. Yes, Roland thought, once final plans and provisions were in place, he would make use of a roomful of their temporary accomplices.

As the door once again shut, Tig turned to face his comrades. Roland took a seat at the table. Janith sat on the windowsill. Tig stood in the center of the room.

"Rat," he said, looking to Roland, "catch Jani up to date."

"I hate when yeh call me that," Janith said. Roland knew that was why Tig used the moniker.

"I hate when you speak out of turn," Tig replied with the quirk of a brow. "Roland?"

"Aye," Roland began. "The pokes left Cully a little more than three months back. We confirmed they have the chest in their possession."

"Do yeh know if the chest actually holds gold?" Janith asked. Roland nodded. "*The* gold?"

Roland looked at Tig. Janith had only joined them a year before, and though the man had always carried his own weight and gotten the job done, neither Tig nor Roland fully trusted the man yet. Time proved a man, and little besides. Time for the dust to settle and the blood to dry . . . . Even a year had not been enough to prove Janith's mettle, not to Roland's satisfaction. Nor to Tig's. And it seemed Janith had yet to grow trust in either Roland or Tig. Roland understood this. An abundance of trust was slow-working poison and nothing more. It would kill any man who didn't keep it in check.

Roland's trust in Tig was different. He'd been with Tig for ten years, since he'd found Roland at nine years living beneath a high porch of a brothel in Gal-Thinny. Tig, five or six years older than Roland, had become a brother to the younger boy. Even so many years later, Roland saw the same look in Tig's eyes as he'd seen when the older boy had discovered him beneath that porch. What's this then? he'd asked as he'd squinted into the dim space. A rat . . . with a knife. Tell me, Rat, would yeh kill me with that knife? he'd asked. Yes, Roland would have killed him, but there had been no need. Even at nine years, Roland had understood the cost of survival, and having a confidante—a partner, an accomplice, a co-conspirator—could mean the difference between life and an orphanage. Gods, imagine if he grew up to become a khamun . . . . So he'd come out from beneath the porch, and he'd gained more than an accomplice: he'd gained a brother. Even then his gut had known the truth of things more times than not, and he'd known he needed Tig. As Tig had needed him.

Tig made no reply to Roland's glance, but Roland hadn't expected one. The two men did not need words or gestures to understand one another.

"Stop with yer eye kissin'," Janith demanded. "Just tell true: is it *the* gold we are lookin' for?"

Roland nodded. "Aye. It was recovered from a ship that run aground just north of Siren's Cove. Its origin remains unknown, but it is said to be cursed. A string of dead men marked the way from the Cove to Cully, where the village governors employed six fighting men to escort the chest, double-bound, to Throm, where an unknown buyer intends to take possession of it."

"But that won't happen, will it," Tig said, and it wasn't a question.

The plan was simple because simple measures always worked better than complicated schemes. They would wait for the pokes to arrive, have the prostitutes strategically placed, along with bribes for the innkeeper who held the poke's reservations. Use food, drink, and sex to distract the men. And milk fern . . . not enough to kill them, only incapacitate them. And once that happened, they would remove the chest to the cellar beneath the inn in which Roland and his fellow reavers now held counsel. By then, festival would be in full swing. Roland, Tig, and Janith would join the revelers as though they'd come to Throm for no other reason. A week or two after Sauingrey, they would head south. The chest would remain buried beneath the inn back in Throm. Only after six months had passed— perhaps more if the pokes remained sore over the loss of their cargo, or if the unknown buyer sought reparations—Roland and Tig would return to collect their bounty. And after that, they would pawn the chest off to outlanders—discreet buyers could be found easily in the ports of Thinny or Galleen—and make away with enough teegs to never need work again, save for the joy of it.

But that would come only after. Just now, they had considerable work ahead of them.

"Like robbin' apples from a blind merchant," Janith said, laughing.

"This will not be easy," Roland said. "These pokes are not trifles. They are trained fighters."

Janith's laugh continued, but any real mirth had left it. Still, Janith's optimism was well placed. The pokes were professionals, that was true. But so was Roland. So were Tig and Janith.

"Do yeh have the food and wine?" Tig asked.

"Aye," Janith said, "and I made a good deal on the meat. Paid nearly nothin' for it." His smile, which revealed the crooked brown teeth of a man unacquainted with hygiene, made his eyes glitter. "The savin's I put to good use, aye. But I may have got a bit of a scratch." And he dug between his legs as though seeking fishing worms in river mud, but his laugh suggested he didn't mind.

"What meat?" Tig asked.

"No worries, Tig. I took care of it," Janith said. "A great deal's a great deal."

"Jani," Tig said, his voice heavy with authority, "what meat?"

"It were a butcher who said he had a mess of meat he needed unloadin', and quick. Said he'd give me best prices to take it off his hands." Janith's grin widened, wicked and hideous. "I negotiated an even better price, if yeh know what I mean."

Tig looked at Roland, then back to Janith. Roland didn't see the problem, but Tig clearly had one.

"How long?" Tig asked.

"A day ago," Janith said. "Mayhap two."

Then to Roland, Tig asked, "How long?"

"The pokes should arrive within five days. Mayhap six if the weather turns."

Tig looked back to Janith. "And what do yeh plan to do with meat a week old?"

Then Roland saw it. It was a good reminder why Tig was their leader. He was the thinker. Janith was a people mover. Roland was brute force. Without a brain, a body can't function. Tig was their company's brain.

"It'll keep," Janith said.

"Jani," Tig began.

"It'll keep, aye," Janith said, and just a touch of petulance came out in the phrase. Roland found Janith mostly reliable, but he loathed the man all the same. "And don't call me Jani."

"Act like a man, and I won't," Tig said.

Janith looked at Roland. He'd never appreciated the friendship Roland shared with Tig. He found it suspect, and often he took the opportunity to voice as much. He'd always seemed to expect them to turn on him, to cut him out of their bounty. Or perhaps just cut his throat while he slept. And his concerns were valid: Tig had no intention of sharing the bounty from the chest's sell with Janith. Roland found the man mostly tolerable, but Tig found him deplorable. In the months leading up to the job, this had only worsened. There had been many men over the years who'd served in Janith's position, and each one had, at some point or another, found himself on the dark side of death. As Tig put it, sometimes you had to clean the house you meant to live in or else it'd fall down around you.

Janith made no reply, instead choosing to grumble beneath his breath. Tig ignored this, looking at Roland.

"The innkeeper has been paid off, and a boy paid to keep watch on the innkeeper," Roland said. "The rooms bein' held for the pokes have been chosen. They'll serve our needs, aye."

"And what of the buyer?" Tig asked, this time to Janith.

"No sign," he said. "Whoever he is, either he keeps a low profile, or he ain't comin'. I've heard no word of him, seen not a stitch of hide nor hair of him, neither. But if he shows up, we'll be ready. But that won't happen till after festival, no ways."

Tig considered all this, weighing it in his head. Roland waited. Tig knew everything was in place. Roland knew his friend wouldn't have entered Throm at all without having total confidence that every detail had been managed. Still, Tig's hesitation made Roland curious. It must be the meat.

After a while, Tig released them with a wave of his hand. "Now we wait. Enjoy yerselves, but not too much. Do yeh hear me, Jani? Caution is the word here on out."

Janith laughed as he made his way for the door. "Aye, caution is my given name, boss. 'Sides, I don't need no bilbee root just now. Not when I gots two rooms full of switch and stick to occupy my time."

He pulled the door shut behind him as he left, his greasy laugh fading down the hallway. Tig looked at Roland.

"I don't like it," he said.

"The meat?" Roland asked. Tig nodded. "Then we make that fool eat it first, just to make sure all's well with it."

Tig nodded, satisfied, it seemed. "Now, Rat, go snatch his nasty pecker outta whatever whore he's trying to stick it in. I reckon it's our turn."

The next several days passed slowly. But that wasn't so bad, Roland guessed. With Sauingrey bearing down on them, Throm was flooded with folken from across the countryside. Drink-saucy eyes stared out from behind masks of devils and creatures, the celebrants crowding every street and back alley of Throm. Blending into the crowd was easy. Keeping an eye out for their quarry was also easy. And there was a bounty of roasted apples and nuts, slow roasted meats and root vegetables, and every kind of divet Roland could imagine to keep their bellies filled. A room full of beautiful bodies to keep their lusts satisfied. And nothing besides but time.

The pokes arrived two days earlier than Roland had expected, but that was just fine. The sooner the job was over, the sooner Roland could return to festival, to blending in and pretending he knew nothing of stolen chests filled with cursed gold coins. That would make eluding the pokes easier . . . the buyer, too. If either caught wind that Roland and Tig were behind the job, blood would spill freely. They all wanted to avoid that as far as possible. Spilling blood was no great task, but making away after could be problematic.

Roland and Janith took the wine and meat to the kitchens of the pokes' inn where they were already making themselves comfortable. They had three rooms for sleeping and one for the chest. This one would serve for the buy. It would also serve Tig's plan quite well. After they had handed off the provisions—including the milk fern to be added to the wine—the cook had opened the cask of meat and grimaced but otherwise made no comment on the ripeness of the fare. Roland took that as a good sign, and the two men left the kitchen to join Tig, leaving the cook under the watchful eye of the innkeeper they'd bribed.

"How goes it?" Roland asked, meeting Tig and Janith in an alley with a view of the inn. All three were dressed in festival garb and smelled of ale. All three were sober as midwives.

"No sign of the buyer," Tig said. "The whores are in place."

"They do a good job, aye," Janith said, his smirk a hideous scar on his face.

Roland had to admit they were good at their job. He only hoped they would remember the coin offered to them—a considerable amount, enough to ensure they asked no questions—and perform their duties with tight lips regarding reavers waiting in dark alleys. The pokes needed to be distracted long enough for the poisoned wine to take effect. And judging by their haggard looks upon their arrival, they all seemed more than eager to get drunk and rut with a beautiful lady or boy. Just as Roland thought this, he saw the cook leave the kitchen with the meat board, followed by two servants carrying bowls of roasted potatoes and flagons of tainted wine.

The following hour passed with incredible slowness, but this was the job. Roland knew how to wait better than anything else, save for bashing skulls. There should be no complications, but he had his axe, just in case. He would be ready no matter what. Once the sign came, he and Tig would make quick work of the chest while Janith sorted the pokes and prostitutes. Movement caught Roland's attention, and he looked up to see a naked girl waving a burning candle from one of the pokes' rooms. This was the sign they'd been waiting for: the pokes were passed out.

Without comment, Tig, Roland, and Janith entered the inn by the back door, taking the servants' stairs up the two flights to the rooms. Transporting the chest from this inn to their own would normally be the trickiest part of the enterprise, but Sauingrey—and the naked prostitutes tossing Hidain tokens from atop the cart holding the well-hidden chest—should make up for any difficulties that might arise.

Upon reaching the correct floor, Tig was greeted by one of the male prostitutes. He nodded and wordlessly led them to a cluster of four rooms: two on the left side of the hall and two on the right. Tig opened the first door. He nodded for Janith to take the next door, which he did. Roland crossed the hall and opened the third door. Inside were two whores and one naked poke. He closed that door and opened the final door: here was the prize. The chest had been stuffed behind a filthy couch and covered with a tarpaulin, but it was easy enough to identify. Roland left the room to join Tig back in the hall. A moment later, Janith joined them.

Using hand gestures, Tig instructed Janith to collect the prostitutes in the third room. Roland went to retrieve the naked poke and put him in the first room. This room was currently occupied by two sleeping men, both naked and drugged. This door—and the door of the second room where the remaining pokes slept—would be locked.

"Kinnit, there have been—"

A quick slap cut off the words, and a fierce rose blossomed on the cheek of the male prostitute who'd met them at the top of the stairs. Tig shook his head. *No words*, he was saying. Tears spilled down the young man's cheeks, but he said no more. Instead, he joined his coworkers in the third room. Tig and Roland entered the fourth room, closing the door behind them. Only then did Tig speak.

"Let's do this right, Rat," he said. "No room for sloppiness."

Roland nodded and began pulling the couch from the wall. He and Tig removed the tarp and then the crate from the corner of the room, placing it on a sturdy table along the opposite wall. They pried off the lid. Inside was a rather small chest, one bound by chains. The keyhole had been sealed with wax, a cock feather and needlework pins fixed within the wax. From the crate issued the strong odors of vinegar and ammonia, and Roland saw salt had been crusted around the rim. No doubt it filled the bottom of the crate as well.

"Someone took no chances," Roland said, pointing at the wax. It was a hex, and from what little Roland understood of such work, the whole of it was both a protective spell and a containment spell.

"Neither will we," Tig said. He placed the lid back atop the crate. "I'll bring the wagon. You and Janith bring down the crate. Send the whores ahead of you."

Roland nodded, and Tig left the room. A moment later, Janith entered.

"Let's see then," he said, moving to the crate and removing the lid.

"Nothin' to see," Roland said, "not yet. Send down the whores."

"You send 'em," Janith said. His greedy eyes peered into the crate before being overcome first by befuddlement and then anger. "Well, that ain't big enough to store a dead cat, is it. I thought we were takin' a proper chest full of gold."

"We are," Roland said. "Leave off, Janith. Stick to the plan."

Roland went into the hall and opened the door to the third room, motioning for the prostitutes to go down and meet Tig in the alley. Then he returned to find Janith with the chest balanced on the corner of the crate, his knife stabbed into the wax of the chest's lock.

"Janith," Roland hissed, closing the door again. "Leave off, milly. There'll be time enough for that after."

"I need to see," Janith said, and Roland saw the man was on the razor-bone edge of losing his temper. He knew an angry Janith would not do, not for this job.

"Aye, and yeh will. Just not now." Roland grabbed Janith by the wrist whose hand worked the knife. Janith turned his smoldering gaze on Roland, but before he could say more, a sound from the hallway stopped him.

Someone was trying the door across the hall. Roland put a finger to his lips and crept closer to the door. From the hallway, he heard someone jiggle the knob of the door directly across. The first room, then.

"Ah, fuck off," a voice said. Then it moved to the second door and tried again. When this door failed to open, the man began shouting. "Open up, Randal. It's not funny."

From behind him, Roland heard Janith mumbling. Roland turned, both hands up in an effort to reason with Janith for silence. Roland had no need to see the man to understand what he was about. Janith meant to cross the hall and dispatch the stranger, and no doubt he would bring out every guest in the inn during the struggle. Roland again shushed Janith, and he saw by the tight set of Janith's jaw that this would not go well. But the door behind him swung open before Janith had a chance to move. Roland spun. In the doorway stood the sixth poke. Later, on the cart between this inn and their own, they would learn from the male prostitute whom Tig had slapped that only one of the fighting men had eaten before drinking themselves silly and sinking their cocks inside any hole they could find, and that one had gotten sick. That one had needed to evacuate his bowels, and that with haste. And so, of all the pokes, he alone had not consumed enough of the tainted wine to pass out. Nor had he been present when Tig, Roland, and Janith came calling.

But just then, Roland knew none of that. He swung, his fist landing solidly in the man's face. Roland felt bone crunch against his knuckles, and the man collapsed into a heap on the floor. He was dead. Roland hadn't meant to kill him, but neither had their plan meant to be discovered. Roland turned to Janith—there was no time for consideration just now— and slapped him across the face. He lifted a finger. Janith lifted his knife. Roland ignored this.

"We stick to the plan. Deviate, and I will stop yer heart." Roland waited for Janith to process this. Janith was angry enough to have stopped thinking clearly. Perhaps it was that the chest was too small. Or perhaps it was that he suspected some double-cross by Roland and Tig. No doubt it would make perfect sense to Janith that, in the brief moments he had been in the room with the whores, Roland and Tig had somehow managed to secret away the real chest, replacing it with a proxy. Or perhaps it was nothing more than the lack of consideration on the poke's part for discovering them in the act, and the inconvenience it had caused Janith. It was impossible to make sense of the man's tempers. And either way, Roland did not have the patience to suss out the source. When Janith said nothing, Roland continued. "Now put that away, and re-lid the crate."

Janith tucked his knife back into its sheath with little more than a grimace as protest and replaced the lid on the crate. Roland tossed the tarp back over it, and the two men hefted the crate onto their shoulders and headed for the stairs.

The trip across the village to their own inn was uneventful, the mad clamor of Sauingrey doing more than its share to blend the three men, the chest, and their retinue of flesh workers into the throng of celebrants. Upon reaching the inn, Tig paid the prostitutes and sent them on their way. Each to the last seemed eager to be released. No doubt they still had time and opportunity to make additional coin during festival. And no doubt they had tired of the company of reavers. By midnight, the crate was buried in the cellar beneath the inn, and Roland and the others were back in their room.

"There was a complication," Roland said. Tig did not respond. Roland continued. "There was another poke. He'd been to the privy."

Tig's face darkened as Roland explained what he'd learned from the prostitute on the cart. After Roland was finished, Tig sighed. "Tell me why." He was not speaking to Roland, but to Janith.

Janith scratched at his wrist and chest. His eyes were fevered and wild. His distemper had yet to reduce, Roland saw. But the man did not answer Tig's statement. Tig went to Janith and grabbed him by his tunic, shaking him.

"Tell me why, gods dammit," he said. "It was perfect. The scheme was perfect. The execution was perfect. So, you tell me why one poke left three rooms full of naked beauties to make shit."

Janith did not hold Tig's gaze. Instead, he pulled away from the man. "Weren't my fault," he stammered.

But it was. Roland knew it. Tig clearly knew it. And Janith knew it. He'd bought spoiled meat so he might pocket the remaining coin. Or rather, to spend the remaining coin on switch and stick, as he'd put it. He continued scratching his chest and wrists, now scratching his neck and crotch as well. A rash of red skin showed above his collar. He was clearly aware of the trouble he'd caused, and no doubt he fretted over what trouble would befall him as a result.

But Roland knew Tig would not harm Janith, not yet. They would wait. They had to. They had to see what would come of the poisoned pokes upon rousing, upon discovering their dead comrade and learning the chest had been stolen. And it would not do for Tig to kill Janith just then. That would risk bringing unwanted attention. The pokes would seek out the prostitutes, and if their tongues were as loose as their legs, blood would be spilled. So they would wait.

The next several days ticked by, each moment of each hour passing in a slow parade of relentless boredom. Any hope Roland had of enjoying festival had been dashed when he felt the man's face crumple against his fist. He and his partners were too wound up to enjoy themselves, and yet each of them made a valiant show of reveling in the wares and temptations filling Throm. But after three days, and the passing of Sauingrey proper, they found they lacked the capacity to pretend any longer. And it wasn't just worry over whether the surviving pokes might stumble upon some scrap of evidence that could lead them to Roland and Tig, but also for the state of Janith. The man was unwell. He'd sworn countless times he had not eaten the spoiled meat himself, but something was deadly wrong with him. And neither Tig nor Roland could account for why. His skin appeared blistered, weeping viscous fluid from a multitude of abrasions. And still he scratched, his fingertips stained crimson.

The three men waited in their room. The inn was quiet around them, but the sounds of carousing still lifted from the street below, a dull cacophony of pain and pleasure.

"What do we do?" Roland asked.

Tig stared at Janith, and Roland saw the hatred in that look. The displeasure. The impatience to kill the man and be rid of him. "We wait one more day," Tig said. "Then we go. We follow the plan. We head south."

"What about me?" Janith asked, his skin syrupy with puss and blood. The abrasions and swollen blisters made him well suited for Sauingrey, the devil's Hidain. He'd scratched large fissures in his neck and arms. No doubt if he'd removed his clothes, Roland might see he'd scored his body head to heel by his endless scratching. It was misery to look at the man. Roland could not imagine how Janith must feel.

"What about you?" Tig asked.

"I need a healer."

"You need a mourner," Tig said. "Or you will soon enough."

Janith made no reply, but soon tears began streaking down his inflamed cheeks. "What is happenin' to me?"

Roland looked at Tig. Tig nodded. Neither spoke.

"Say true! What is happenin' to me, aye?" Roland heard the fear and panic in Janith's voice. Roland removed his knife and stood. "Roland," Janith said, and he sounded like a child just then. His voice was thin and warbly. "Roland, please," he said, holding up his hands as if to fend off the approaching brute.

"I'll not make a show of it," Roland said, "but it can't be helped."

Janith clamored to his feet, backpedaling to bump against the far wall and slide to the floor. "No, Roland. Tig, hear me. I'm feelin' better. It'll be okay. I'll be fine. Just don't . . ."

"It's too late for that," Roland said. His voice was quiet and controlled. He approached Janith, who trembled. "Yeh shouldn't have been careless, Janith. Yeh shoulda stuck to the plan."

"But wait!" Janith cried. Realizing how loud he'd spoken, he quieted. "Wait, Roland," he whispered. "Wait, just wait. There's no harm done. No harm at all . . ."

"Shhh," Tig said, but Janith didn't.

"Aye, yeh can have my cut. I'll not take a single teeg," Janith promised, working to stand again. His legs shook beneath him. Roland wondered how the man remained capable of sitting up, much less standing. He looked palsied.

"Quiet," Tig said.

Roland took Janith by the hair and tilted his head back, revealing the knot of his throat as it bounced against the man's gasps.

"Roland, quiet!" Tig snapped, and Roland turned to look at his friend, his knife already biting into Janith's flesh.

Tig stood, his stance wary. He was facing the door.

"What is it?" Roland asked. Tig did not reply. Roland released Janith, who fell to the floor, his choking gratitude over even a moment's reprieve from execution an evident balm. Roland took a step forward, but just then the door to their room exploded in a spray of splinters and dust. As the debris settled, Roland came alongside Tig.

In the doorway was the small frame of a woman. She was black as midnight, and Roland could not tell if she was a hundred years or thirty. She had the look of age but moved with the vigor of youth.

"I am come to claim what is mine," she said, her voice thick and round. She was not from Carde. Not from Mor-Thandak, Roland guessed. But she did not appear to be an outlander; sea folken had a certain look. A certain way. This woman was different. And as unaccountable as it seemed, Roland feared her.

"Who are you?" Tig asked.

"The last person you will see alive if you do not give me what is mine."

She walked into the room. Now that the dust and debris had further settled, Roland studied the woman. She was old, but not so old as first he'd imagined. She was a sawdust witch, one not to be trifled with. Of that he could clearly see.

"Please," Janith said, his voice a whisper. "Help me."

"Aye," the woman said. "I will help you."

Before Roland could make sense of it, the woman had removed a knife from within her cloak and flung it across the room. It buried itself to the hilt in Janith's skull. Her eyes then returned to Roland and Tig.

"My chest . . . . Where is it?"

"Who are you?" Tig repeated.

"I am angry. That is who I am," the woman said. "And I am impatient."

She removed another knife, and Roland saw it was a dagger with a long, thin blade. He'd seen the like before. It was foreign, and deadly. But only if one knew how to wield it. This witch knew how.

"We do not have yer chest," Tig said, but the woman waved this away and stepped closer.

"Listen to me," she said, speaking low and swift. "Listen to Marta, and mayhap you will live. Your friend was dead the moment he broke the seal. That moment he became infected by the curse. The curse is insatiable. Even now, it is burning its way through what remains of the defenses put in place by the warlock in Cully. I know his work. He is good, but the curse is strong and thirsty." She stepped closer, and Roland felt the skin on his neck tighten. "With the seal broken by your stupid, greedy friend, the curse will escape the chest, and soon. And then it will consume this village. Where is it?"

Roland stepped forward, ignoring Tig's hiss. "The cellar, buried the full height of a man."

The woman—Marta, she'd called herself—did not speak. Rather, she studied Roland. Tig raised another complaint, but Marta waved her hand and puffed out a breath. Tig's words fell away like stones from his mouth.

"You are a witch," Roland said.

Marta smiled. "And you are a brute. What is your name?"

"My name is Tig," Tig began, but again Marta waved her hand and huffed. But this time, Tig fell backward onto his ass, his eyes wide with disbelief.

"I will ask again, young brute. What is your name?"

Roland looked from the witch to his friend, offering Tig his hand. "Roland."

"Listen to me, Roland. You will help me. Aye, your friend can help, too, but I do not like the look of that one. Tig, is it? I do not need a blade to kill, Tig. Do you believe me?"

Tig nodded. The man cleared his throat and said, "Aye, I believe yeh. You are the buyer come to take possession of the chest."

"Buyer," Marta said and laughed. "There is no buyer. Buying implies payment. I would not pay for this curse."

"You set up the governors in Cully," Tig said. "You meant to steal the chest."

"Aye, but thanks to you two, I no longer have to. But we have to act fast. I can smell the curse. It grows worse with every moment we linger here." She turned toward the door, but stopped, looking back over her shoulder at Roland. "You will no doubt still want your coin. But I tell you, you would never have survived long enough to sell the chest. Your curiosity to see inside it would have been far too much. You would have rotted alongside your friend, likely before you even left Throm with your prize. Dead men have no use for coin. Be grateful you still have life . . . for now."

She turned and left the room.

"What make you of this?" Roland asked.

Tig didn't answer. Instead, he studied the empty doorway. Then he sighed. "It seems what I make of it no longer matters." He followed after the witch, and Roland fell in behind him.

The woman was small and old, but quick. She'd made it halfway down the stairs before they reached her.

"Roland," she said, without turning to look at him, "stay close beside me. I may have need of your strength."

"I am the leader here," Tig said. "We follow yeh only to see if there be any truth in what yeh say."

The woman stopped and turned. "Leaders do not interest me . . . . And you are not my leader. I speak to him because he sees me. You do not."

"I see you?" Roland said, confused. Marta nodded. "I am no seer, if that is what yeh mean."

Marta chuckled. "Seers are not the only ones who see, Roland." Then she fixed her eyes on Tig. "And that truth you speak of, I feel it turning your bowels to jelly." Roland saw the man's wide shoulders fold in on themselves. It was slight, but clear enough. The witch continued. "This chest has never sat right in your gut, has it? You could have taken it in Gal-Cully. You could have taken it at any point on the road between there and here with no worry of witnesses. Why didn't you? You waited until Throm because something told you to leave it be." She turned her eyes to Roland, then back to Tig. "Do I say true?"

Tig didn't answer. Roland did not think Marta had the truth of it. Tig shared most everything with Roland when it came to jobs. His policy had always been full disclosure—with Roland, at least. But now Roland wondered if his friend had harbored secret concerns over the chest. Perhaps some deep vein of superstition ran through Tig, deeper than the man was willing to confess, even to his brother. For Tig's reaction to the witch's words made Roland worry.

"How come you to know so much about the chest?" Roland asked.

Marta started moving—they had reached the bottom of the servants' stairs, and now she made her way down the hallway toward the trap that led to the cellar—but she answered without hesitation. "It is from my home country, very far from here. It is an old and angry curse, one that remained buried for many ages. When I was a young woman, it was revived. I was feistier then, but stupider also. I did not respect its power. I do now. It nearly cost me my life, but I was able to secure it again. To seal it away.

"I knew a day would come when I would have to answer to it, and I have prepared. I believe I have found a way to destroy it, to break apart the curse's power by releasing it. That is what it wants: release . . . but it does not know it."

Tig scoffed. "Yeh speak as if it is sentient. As if it were thinkin' and feelin' . . . ."

Again, Marta stopped and turned. "I do not like you. Stay out of my way."

"Like has little to do with it, aye?"

Tig's challenge was left unmet, for Marta turned to Roland. "Close, remember? Stay close." Roland nodded.

"What will happen to the gold once the curse is released?" Tig asked.

Marta barked a laugh. Then another. "Wouldn't you like to know?" Then she bent and threw open the trap. Turning back to Tig, she said, "After you, leader . . . ."

The cellar was dark and damp. It smelled of mildew and earth. Candles fixed in sconces along one wall suddenly sprang to life with flame.

"Show me," Marta said. She was speaking to Roland. Her deference to him made little sense. He'd done nothing to win her favor, and Tig had done nothing to deter it. Not that Roland could see. But no matter.

He led her to the farthest corner. The space was not large, but neither was it cramped. Roland could stand to his full height without fear of bumping his head, which was surprising. He was a big man, and used to finding ceilings too low for his stature. A cellar would no doubt be tighter, but that wasn't the case here.

The ground appeared almost entirely undisturbed beyond the crates and boxes that had been forgotten here, each of them wearing the gauzy skirts of cobwebs and dust. Roland and Tig had done a good job making it difficult to mark where they had buried the chest, and they had buried it deep. The ground was not hard, but Roland was not looking forward to digging it up again.

"We should not have to dig it up," Marta said, her words sending a shiver through Roland's veins.

"Why not?" Tig asked. "Don't yeh need to redo the seal?"

Marta waved the question away. "That seal is dead. And I do not mean to seal the chest shut, but to release the curse back into the elhwith from where it came."

Marta brought forth a bundle from within her robes and unrolled it, laying it flat atop one of the nearby boxes. She handed a large jar of salt to Roland and a similar jar of vinegar to Tig.

"With the salt, make a circle around where the chest is buried. Be absolutely certain to complete the circle and to ensure the chest is within the circle, beneath it. Then you make a wider circle with the vinegar. I will prepare the rest."

"What is this for?" Tig asked, and Roland had to suppress the urge to silence his friend and brother. "Will the vinegar and salt contain it? Or release it? Or whatever the fuck yeh mean to do to it?"

Marta barked another laugh. "It will try, but no. It will not, not for long. Only blood will do that."

Roland froze, his circle of salt only just started. Marta saw this and motioned for him to continue. Roland did not. Instead, he stood to face her.

"What blood? I do not want anythin' to do with blood magic," he said.

"And neither do I," replied the witch. "But a blood oath is the only hope we have." And now she, too, stopped her progress and turned to face Roland. He felt ice penetrate the length of his spine. "And it is a meager hope, I warn you. If it does not hold, we will not leave this cellar."

Then she returned her attention to her roll of supplies. The ice Roland had felt now branched out, engulfing his ribs to freeze his lungs, but he did what he was told. He finished the circle of salt. Tig was right behind him with his jar of vinegar. The scent was overwhelming in the confined space, and Roland's eyes burned.

"Use it all," the witch directed. Roland used what salt remained in the jar to reinforce the circle. Tig did the same with the vinegar.

This appeared to satisfy the witch. She had brought out a variety of trinkets and bones, and now she used these to create a shape in the center of the circle. To Roland's untrained eyes, it appeared to be a rune of sorts. One he did not recognize. While she did this, the witch spoke an incantation in a language he did not know. Perhaps she spoke lynthian. Perhaps she spoke the language of her home country. Or perhaps she spoke a secret language of witches. Regardless, Roland did not want to know of what she spoke.

"Close," she said. "Stay close, Roland."

Hearing his name slide from the witch's lips so easily made Roland want to break and run. Though he'd not shown it, he had felt fear often in his lifetime—but he could not remember a time since Tig had found him beneath that porch in Gal-Thinny where fear had come so close to mastering him. It took incredible resolve to stay put when every part of him wanted to flee, not just the cellar, but all of Throm.

Rather than running away, he stepped closer. He stepped inside the circle to stand beside Marta.

"I am an Eri," the woman said, as if this fact would set Roland's nerves at ease. He knew little of the Eri, and certainly not enough to be comforted by this admission. Marta went on. "I suggest you pray to whatever gods you trust in for aid just now. I will do the same."

Roland felt something brush against him and looked down just as the woman took his hand into her own. She squeezed it.

"Eri-Sofia be mindful of us," the witch said, her voice quiet yet firm. "Eri-Timley guide us. Help us see true. Eri-Staint hold the door and make a way, should a way out be needed."

Roland swallowed the knot that had formed in his throat. Feeling obligated to follow suit, he prayed, "Gods save us, lest we get fucked."

A noise turned his insides to jelly before he recognized its source. It came from the Eri. It was a soft chuckle. She turned to look at him.

"Aye, simple faith is the best sort." Then she looked at Tig. "And you?"

"I trust in myself," Tig declared.

"Suit yourself," the Eri replied. Then she returned her attention to the earth beneath her feet.

Once again, she began speaking her incantation. Even though Roland could not understand the words, he felt their gravity push and pull against him. He felt them swim through his head. He worried they might undo him. His feet began to itch. He ignored this amid all the other stimulations, but as the Eri continued speaking, the itch intensified. Soon, he saw it for what it was. The ground beneath his feet was vibrating.

"Marta," he said, his throat so dry the word came out as a growl. "Eri?"

The Eri did not respond, but her grip on his hand tightened. Her voice still uttered the incantation, but it became strained. Soon, it no longer seemed that she spoke voluntarily but rather as if the incantation demanded to be spoken. As if it had taken control of her voice. The itch in Roland's feet intensified further, bordering on pain.

He studied the ground beneath them. The bones and trinkets making up the rune had sunk into the soil. He saw the grains of dirt shifting, pressed away from the center like water flowing down flat rock. Or like the skin of a recently dead snake, Roland thought, and that seemed more true. Neither image gave solace, and Roland thought that if something did not happen soon, he might run screaming from the cellar, after all. And somehow, through all of this, Roland felt the unnerving tickle of another concern: if they were to perform blood magic, from where would the blood come?

The candle nearest them fluttered out, followed by a second. Only two remained. The vibrations in the ground ceased, as did the ministrations of the witch. Roland waited, his breath so loud in his ears he could hear little besides. Then some small nerve in the back of his mind sprang to life, and without thinking, he grabbed the tiny woman by the back of her robe and flung her out of the circle and across the darkened cellar. Not a moment later, the ground where she'd been standing fell away, a gaping throat of darkness bearing down into the depths. A malevolent pinprick of flame deep within it looked up with a hungry gaze.

Roland stumbled backward.

"It wakes," Marta said from across the cellar, winded.

Roland crawled out of the circle, careful not to disturb the salt and vinegar, though what good either might do against that baleful eye, he could not imagine.

"What do we do?" he asked.

"Run," Tig said, turning to do just that. In the failing candlelight, Roland saw the glint of Marta's blade just before it sliced Tig's throat into a yawning grimace. Tig fell to his knees, gurgling.

"Take him," Marta yelled. "Take him now."

Roland felt his stomach churn, and he thought he might vomit, but he did as told. There was no time to consider his friend's murder. He reached for Tig, taking hold of his would-be brother by the collar. He hoisted the man close to the circle. Then Marta was there, guiding him.

They held Tig's bleeding neck over the hole, and Roland saw the glowing eye pulse as the first of the blood spattered into the darkness.

"Blood speaks truth, aye," Marta said. "And do you see it, ancient one? Do you taste it? Would you be satiated with one last drink? Or would you be glad to be freed, once and for all?"

At this, the hole yawned, and Tig's body was sucked into its depths. Roland fell backward against a nearby crate, wanting more than anything to be hidden inside it. Marta stepped closer to the hole, bending her body over it to glare at the curse within.

"I am Eri-Marta. I am the survivor who gave you your name, who made you anew. Who gave you a second life. Who led to your imprisonment in this realm. And now I am come to balance the scales. To return you to that place from whence you came. To release you back into the elhwith, back into the other. Back. Back you must go. And will you defy me? Or would you go gladly?"

The inn shook above them. For that matter, perhaps all of Throm shook, Roland could not say. He stepped close to the Eri, ready to grab her should she need his assistance. This was madness, but this tiny witch woman was the only hope of survival Roland could see.

"Aye, very well then," she said.

From within her robe, Marta pulled a small round object. In the meager candlelight, Roland saw it was a silver bowl. A seeing bowl, he thought. Marta held it aloft.

Sounds came from her throat then, not so much from her mouth. And though Roland thought she spoke words he might know and understand under normal circumstances, just then they were squirrelly in his head. He took hold of the woman's robe, just in case, but he had to squint his eyes against a seething, blinding light. It reached from within the hole and burned its way through the wood of the ceiling. Roland heard screaming from the room above, but Marta's voice peeled louder. Then the wind came. It stirred not only the earth but also the crates and boxes in the cellar. Roland felt the inn above them tremble. And still the Eri's screams pierced through the night and into what lay beyond it.

Roland lost his balance and fell to one knee, but he held fast to the Eri's robe. Only from this vantage did he see that the Eri no longer stood on the ground. She flew above it, hovering over the hole, surrounded by the light issuing from within it. He felt the wind pulling on her, and Roland reached for her with his free hand, holding fast with both. Marta continued crying out her incantation.

The light widened. The inn above them tore up and away into the night sky. The walls remained, but a broad cylinder of nothing reached up through the heart of the building. Rain—new rain, Roland guessed, for it hadn't been raining earlier—cascaded down through the gaping heart of the building, saturating his clothes and that of the Eri. Still, the witch continued her cries. The shaking around them grew. The light burned Roland's eyes so that squinting was no longer enough. He screwed them shut as a wail forced its way out of his throat.

He felt like his arms were being ripped free from his body. He felt the light scalding the skin of his hands and arms. He heard the witch's words. He felt them like darning needles in his brain. Then all went still, all save the witch.

Marta fell, and as she did, her velocity nearly pulled Roland into the hole after her. But he managed to pull her up and out, rolling onto his back. For a long moment, neither moved nor spoke, Roland's breaths coming in great gasps, the witch riding his chest like a sleeping child on a mule.

Finally, Roland pushed her off him and rolled to his side.

"Is it . . . ?" he tried but failed to finish. "Are we . . . ?"

Marta began laughing. Her chuckle grew into a mad cackle.

"Damn you, woman, did it work?" Roland demanded.

"We yet live, don't we?" the witch asked, her maniacal laughter returning.

"Yeh thought we'd die, didn't yeh," Roland spat, rolling to his knees as the mad woman's fit of laughter tapered. "Great fuckin' pig shit . . . I thought we were dyin'." With a huff, Roland stood and took two steps before collapsing face-first into the dank earth. He rolled again to his side, or tried. But all his strength had fled. He felt two small hands grip his shoulders and turn him over. The witch was small, but she was strong, it seemed.

"No, Roland," she said. "Wait. I have something that will help you regain your strength."

Then she turned to grab a bottle from her things. It took her several moments to find it, the wind having reset the contents of the room. And while she searched, the rain fell steadily into Roland's face. He opened his mouth and allowed it to wet his parched throat. He had loved nothing so much as that rain in his full life, he realized. After an age, Marta returned and poured the contents of a small bottle into his mouth. He swallowed the sweet, tangy concoction and was surprised to find a modicum of strength return to his limbs. He sat up.

"What will you do now?" she asked him.

"Why did you kill my friend?" he demanded.

Marta shook her head. "He was already dead."

"No, he wasn't," Roland began. But then he saw what his mind had ignored earlier. How, when they had buried the chest, still secreted within the crate, Tig had lifted the crate's lid to peer inside. Had reached in to stroke the chest. It had been brief, but something had changed in his friend then. And hadn't he started scratching his chest? Yes, Roland thought he had.

But then again, Roland was not certain if he'd seen this for true, or if it was easier, after the fact, for his mind to paint in the sight rather than facing—and in part owning—his friend and brother's fate.

"It is as I say," Marta said. "He was already dead. But not you. And why is that? Why did you not reach inside the crate? Were you not curious, or did you see enough to warn you against it?"

Roland shrugged, falling back to lay flat on his back again. He was exhausted.

"What will you do now?" she asked again.

"Leave," Roland said. "Just as soon as I can stand up."

Marta spat another laugh. "You will stand soon enough, but you will not leave. Not for some time."

"And why do yeh say that?"

"Because," Eri-Marta answered, "the cost of blood is steep. We performed a blood oath this night. It will take your life if you do not pay it back."

"What?" Roland shouted as he sat up so fast, his vision flipped. He shut his eyes and fell again to the ground. "What does that mean?"

"Do not worry about it," the Eri said with a wave of her hand. "I will take care of you. I will take care of us both. You will have to stay, for some time at least. A year, mayhap more."

"I will not stay a day longer than I have to," Roland said, but even as he did, he knew this was untrue.

Everything had changed. Tig was dead. Their job had failed. Roland felt he may not be suitable for reaver work any longer, and if he was, how would he begin again without Tig? And the way he felt just then, he wondered if he would ever fully recover.

"Aye, but there are things beside pain and debts to blood magic that might keep you here, Roland." Marta placed her palm against his chest. "Take deep breaths," she instructed. "Slow and deep. This will help. The tonic is working. Soon we can return to my hut. But for now, breathe slow and deep."

Roland did as she said. He felt himself calming, felt heat returning to his limbs. People clamored in the ruined inn above them, their superstitions ensuring they ward against whatever Sauingrey devils had brought such destruction. Roland granted Sauingrey had once again hid them and their work. Still, they had to leave the cellar soon, or they may be forced to answer difficult questions. He looked again at the witch, and he guessed she might have a remedy for curious onlookers or angry regents. Still, best not to find out.

But before they left, Roland needed one more answer. "What of the gold?" he asked.

Eri-Marta's grin was wicked. "There was no gold. Only a tempting illusion of it." Roland did not understand, and it must have been obvious on his face. "Honey attracts flies, aye?" Marta explained. "Gold attracts greedy men, even cursed gold. And greedy men satiate thirsty curses." She reached a dark hand out to pat his forearm. "Sorry about your friend."

They remained quiet for several moments.

"Roland, I could use a man like you," Marta said. "Sometimes my work requires lifting heavy things."

Roland scoffed, then he surprised himself with a laugh. And the laugh kept coming. "Aye," Roland said after a time. "I bet you do."

Roland pulled on his pipe, but it was still out. The rain fell harder now, but the door to the barn remained closed. He almost struck a match but feared the boy would see from inside the barn. Instead, he tucked the pipe inside its pouch and leaned back against the house.

"Only then can a man's mettle be measured . . . ," he whispered.

The memory still swam through his emotions, leaving confusion in its wake. He had stayed on with Marta after that, and not just for a year. He worked as her muscle for several years, and it had been during that time he had spied a lovely young farmer's daughter named Leah. Despite his time with Marta, only then had Roland become truly acquainted with the powers of magic, for Leah had mesmerized his mind and heart entirely. That spell yet held, so many years later. She had begun a transformation in him even with her very first glance. It had been a long while since he'd seen Eri-Marta. Roland left being a brigand behind to become a husband and father instead, a respectable farmer and member of their little community. This life was one he'd grown to love . . . and now a new shadow lay heavy upon it.

Roland knew rascals and criminals when he saw them. He had been one. Eliot was neither. What Eliot was felt somehow worse. The boy had been painfully scarred by things Roland could only imagine, and his gut told him Eliot needed someone. Eliot needed a friend . . . . He needed a father. But what might that cost? *Only once the dust has settled, and the blood dried . . . .*

Roland hated the truth of it, but he had no choice. The boy could not stay. Whatever devils roosted in Eliot's head would come out in time. Leah and Cora were what mattered, not the stray boy.

Eliot would be on his own. The idea twisted Roland's gut, but it was the only way. He stood, glancing at the sky. The rain would be gone by morning. He'd hoped for a little more. The fields could use it. But when had anything ever been so simple?

Roland looked again at the barn. Come first light, he'd tell the boy. He'd send Eliot on his way. For now, he could only wish the boy quiet dreams. "Sleep, Rat," Roland said. "We will deal with tomorrow tomorrow. For now, sleep."

Author's Note

The following note has mild spoilers for book two, *A Greedy Shadow*.

I knew before writing a page of *A Greedy Shadow* that Eliot would be haunted by a new darkness: dark calls to dark, after all. His stains—the residue left over from his kohlas—would not go away. An extraordinary and horrifying ordeal like his cumatu leaves permanent scars, and in this case, not just those on Eliot's skin. But I admit: I struggled with the idea that Eliot would have to face off against a cubare, or rather, a sex demon. There seemed to be no more humiliating challenge he could face, but that's why it was necessary. I knew Eliot would be stripped of his dignity and self-worth, being reduced—in his own reflection, at least—to a hideous shell of a man. Therefore, his demoralizing had to be acute and total. As I reflected on my own experiences, it became obvious that this metaphorical stripping would be best demonstrated by the very literal stripping imposed upon Eliot and all the other demoralizing violences exacted upon him by the cubare.

I grew up in a small, conservative southern-American town in the 1980s. My fundamentalist church taught me sex was an ugly thing that should be kept secret, that the "ways of the flesh" could leave me with a "reprobate mind." Rather than learning a healthy respect for my sexuality and that of others, I was confused and often petrified. Even feeling sexual attraction often made me feel like an "abomination" for urges I had no control over and should not have felt ashamed of. In a way, the cubare represents the internalized fear of being a deviant that can lead to a deep-seated, debilitating insecurity in such an environment.

That's why I believe interactions like those between Roland and Leah with Eliot have such an emotive power. You must understand: I love this boy. He is very real to me. And I hate how vulnerable he is. I hate how his body seems to betray him. I hate how he asks for none of the bad that happens to him, and that he has little control over how it marks him. It breaks my heart. But the most important thing in this scene isn't what Eliot experiences. Roland gets a good look at just how disturbed Eliot is, but Roland, too, loves the boy, even if he does not yet know it. Roland and Leah's love for Eliot is a big reason why his story is so beautiful to me. Love like that has a magic all its own.

But it demands an explanation: if Roland witnessed the depths of Eliot's stains, how could he allow the troubled boy to remain so near to his family? In this scene, Roland struggles against his acceptance of Eliot, but he also struggles against a long-buried memory of his own reprobations. As we look back with him into that memory, he sees a shadow of Eliot in himself, only with stark differences. Roland had not chosen his condition at nine when Tig found him, but he chose how he would respond afterward. What sort of man he would become. He would choose again in the wake of his and Tig's attempt to steal a cursed chest of gold. Eliot did the same, but his choices—so far—had been better than Roland's at a similar age, or so Roland believes. Does this make up for the risks Eliot brings to Roland's family? By the end of this scene, Roland has determined it does not, but a lot can change over the course of a single night.

The scene where Eliot skulks naked out of the barn while Roland smokes on the porch happens after Eliot has been on Roland's farm for around two months. We see the scene from Eliot's point-of-view in chapter two of *A Greedy Shadow.* The memory of Roland's heist with Tig and Janith happened nearly thirty years before.

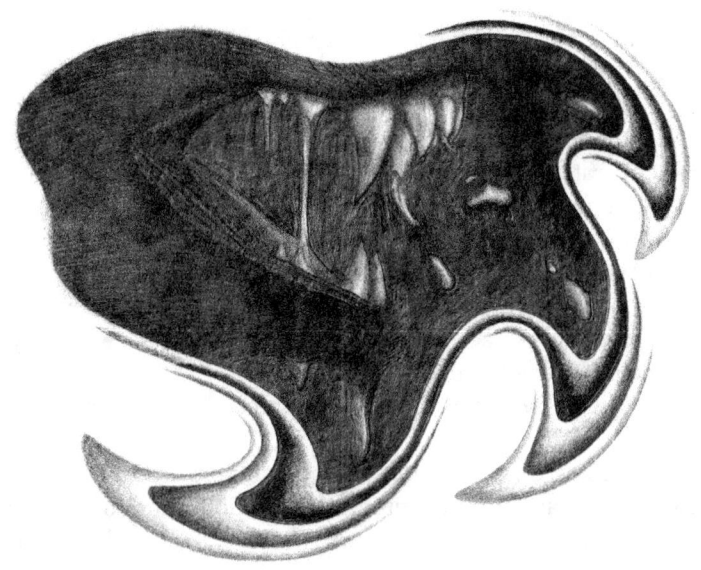

A LION AMONG WOLVES

As a boy of six years, Dathan had two favorite things: one was roaming the hills and forests with his father and grandfather, hunting rabbits. The second was listening to his grandfather tell stories.

"Pooba, tell me a story!" Dathan had climbed into his grandfather's lap, and for all the world, he looked like a gopher in the arms of a grizzly. The storm outside buffeted. The world was dark except for the occasional blast of lightning, each one transforming a square of night into day. It was a good night for stories . . . .

Back and back, many a many ago, a man came from the mountains to seek out and cleanse an infection that had taken root across the land. His purpose was simple: find the infection and remove it the way one might a rotting tooth. Simple though it may seem, the task would not be easy. It would be dangerous. He risked his life and body . . . and perhaps worse, his soul. But he accepted these risks. They filled him with nervous energy: he was exhilarated.

When he found the secret place, tucked beneath a large mound of earth protruding from a larger hill, he walked right in as if it were home. At its entrance was an abandoned metal grate. Twisted and rusty with age, it was the decaying vestiges of a long-dead city, one that once sat atop the large hill like a sentinel keeping watch. He made his way past this and stepped into the jowls of the cave.

The place was wet and stank of rotting food and human waste. And stagnation. He splashed his way through a pool of rancid water, the stench increasing for a few interminable moments. Luckily for him, it mellowed eventually. It never quite dissipated, but it dulled enough to stop burning his nostrils. After a time, perhaps he wouldn't smell it at all.

He entered a large, vaulted room deep within the cave. This had been carved there, that much was certain. An ancient room that many peoples had inhabited through the ages. Some good, others quite bad. This chamber had likely been a weapons store in some distant past. There were scores of passageways that led away from this central hub, each one arched and dully lit with torches. The floor was a network of stone brick. The air was cold, still and sweet with mildew.

"Pooba. We don't *care* 'bout the cave! Where are the monsters?"

"Oh, aye. Sorry, lad. I get carried away with the structure. I used to work with stone." Roland sniffed, assuming the air of a teacher . . . though he and Dathan both knew he'd never worked with stone. "Just a little here and there, mind. Fascinatin', it is. Yeh see, boy, the construction of such a space could only—"

"Pooba!"

"Right. As yeh wish, lord Gopher."

Dathan smiled—he loved when Roland called him lord Gopher—and settled deeper into his grandfather's lap, one leg thrown over Roland's arm as if over the arm of a chair. His head nestled in the crook of the great man's other elbow. A perfect fit.

Dathan's eyes were wide and his mouth agape, a smile curling its corners, as Roland continued his story.

The room was filled—wall to wall—with scrawny, naked men. Their brown skin was a plexus of tattoos. Runes, most like. Strange markings and words of a language no man knew. Not real men, at least. Their bodies were so tight with lean muscle, they were pulled into an unnatural, bent posture. This gave them the appearance of constant readiness, as if they were always about to lunge. And so they were. Even when they were completely still, raw energy imbued their stance, causing their muscles to quiver, implying ceaseless motion. Like water flowed just beneath their taught skin.

They were dark men with dark, matted hair and dark eyes. In addition to their tattoos, they were covered in hideous scars: tokens of violent, reprobate lives. The whites of their eyes were stained yellow and their fingertips a deep brick color as though dyed with blood. They looked at the intruder with anger. Of course they did. He did not belong.

"Tell me his name, Pooba."

"Oh, I don't recollect I know his name—"

"Pooba. Yeh know his name."

"Aye, I do," Roland said, nodding. "His name were Geoffry."

"Pooba! No!"

"Aye, I 'spect yer right. His name was Barnabas?" Roland said, scratching his chin.

"No, Pooba. His name starts with a *D*."

This story was older than the hills, and the hero's name did *not* start with a *D*. But at some point, Roland had personalized it for the boy. Now, there was nothing for it.

"Oh, aye," Roland continued, as if suddenly remembering. "Donovan. That were it!"

"Pooba, I will *hurt* yeh, so I will." And Dathan began to growl, shifting his position on his grandfather's lap to adopt that of a predatory cat.

Roland rumbled in laughter. "Aye, aye . . . yer right, boy. Yer right. Keep yer breeches on. I know his name. His name were . . ."

Dathan looked at the room before him, filled with a horde of fierce, feral men. Though the cave was damp and cold, their bodies were covered in a sheet of sweat as though heated from within. Dathan stood watching. He didn't give them a chance to speak.

"I am come to tell you your time is soon up."

A few of the men snarled. Another laughed outright. Most growled low, guttural sounds that reminded Dathan of great stones scraping against each other. Barks came from several men as if thrown from their throats. Then one of the men stepped forward, and the room fell silent.

This must be their leader, Dathan thought. The one in charge would likely be the one who spawned the most fear in the others. Or the one who could stay alive the longest. Any man who could control—much less wield—the mass of lunatics surrounding them, even for a short time, was worthy of careful consideration.

Dathan regarded him. This man carried himself with an authority that seemed palpable, even if self-appointed. He came so close, Dathan felt heat from the man's body. *No wonder they're sweating,* Dathan thought. *They are scorching.* He sniffed Dathan like a dog.

The leader moved back one step. Then two. His body began to twitch all over, as if in a fit, causing his sweat to spray out in a fine mist. As Dathan watched, it seemed as though the leader's body began melting, sweat coursing across his tattooed body. His skin began to dance, clenching in and out of shape. Dathan smelled the rank scent of burning hair. Then, in a blink, the man before him was no longer a man. His body stood nearly erect, halfway between human and beast. His face was contorted into a sneering half snout, the mouth filled with large teeth the size of nails. Hair covered him except in the center of his chest and abdomen. His genitals hung between his legs like a dark pendulum.

He was wolfenkind.

The rest of the pack followed him in the change. The place filled with the burning scent, so strong it burned Dathan's eyes. To the last, they each transformed, surrounding him. Fifty manwolves, perhaps more. There had to be more. Dathan only saw the males of the pack. The women and children were somewhere else. That was ironic, that only the men would be allowed for this spectacle. After all, a woman made them what they were: their original alpha had been a bitch, one known for her insatiable lust for blood.

Dathan watched, unimpressed and unafraid of their terrible shift. Instead, he took two steps toward the pack leader. Dathan was a tall man, but still he had to look up to meet the creature's eyes.

Dathan repeated, "I am come to tell you your time is soon up."

The pack began laughing. The incredulous laugh turned into a guttural, grating hum. The hum turned into obscene howls. The leader never took his eyes from Dathan's, so he must have seen Dathan as he began removing his own clothing. Soon, Dathan stood in the midst of the heaving mass of beasts, naked himself. Naked and unprotected. When his change came, the wolfenkind were not ready.

At first, Dathan quivered. Then he shuddered. Soon, his own body was covered in sweat and twitching all over, just as the others had been. While theirs had exploded into mass and black fur, though, Dathan's change turned him gold.

His body transformed into the wide set haunches of a lion with a magnificent golden mane and golden eyes that burned like the sun. He did not stand erect like a man. He did not need to, for even on all fours, he stood eye to eye with the beast before him.

Dathan was a lion among wolves. A leoman, something of legend in which even the wolfenkind didn't fully believe.

The nearest wolfenkind lunged, yapping. Dathan leapt out of his way, but the creature still caught his jaw with a massive claw. It was a deep scratch but began healing straight away. A very human gasp came from the pack at this. The wolf attacked again, but Dathan struck back. A new scratch, along Dathan's flank this time, healed itself and was gone before the wolf's head stopped trundling along the cobbles. Its body, now headless, deformed in the midst of a grotesque half-change before growing still.

Dathan growled at the silent pack of wolves—*see me,* this growl said, *see true*—then he transformed back into a man. Not so quick to follow, the wolves glowered at him. Not a one made a move against him. Finally, the pack leader changed as well. As a man again, he spoke to Dathan for the first time.

"One of you cannot stop all of us."

"Agreed. But you cannot kill me and live. Not all of you, leastways. Which among you are willing to die?"

Both were correct, and neither were willing to disagree. They stared at each other. Dathan knew they could overpower him, and he would die at their hands, but they would pay a high price. He couldn't kill all of them, that much was true, but he could kill many of them. Their leader, at least, knew as much. The room, though cavernous, was not big enough to allow for an open fight. Only so many of them could come at Dathan at once. Those who did stood a grave chance of finding themselves divided into pieces. It would take time and many casualties to overcome the lion.

But Dathan wasn't there to fight, not yet. They all saw that. He was there to deliver a message. The message had been delivered: your time is soon up.

Most of the other wolves had changed back. After several moments, the leader grunted, and some of the others came to Dathan and bound him with chains. Dathan let them. They put a cuff around his throat and a large chain tight around his waist. These were connected with another long leash of chain. The leader held this. Dathan's arms and legs were left free.

Quick like lightning, the mass of smelly men were wolves again, yapping and howling. From the darkness of the corridors, Dathan saw others coming. *These must be the women,* he guessed. In a furious rush, the wolfenkind left the place then, Dathan being dragged along with them. They flew across the land at a pace so quick, Dathan, in his human form, could not match their speed. Instead he rode the back of his chain master, wrapping his legs around the beast's furry waist and holding on to its dirty neck. They came at last to a hill overlooking a village in the valley below. Dathan was chained to a tree, allowing him a perfect view of the slaughter that happened there.

The men and women of the village ran before the wolves, shielding their children and wielding their weapons and fire torches in an impotent attempt to protect themselves against the onslaught. There was no use. Even if only a handful, the wolves could have tended neatly to the small village, but this was not a handful of wolfenkind. It was a horde. The melee was over in minutes, but the carnage would remain: not a single person remained alive in the village.

Dathan was furious, but he could do nothing to change what happened. And he could not have prevented it. That had not been his purpose for coming. He'd brought a message. That was all. Their end would come, but he could not bring it on his own. He thought then of changing, of taking down as many of the creatures as he could. Perhaps he could take most of them. But no. He knew there was a better way.

Dathan mourned those who died in the valley. He silently sang prayers for them. He preserved his focus against despair with the salt of truth: the vile beasts were almost at their end. Their time was soon up. Nothing could prevent that.

The wolves returned to their human shape, their flesh smeared with blood and gore. Lethargic, they walked back to their lair. The trip, much slower this time, lasted all through the rest of the night. They were in no hurry, their hunger slaked and their bodies heavy from their feast. Some of the men had sacks slung over their backs. This was presumably food for the cubs back in the cave: dead bodies. The pack had also taken several live victims prisoner. These would serve as training for the young ones. The realization of this sent a visible shudder through Dathan. The man holding his chain looked at him skeptically. He knew that shudder.

The chain around Dathan's neck was meant to stymy any attempt he might make to change. It fit comfortably around his human neck, but the wolves were certain it would choke the lion. Dathan, however, knew the chain would snap clean. He could certainly do damage to this brood in that moment. They ambled as though drunk. And in truth, they were drunk: drunk on blood and fear. Dathan could take out half of them before they understood what was happening. But no. Still no. He would not. The time would come, but not now. By the first signs of morning light, they had returned to the cave.

The pack slumbered for days after. A state of near hibernation came over them. Dathan was kept chained to the wall. He refused to eat meat the wolfenkind offered him, certain it was human flesh. He lived instead on the rats infesting the cave, of which there was a bounty. He followed the plan. He waited. On two other occasions, the pack took him on a hunt. Once they ransacked another village. Once they destroyed a traveling caravan. In both cases, they left behind a butcher's work. With each slaughter, Dathan became more and more hungry for the wolfenkind's slaughter; he would take great pleasure during their own massacre.

"What happened to the others?" Dathan, the seriously rapt child of six, asked.

"The other what, boy?" Roland pulled Dathan, who had drifted during the telling of the tale, square once again in his lap.

"The prisoners. What happened to 'em, Pooba?"

Roland thought it over. "I think yeh know what happened to 'em, Gopher."

"Aye. But I would set 'em free."

"Aren't yeh listening, boy?"

"Aye, I'm listenin'. And if it were me, I'd set those prisoners free."

Roland's bedtime tale had suddenly become an issue of moral judgment. "True, that seems to be the right thing to do," Roland said slowly. "But sometimes what seems like the right thing to do ain't always it."

Dathan sat up so he could better look at Roland. "Yer sayin' sometimes it's good to let folken get et by wolfenkind?" The last word was big and clumsy on the child's tongue.

Roland thought hard, swallowing uncomfortably against the boy's question. Dathan had many difficult questions, questions with complex nuance and moral counterbalances. He was as inquisitive as any child, and this was just fine—even as it could be tricksy to navigate during Dathan's more high-minded inquests. Finally, Roland found his answer.

"Boy, sometimes a man's gotta know where his limitations are. Aye, he could've saved those handful of prisoners, but his goal wasn't to save a handful. It were to save all of 'em. All the people. Yeh know how the story ends." The gopher was focusing on the details of a story told so many times, it should no longer contain any mysteries whatsoever. And a tale told for children, even a morality tale such as this one, needed its truths gripped with a loose fist, accounting for the ebb and flow of narrative. But such realities were difficult to explain to a very literal boy of six years. "Yeh've heard this one enough by now to just enjoy it through to the end, aye?"

"Pooba," Dathan answered, his voice reasonable but firm. "Yeh just said he didn't save 'em. How could he save all of 'em if some of 'em got et?"

Roland closed his eyes, sighing. Dathan's six-year-old logic had no room for the complexities of the gray areas of morality. And the story hadn't been written for such scrutiny. It was a story to frighten children into sleeping through the night, an allegory, perhaps, for what happens when little boys let their wild sides have the better parts of them. If scrutinized closely, the story fell apart. Roland understood this. He also understood the story was like a candied shell meant to hide a morsel of truth hidden inside. It was not meant to be taken seriously. Why warn the feral beasts of their imminent doom, for example? Why not storm the hidden vaults of the wolf caves with an army and slaughter each creature to the last, including their whining pups? Ah, but that wouldn't make for an interesting tale, and Roland would never pose such questions to

Dathan . . . not questions that might unravel the boy's favorite scary story. There was, of course, no such thing as wolfenkind. Or leomen, either, for that matter. But there was good and bad, light and dark. There were monsters, more than the world's share in Roland's estimation. But there weren't just monsters. True, sometimes the monsters won. Often times, even. But sometimes, those same monsters got eaten themselves.

But how could he explain all of that to a child, even one as pensive as Dathan?

"Dathan," Roland began, a bit more sober than before. "Look at it like this. Last spring, when the river rose and we dug out that nest of chucks that burrowed in too close, what'd we do?"

"We moved 'em. We didn't eat 'em." Dathan's face was pinched. He was yet to see the connection.

"Aye, but what happened to the little'ns?"

"Some died. Three of 'em."

"Aye," Roland said slowly, "and didn't we know they'd die, like as not? Too young to move?"

Dathan stirred, defensiveness in his body language. When he spoke, Roland heard it in the boy's voice. "Aye, but if they stayed, they'd all die. They'd drown in the river."

"Right, boy. That's right. Now, think of the wolfenkind as a swelling river."

The boy's eyes lit up with understanding. "Aye, I see it, Pooba. I see it."

Roland's eyes filled with warm tears and his face with a smile, and he was surprised to be thus moved over such a commonplace occurrence. Roland's love for Dathan had no bottom. It had no lid or limit.

"Good," Roland rumbled. "Now do yeh want to hear this tale, or do yeh want yer grumpy grandfather to turn into a wolf himself and eat yeh up?"

"A bear, Pooba," the boy laughed. "Yer the bear. I'm the gopher."

"Right yeh are. Very right."

Dathan settled back into his roost in the bear's lap, once again content, and Roland picked up his tale.

Weeks passed, the wolfenkind swinging between violent attacks and lethargic hibernation. A restlessness grew in the pack. They stopped hunting. They slept less and less. More agitated and aggressive, they often tussled with each other. Their hunger grew, their fasting intentional. The younger members would nip and snap at each other, some in human state, some in wolfen state. The adults were brooding with fitful energy. The pack was on edge.

It was the moon, Dathan knew. And Sauingrey.

As the orb grew fuller in the night sky and the season grew colder, the wolf state became more pronounced. The pack hunched even further in their drawn, upright stances. Their yellow eyes seemed to sink deeper into their animal skulls. Their jaws dripped with constant salivation. All this was evident even in their human form. This angst was leading up to the full moon and the pack's lunar festival on the eve of their new year, a time known as Sauingrey.

Legend asserted Sauingrey marked the ancient battle of the Monkshood when the goddess Dal-Reeahs was cast down into the transient pit by the druids who had once worshipped her, ending her violent rule. But Dal-Reeahs had a faithful following. As she fell, she spoke over them an incantation, binding their humanity to her own exiled form. What was left of them was a human-animal hybrid embodying the ferocity of their lordess: the wolfenkind. These turned on the druids, ate their flesh, and drank their blood. Still, the work had been accomplished. Dal-Reeahs was displaced.

Each year thereafter, Sauingrey stood as the marker between the wolfenkind's old year and the new. This was not the same new year as celebrated by the rest of the world. The wolves considered themselves distinctly separate. This new year marked the moment between when their lordess had reigned and when she had been cast down, the beginning of what they called the deep winter. Sauingrey was celebrated in preparation for when Dal-Reeahs, their lordess, would be liberated and return to them. Festival sacrifices were thought to feed her in her exiled state. The whole pack went out together on Sauingrey—men, women, and children— on the eve of deep winter, to begin a riot of murder and destruction. The weeks of fasting before festival made them mad with hunger, but they did not simply eat their victims: the point was carnage, not feasting. Festival would last several days while the pack worked their way from village to village, town to town, leaving a trail of blood and viscera behind them.

This happened every Sauingrey, but this year was different. It was also a full moon. It was believed there was always more magic when the Pregnant Moon broke on one of the Hidain, but more so when it broke on

Sauingrey. Though not as strong as the Drodein, when it is believed by the Monkshood their queen will ultimately return in power, a full moon during Sauingrey was a special time for the wolfenkind. A Poison Moon, they called it. Their fasting was even more intense than typical during a Poison Moon. Their feasting and carnage would mirror this.

On the first day of Sauingrey, the pack abandoned the cave. The moon was full to bursting, like a breast full of milk. The wolves were feverish. They flew across the countryside. They had to travel far since no sensible folken would live so close to a pack of killers. Folken didn't believe in the Monkshood, as the wolfenkind were known, not truly. They were creatures out of myth, but myth is difficult to dismiss when it is eating you.

The moon's light eventually brought the pack to a homestead: a large farm with several families, but not quite a village. The folken had sealed their windows and doors against the night. Everyone knew the perils of Sauingrey, though many believed these were mostly legends. The children would often dress like animals—goats, dogs, wolves—and go from house to house asking for gifts. In the more superstitious communities, such as this one, this was not for fun. It was an act of coalescence. The animals going door to door this night were not children in costume, however. Though some of them were, indeed, children: this was the one time of year when the cubs of the pack were allowed to join the rest in slaughter.

The rampage ended quickly, and the pack moved on.

Hours later, they came upon a village, but it was abandoned. The pack moved on. In time, they came to another village with a large, broad wall surrounding it. Inside, the village was ripe with humanity. Afterward, when the place stank sweet of death and rattled with blood-splattered fricks dangling from windowsills and doorjambs—Hidain tokens meant to ward against the presence of evil, but having failed—the wolfenkind moved on into the growing light of morning. The silver blue light of the full moon made the night very bright, but now the earliest edge of morning reached them, a warm hue growing on the horizon. Dathan, who had again ridden the back of one of his captors during the more furious flights, now walked in their midst, sickened. Moving at a slower pace, the pack had mostly returned to human form. Glutted and stuffed, they were languid. Many still bore wolfish features, too lazy from their feasting to pull themselves into either one shape or the other. The sight of gore on the men's bodies was bad, but on that of the children, it was painful for Dathan to see. And the women, whose solid bodies might have been exquisitely attractive in other circumstances, were perverse to him now, gowned, as they were, in the manifest cruelty of death. Dathan was a leoman. He was a carnivore . . . but he was not a monster. The sight of the women and children turned his stomach. The sight of the men turned his anger.

They were crossing an open field when Dathan sensed it. His skin prickled, the hair on his naked body standing on end, and not from cold. He stood still. The act of stopping was so sudden the wolfenkind holding Dathan's chain in its tight, half-wolf grip was snatched nearly off his feet. The creature pulled the chain to force Dathan to keep moving, except Dathan did not move. Instead, he took the chain in his hands and yanked the wolfenkind to him, snapping his neck like a twig. Dathan closed his eyes then and breathed in deep.

The pack surrounded Dathan, many changing into wolf form. When Dathan's eyes reopened, they were glowing gold. His body swiftly grew, shifting into his lion form. It happened so suddenly, the pack was dumbstruck. The metal rings around his neck and waist fell away from him like tree bark. Those who had seen Dathan change before had seen it only once. And that had been less than half the pack. These recovered more quickly than the others. One by one, the pack all began to change.

The leader walked up to Dathan, a wolf confronting a lion. "You cannot kill us all." He said this as if only a little reminder was needed. Perhaps he thought this was so.

"No," Dathan replied, his voice a deep resonant growl. "But they can."

The leader's eyes narrowed, confused. Then they sprang wide with understanding and dawning fear.

The hills surrounding the valley were wreathed by an army of people—men, women, and children—each one of them with golden hair and golden eyes. Tall and regal, beautiful and strong, they looked down into the field of wolves surrounding a single lion, their eyes betraying the sense of disgust they felt.

The wolves howled to intimidate the folken looking down at them. They nipped and barked, the young ones cowering behind quivering hind legs. As the sun mounted the crest of the eastern horizon, the people crowning the hills began to shake. One might have thought their shaking was from fear. It was not. For suddenly, the hillside was covered with golden lions, their eyes shining bright like the coming sun. Their roar was a coming storm.

The wolves fell on themselves in hysterical panic. In the frenzy, they did not think. They simply slashed and bit in such a fashion that, by the time the pride made it down into their midst, the work was half complete:

the wolves had nearly destroyed themselves. But they did not work alone. Dathan bathed in their blood.

Soon, the field was quiet. The air was clean. The sun was shining. Not a wolf was left alive, or in one piece. Somewhere, Dal-Reeahs wailed in her primordial tomb. Her sacred Sauingrey had been used against her.

Dathan roared in triumph.

One might expect a boy of six would be asleep by the end of such a long story, cradled as he was in his grandfather's lap on a late stormy night. Or be cringing in fright from such a heinous tale. But listening to his grandfather tell a story, especially *that* story, was one of Dathan's two favorite things in the world. He was wide-eyed and wide awake when Roland finished. Instantly, Dathan was up and running throughout the room, growling and pouncing like a lion. He was Dathan, the leoman.

Leah peeked her head in from the kitchen. "Nice, lover," she said, winking at her husband. "It's good yeh got that boy coiled tighter than a spring at bedtime. Well done." Roland winked back, smiling.

"Nothin' his da' and ma' can't tend to," Roland said.

The storm outside had spent itself during the last moments of Roland's tale and was now crawling along in its grumpy fashion, away from the farm. Dathan's storm would have to spend itself in like manner: by running its course.

Dathan stopped suddenly. "Pooba?"

"Aye?"

"What took the other leomen so long?"

Roland smiled. *Leomen* sounded a lot like *lemon* in Dathan's voice. "What do yeh mean, boy?"

"If only they'd come sooner, mayhap the others could've been saved."

Perhaps Dathan's curiosity in grown-up matters was a testament to something marking him as unique. Roland couldn't say. But this thought did not fill Roland with pride so much as dread, and he couldn't say exactly why.

Roland understood Sauingrey had been used against Dal-Reeahs's magic, that in using its magic against the wolfenkind, it marred the magic somehow. Or that was the idea, thin as it might be. But explaining that to a six-year-old might require a bit of magic, as well. Roland was fresh out.

Roland looked at Dathan. "Boy, I'm pert near an old man, and it's pert near too late to think. Save yer yammerin' and curiosity for a time when I'm not most dead."

Still, Roland didn't mind Dathan's endless questions. The boy was curious, and his curiosity was a joyous, happy thing. There was nothing more Roland wanted than good things and happy times for his grandson. But, every once in a while, darker thoughts crept in.

Good and happy were abundant now, but, one day, the boy would be a man. Trouble had a way of finding men. And sometimes, as in the story of the lion among wolves, monsters get to eat the children . . . .

Author's Note

This scene serves two functions in the anthology: first, it shares a mythological tale about a group of wolfenkind who worship the fallen witch—the "True Witch"—Dal-Reeahs, and of a separate group of leomen who stand against them. Second, it shows the interactions between grandfather Roland and his rambunctious grandson, Dathan.

I should point out there are a fair amount of references to the witch Dal-Reeahs in the wolfenkind story. As a folkentale, we must assume the story is fiction. However, much of the fiction from many folk tales in our world is based on a germ of truth, perceived or otherwise, so perhaps the same would be true here. That isn't to say the story within this scene is true. It only suggests that those from whom the story originated believed at some point it was true.

The thing I most enjoy about this scene is the joyful frustration Dathan has as Roland is telling the story, and all the questions his six-year-old mind needs answers for. It is reminiscent of my dad telling me stories as a child.

My dad would read me and my brother stories from children's books most nights before bed, but he rarely—if ever—read them as written. Rather, he made them up as he went. When I was too young to read the words on the page and could only judge the pictures, I somehow always knew when he was recreating the story. He did it intentionally to irk me and my brother, but especially me, I think. Brian—my older brother by five years—could read just fine, and he wasn't the "rambunctious" kid I was. I had a short fuse and was prone to emotional explosions—I'm a Sagittarius—but I always loved stories. And secretly I loved that the stories my dad read us always changed . . . the ending was never the same from one telling to the next. I think this made me fall in love not only with stories but with storytelling at a very young age. I would, like Dathan, scale the mountain of my dad's body and demand retribution, or at least that he stick to the words on the page, but in the end, my dad always told the story how he wanted, and I always loved it. Perhaps that rubbed off on me. I tell stories the same way.

Elements of this scene exist in chapter twenty-Seven of *A Greedy Shadow,* but here it is in its entirety. I left out most of what you can find in *Shadow* to prevent redundancy, but it was difficult to do so. I love Dathan's interactions with Roland. For reference, Dathan is six years old. Also, the leomen story is based on a vivid dream I had. Obviously, I was the leoman.

III

PART THREE: SONGS

Poetry and music are often the colors that invigorate the tapestry of a culture, giving it depth and texture. While building the world of the Glint, I have leaned heavily on these to make the land and its people more realistic. I want to give insight into where the songs of this series come from outside of the story and a context for their origins within the story.

Even though this section is called Songs, I am including any song or poem that lives in the first three books. I wrote some of those that follow while I was in the ebb and flow of the story, following the current in and out of lyrics as needed. But many of these were originally written during my own musings while sitting at my piano. I am a classically trained vocalist and have been in a couple of bands over the years, so writing songs was something I did often.

Moving into 2016, a priority for me was to invest a more appropriate level of time and energy into writing books, leading to the completion of the manuscript version of *Scarecrow* that I'd been tinkering with on and off for about ten years. That manuscript would later be dissected by my editor and rewritten by me into two novels, *The Scarecrow Hunters* and *A Greedy Shadow* (2020). In 2017, I began writing *The Singing Bones*. By then, I'd not written a song in several years, and those gears were quite rusty. For me, writing poetry, including song lyrics, is a very different process from writing prose. It requires a separate type of creative energy. Because I had been out of practice for so long, writing songs for Grey felt cumbersome at best. At worst, everything new I wrote simply sucked.

I had an archive of songs to pull concepts from, and similar to Grey in *The Singing Bones*, I had often leaned into the natural world around me to inspire the lyrics. That is how I found Grey's lyrical "voice." The first example of this type of repurposing (or rather, finding a forever home in this series for an orphaned lyric) is a song that first appeared in the 2016 manuscript of *Scarecrow* and, in large part, inspired *Bones* . . . or at the very least, the character of Grey. The song is "Edön Grey," and originally it was a lullaby I wrote for my cousin's firstborn. Eden Grace was her name, but she became Ben instead. Thus, the lullaby I wrote had no baby to call its own. Then I saw Grey coming out of the mist . . . .

I have included very simple musical notations, like key and tempo, just for fun. I have also included a brief synopsis of the origins of the songs within the world of the Glint. An author's note follows select pieces as I deem them worthwhile. The pieces are in the order they appear in the books. Also worth mentioning: I've noted the first chapter of the first book in which a song is referenced, even in part, but I did not list its every occurrence in the series. I've also included each song in its entirety here and in the format it was written to be performed, not necessarily as the characters perform it in the books.

MAGIC GLASS

BOOK ONE: *The Scarecrow Hunters*
CHAPTER SIX: The Smoking Man

CHILDREN'S SONG

TEMPO: moderato, 108 bpm, 4/4 time

ORIGIN: This tune was written by Lightfoot and is based on ancient lynthian scrip. In particular, it draws heavily on the epic historical poem "The Valiant." Lightfoot would not have written the song to be passed down or even shared with others. Rather, it seems most likely his intention was for personal enjoyment, or perhaps as a bit of soft spell work. Because of its source material, it includes many allusions to the foundational mythologies of most belief systems in the land of the Glint. It has no musical notation or accompaniment. (For more insight, see "The Valiant," first, second, and third staves, included later in this section.)

A TALE OF TALES
I HAVE TO TELL
A MERRY TALE IT BE
A STORY OF OLD
AND ONE SO BOLD
AS EVER A TALE THEY'LL BE

THE FIRE KINDLES
IN A POT
A POT OF GLASS AND TREE
IT BURNS TO LIGHT
THE WORLD ALIGHT
IT SHINES ON ME AND THEE

THAT MAGIC GLASS
THAT SACRED BOUGH
IT SETS OUR MARROW FREE

And showers down
In endless round
All good and lovely things

A tree sprung forth
From river mouth
And stretched, towering
The sandy bed
A cryst'line bed
Gave us gifts like these:

Up from the glass
That formed the bowl
A light was loosed and see!
The world became
Awash, ablaze
Bounded by the three

It showers down
In endless round
A pitch to make us free
As ever a song
Could carry along
The hearts of those who sing

EDÖN GREY

BOOK ONE: *The Scarecrow Hunters*
CHAPTER SIX: The Smoking Man

LULLABY

KEY: G major

TEMPO: adagio, 72 bpm, 4⁄4 time

ORIGIN: The author of this tune is Lightfoot. Though it draws a great deal of figurative language inspired by the Edöné, his specific muse was the girl, Grey.

FIREFLIES
SWIMMING IN MOONLIGHT
TEASING TWILIGHT'S DUSTY SHADES
NIGHT SONGS
TICKLE TIME SINCE GONE
TO THE SMILE OF EDÖN GREY

THE WILLOW WEEPS
THE MELODY
OF SWEET MEM'RY'S LOVELY STRAIN
THE HUMMING BROOK GOES
AND THE THISTLE KNOWS
THE SECRET OF EDÖN GREY

FAYLEE TALES WISH FOR THE MAGIC
AND MAKE-BELIEVE WANTS TO DREAM SUCH DREAMS
AS THE CREATURES OF THE FOREST LINGER
LINGER WHILE EDÖN SINGS

DANDELI'NS
DRINK IN THE MILKY NIGHT

As the moon shines down his violet haze
Laced with stardust
The singing breeze must
Go the way of Edön Grey

Very soon
The sleepy moon
Follows the stars' parade
As the golden glow
Warms both lilies and thorns
To delight of Edön Grey

Enchanted, the little ones they slumber
As the weaver spins softly night's seams
And fire leans gently from star field to kiss
To kiss little Edön sweet

Author's Note

As mentioned in the introduction to this section, this was written independent of the *Glint & Shade* series. However, I always wanted to expand the "story" of the song, even though I didn't know Grey's full story (or even that her name was Grey) when I wrote the song. Or that her story was part of Eliot and Dathan's. This is one of my favorite lyrics I've written over the years, and I recorded the original version of the song and included it, along with "Forest Music," on an album in 2004.

BLOOD MOON

BOOK ONE: *The Scarecrow Hunters*
CHAPTER SEVEN: Infected

CHILDREN'S ROUND

TEMPO: allegro, 150 bpm

ORIGIN: Similar to children's rounds Eliot would no doubt have been exposed to before his seventh birthday, this round is the product of such children's tunes being re-spun through the webbing of nightmare. It has no musical notation or accompaniment.

> WHEN THE MOON TURNS TO BLOOD
> THE BOYS ALL EAT THE WORMY MEAT
> WHEN THE MOON TURNS TO BLOOD
> THE BOYS ALL EAT THE WORMY MEAT

THE VALIANT,

FIRST, SECOND, AND THIRD STAVES

BOOK ONE: *The Scarecrow Hunters*
INTERLUDE: The Valiant, first stave

BOOK TWO: *A Greedy Shadow*
INTERLUDE: The Valiant, second stave

BOOK THREE: *The Singing Bones*
INTERLUDE: The Valiant, third stave

EPIC POEM

ORIGIN: This poem is sacred scrip and would have been written in lynthian. This is a psalm recording a religious history that has been, on some level, adopted and adapted by most major religious and people groups within the series. Though the original author is unknown, rather than an individual penning the words, it would most likely have been the product of a religious group known as the Order of Light. It has no musical notation or accompaniment.

—First Stave: The Canvas—

THE HUNGRY ARE KNOWN BY WAY THEY EAT
THE THIRSTY BY WAY THEY TAKE A DRINK
THE CRUEL BY WAY THEY TAKE

THE LONELY BY WAY THEY LAY IN WAIT
THE LUSTY BY WAY THEY TASTE THE SWEET
THE SWEET BY WAY THEY TASTE

THE DARK IS KNOWN BY WAY IT HIDES
THE SÖKLYN BY WAY THEY SHINE AT NIGHT
THE LIGHT BY WAY IT SHINES

THE STRONG BY WAY THEY LOVE
THE WEAK BY WAY THEY HATE
THE LIVING BY WAY THEY LIVE
THE HORDE BY WAY THEY DIE

THE FAYE, THE BRUTE, THE DAHNEE
KNOWN BY WAY THEY SHINE
THE BABE, THE SICK, THE DUMAS
KNOWN BY WAY THEY CRY

SO IT IS, SO IT WILL BE
SO IT WAS, BACK AND BACK
AND ON AND ON

AND THE DRAGON'S FIRE SHONE BRIGHT
AS IT CHASED ACROSS THE NIGHT SKY
THE COMET'S TAIL . . .
AND ALL THE WORLD TREMBLED IN THEIR WAKE.

—Second Stave: The Coming—

Light cleav'd the night
Sky burn'd to ash
With tooth and claw and flame
They came in might

Hills receiv'd them
A womb prepared
A bed for their coming
Home for their light

Mother Dal-Reeahs
Dragon, her prize
A symbiont coupling
Garland of peace

But love faltered
The good peace fail'd
Vi'lence bled the fissure.
Dark fill'd the crease

War crowded the belly
Night fill'd the day
The Witch lost her lover
Dragon, his way

—The Darkness—

Shadow defined
Chaos as king
All then lost in darkness
Crav'd a new light

An order grew
A harden'd hope
Resisting the desert,
Men sought the Bright

197

THE WITCH LOST FAITH
FEEDING DESPAIR
HER BROKEN HEART SILENC'D:
HOPE DISPLACED

THE SERPENT GREW
EATING HER GRACE
AH! DAMNABLE CREATURE
WHAT EMPTY WRAITH

THE FOLKEN CRIED OUT,
"GIVE US THE WAY!"
A SECRET WAS KINDLED
TO DRAW THE DAY

Come, they said, come now
But none knew just how
To bring light or flame
To burn night and pain

Come dawn
Come light
Come on
Burn bright
For all men live in shadow
All women live in fear
All children weep in slumber
With darkness so near

Come flame
Come home
Give name
To home
All fathers to find the path
All mothers to laugh or sing
All sons to follow aft'
All daughters, beckoning

Come, they said, come now
We do not know how
To bring light or flame
To burn night or pain

But come, yes come . . .
We welcome you home.

Author's Note

This is an epic poem that aims to encapsulate the foundational mythology on which the *Glint & Shade* series hinges. It is a work in progress, so more staves will appear in future books. I wrote the earliest complete version of this poem while I studied music in college in 1998.

WASH OVER

BOOK TWO: *A Greedy Shadow*
CHAPTER TEN: The Singing Bird Will Come

FOLKEN SONG

KEY: C Major

TEMPO: andante, 78 bpm, 4/4 time

ORIGIN: This song grew out of a folkentale about two lovers separated by war, one doomed to death and the other doomed to live without her lover. As is true of many such stories, love is shown to transcend the limitations of the physical world, in this case creating a bridge between the physical and spiritual planes over which the lovers can reunite.

I HAVE A GREEN BOUGH IN MY HEART.
IT TAKES ONE TO MAKE A GARDEN AND
IT SMELLS LIKE RAIN TO ME AND
YOU WASH OVER.
THE SINGING BIRD WILL COME.

TEARS ARE ROLLING LIKE A RIVER AND
THE SONG OF THE MORNING
TURNS AND TURNS MY HEART AND
YOU WASH OVER.
YOU WASH OVER.

IF THE SUN HAS TO SET,
THEN LET IT SET.
I'LL WHISPER WITH THE STARS
TILL I FORGET THE DARK.

IF THE STORM HAS TO COME,
THEN LET IT COME.

I'LL RUN IN THE RAIN,
AND I'LL LAUGH WHEN I'M DONE.

AND IF MY HEART HAS TO WEEP,
I'LL CRY WHEN I SING.
BUT I'LL SING, AND
I'LL REMEMBER YOU LOVE ME.

I PLANT SEEDS OF HOPE.
SING THEM DEEP INTO THE EARTH AND
BELIEVE THAT LIFE WILL COME, AND
YOU WASH OVER.
THE SINGING BIRD WILL COME.

THE BODY IS STRETCHING, AND
YOUR STORM IS BEAUTIFUL, AND I CAN
FEEL SOMETHING DEEPER, GROWING.
YOU WASH OVER.
YOU WASH OVER.

Author's Note

Though I haven't written the story version of this song yet, Cora tells it to Eliot in chapter ten of *A Greedy Shadow.*

RIVER

BOOK THREE: *The Singing Bones*
CHAPTER THREE: Song In The Night

FRULAY HYMN

KEY: C Major

TEMPO: andante, 85 bpm, 4/4 time

ORIGIN: Songs of the Edöné typically originate from one of two forms, or rather, a combination of the two. Bally hymns are those which are passed down through the mantle of a mother's Edönic identity to her daughter. The other type is known as frulay hymns and is more specific to the singer. This song, a frulay hymn, seems to spring from Grey's Edönic mantle as a part of her specific identity within her heritage. As with most Edön, Grey will, in time, identify with a token personification of the natural world, that element with which she most identifies. In Grey's case, her token is water. This song would be an early indication of that connection. Token hymns such as this one would be birthed within an Edön and grow as they do, in time becoming a sort of anthem by which they live. Within the Edönic community, other Edön may perform such a song upon her passing—assuming the author shared it with others. The Edön do not often congregate together, as do other religious orders, thus limiting such sharing. However, anthems would be shared with daughters during their Edönic tutelage leading into their quickening.

SING TO ME, RIVER
RUNNING ON AND ON
DESPERATE, BUT NOT UNHAPPY
SATISFIED IN LONGING
RIVER, SING YOUR SONG

SING TO ME, RIVER, I KNOW ALL THE WORDS
RUNNING ON BUT NOT CATCHING

I hope in what I'm wanting
It's in your song

I know freedom when I taste it
I know love when it takes my hand
I can't help but sing along
When I hear your song

Sing to me, wanderer
Of the open places
Where you've been

Traveler, you are the opening
You are the coming
The song of the wind

Sing to me, wind and trees
Sunshine, dazzling—sing
Sing to me, height and deep
Come now, opening
Your song is in me

Sing to me, river
Lift me up, move me on
My friend, my brother
Sing in me your song

Sing into me the Wild One
Teach me her name, teach me her song
We are one, You are Companion
I see your faces, I know them all

Author's Note

I wrote the opening lines of this song while white water rafting with my friend, Jonathan. It sprang from my mouth while I was on the water, battling against (or with) the current, being beaten down by the river's furious passion . . . . I loved it. I kept singing aloud, "Sing to me, river!" My fellow rafters were not amused, especially Jonathan, who has a unique loathing of being splashed with cold water.

HINKY DINKY

BOOK THREE: *The Singing Bones*
CHAPTER SIX: Storm Dance

CHILDREN'S RHYME

TEMPO: moderato, 110 bpm

ORIGIN: This song, in its earliest stages, existed within the children's story, "Leo and the Magic Bean." The story was eventually reforged as a song.

COME IN CLOSE, SIT A SPELL, CHILD
LEND ME YER LIST'NERS, LISTEN AWHILE
HINKY DINKY DOODLY-DOO

I'LL TELL YEH A TALE, A STANGE'NE BUT TRUE'NE
'BOUT A LITTLE BOY MUCH LIKE YOU'NE
WINKY TINKY WHITTLY-TOO

LISTEN CLOSE, THOUGH STRANGE IT SEEMS
I'LL TELL YEH OF LEO AND HIS MAGIC BEAN
HINKY DINKY, WINKY WHITTLY-TOO

A BEAN'S A BEAN'S A BEAN'S A BEAN
BUT SOMETIMES A BEAN'S NOT WHAT IT SEEMS
HINKY DINKY DOODLY-DOO

SOMETIMES A WALL'S JUST HIDE-N-FETCH
SOMETIMES A WISH A DREAM GOT STRETCHED
WINKY TINKY WHITTLY-TOO

MAYHAP A BIRD'S A FROG GROWN WINGS
MAYHAP A STORM'S A BEAUTIFUL THING
HINKY DINKY, WINKY WHITTLY-TOO

SOMETIMES THE WIND'S JUST SINGIN' A SONG
AND SOMETIMES A BEAN'S NO BEAN AT ALL
HINKY DINKY DOODLY-DOO

LEO LEARNT MAGIC WEREN'T IN HIS BEAN
FOR BEANS AREN'T REALLY MAGICAL THINGS
WINKY TINKY WHITTLY-TOO

BUT MAGIC THERE WAS, THE SECRET IS THIS:
SO OPEN THOSE LIST'NERS WIDE AS THEY GIT
HINKY DINKY, WINKY WHITTLY-TOO

MAGIC SPELLS YEH MIGHT PREFER
BUT BELIEVIN' HEARTS ARE MAGICKER
HINKY DINKY DOODLY-DOO

IT'S HOPIN' AND SIMPLE TRUSTIN' YEH SEE
WHAT PULLS A STUNNER UP FROM DREAMS
WINKY TINKY WHITTLY-TOO

O' THE STUFF OF MAGIC YER DREAMS ARE MADE
SO LET'EM HAVE THEIR HEARTY WAY
HINKY DINKY, WINKY WHITTLY-TOO

GIVE'EM THEIR WINGS, A DREAM'S NOT TO WASTE
GIVE'EM THEIR SKY TO FLY, FLY AWAY
HINKY DINKY, WINKY TINKY DOODLY-WHITTLY-TOO

Author's Note

I confess I find writing children's songs very enjoyable. One of my favorite aspects of this song is that the refrain at the end of each stanza varies throughout, and by the end, each variation stacks into a single line containing all of them. Another aspect that I love is that it is a song version of "Leo and the Magic Bean." It makes sense to me that a children's story would be adapted as a song, especially considering most of these stories would be passed down orally rather than written. Another example of this is "Wash Over."

OLE CLYDEL

BOOK THREE: *The Singing Bones*
INTERLUDE: No Rainbow For Evening

CHILDREN'S RHYME

TEMPO: moderato, 115 bpm

ORIGIN: A children's tune, this would have been sung by and to children for entertainment and perhaps very basic educational purposes, particularly with young children. The inspiration for the song, however, was a tragic famine that decimated the population many generations before, though that origin would have been mostly forgotten by Eliot's time. Regardless, the original intention of the song was to ease the pain of children and, in particular, to help them make peace with the ever-constant presence of suffering. The "evening rainbow" was a euphemism for death, suggesting it was not an ugly thing to be feared but rather a natural part of life. This tune has no musical notation or accompaniment.

CLYDEL, DUMP AND SEE THE ROOST
BE THE ROOST A HEN OR GOOSE
DUMP YER POT AND HOLD YER SPOT
TILL RAINBOW COMES AT EVENIN'

CLYDEL, JUMP AND SEE THE BEND
BE THE BEND A RIVERBED
POUR YER BOWL AND HOPE FOR MORE
TILL RAINBOW COMES AT EVENIN'

CLYDEL, THUMP YER BRAWNY TRUNK
BE YER TRUNK AN AIRY BUNK
POUR YER HEART WITH ALL YER HEART
TILL RAINBOW COMES AT EVENIN'

CLYDEL, CAN YOU SEE THE ROOST
BE THE ROOST A HEN OR GOOSE

CAN YOU GRAB THE BEARDED HAG
TILL RAINBOW COMES AT EVENIN'

(Eliot's fever begins to alter the lyrics.)

CLYDEL, WILL YOU DIE TODAY?
DIE THE WAY THE OLD ONES SAY
EATEN UP SWALLOWED DOWN
NO RAINBOW FOR YER EVENIN'

CLYDEL, EAT THE BOY OF SPRING
GOBBLE UP EVERYTHING
SPIKE HIS SKULL AND BLEED HIM FULL
TILL NOTHIN'S LEFT AT EVENIN'

CLYDEL, GIVE YOUR SON AWAY
HE'LL COME BACK ANOTHER DAY
WITH EYES OF BLACK AND SOUL OF BLACK
HE'LL BE JUST LIKE HIS FATHER

CLYDEL, DATHAN DESERVES TO DIE
HE WILL DIE HE WILL DIE
IT IS HIS RIGHT TO DIE TONIGHT
HE'LL NOT LIVE PAST THIS EVENIN'

Author's Note

This children's tune was originally included in a chapter of *The Scarecrow Hunters* (2016). In it, Eliot's fear over Dathan's seventh birthday caused him to have an emotional breakdown. In this earlier manuscript, Dathan actually celebrated his seventh birthday with his family, a detail that changed with *A Greedy Shadow*. In rewriting the original manuscript into two books, this song was lost, but I was very pleased to find it again. Now it lives in an interlude for book three, *The Singing Bones*. A portion of the original scene remains intact with it, though with a very new and disturbing context.

You will notice a delineation about halfway through where Eliot's mental instability alters the words in his mind, turning them horrific.

At that point, the rhyme scheme and tempo deteriorate as Eliot's fear escalates to a fever pitch. I considered leaving this bit out herein, since it is not an actual part of the song but rather a construction of Eliot's fevered state. However, I find its diabolical twisting of the original far too fun to omit.

If children performed the song (without the emotional breakdown, of course), they would act it out with hand gestures and body movement and would incorporate claps and stomps.

SPIRIT OF HOME

BOOK THREE: *The Singing Bones*
INTERLUDE: No Rainbow For Evening

TRADITIONAL FOLKEN ELWHEY SONG

KEY: A flat

TEMPO: largo, 52 bpm, 4/4 time

ORIGIN: Elwhey songs are traditional spiritual tunes and generally reflect adherents' personal reflections and experiences. A type of hymn, these songs often use passages of paraphrased scrip, but not always. Rather than formal spiritual texts, elwhey tunes are very personal, reflecting the human struggles and victories of those singing.

SPIRIT OF HOME, COME HOME TO ME
FIND ME IN THE DARK—I CAN'T SEE
PUSH OUT THE DARK, PUSH OUT OF ME
BREAK THE COLD, ONLY YOU HOLD ME
SPIRIT OF HOME, COME HOME

I DO NOT KNOW HOW I GOT HERE
I KNOW YOU WILL NOT LEAVE ME HERE
IF I CAN HEAR, YOU WILL HOLD ME
MY HEART WILL WAKE FROM ALL DARK DREAMS
SPIRIT OF HOME, COME HOME

I WILL LET GO, LET YOU HOLD ME
I'M NOT ALONE, COME HOME TO ME
TAKE HOLD MY HAND, MY BROKEN WING
MY BARREN HEART MAY LEARN TO SING
SPIRIT OF HOME, COME HOME

Author's Note

Elwhey tunes are closer in concept to the spirituals sung by enslaved Africans on plantations of the deep south rather than liturgical hymns written by Charles Wesley, Fanny Crosby, or other famous hymnodists throughout history. Elwhey tunes are to formal church music what the blues are to classical arias. They would be passed down orally, many not written down at all, and have a more direct connection to the faith of those singing than other spiritual songs that highlight the higher concepts of the religion. Because of this, they tend to be more emotive and often more personal.

This tune began as a song I wrote during a time of intercession on behalf of a friend. I often found sitting at my piano was a great way to find the "wings" for my prayer, and this is an excellent example of that. Much of the song is sung to the chord progression from Ab to C minor—in my opinion, the most haunting chord progression and, thus, my favorite. The song is very slow, the melody fluid. These elements give the tune a heightened feeling of longing.

FOREST MUSIC

BOOK THREE: *The Singing Bones*
CHAPTER SEVENTEEN: Traigen

BALLY HYMN

KEY: B flat

TEMPO: andante, 105 bpm, 4/4 time

ORIGIN: This is an example of an Edönic hymn that is part of the heritage passed down generationally between Edön mothers and their daughters, known as bally hymns. Bally hymns will almost always be influenced by the personal experiences and leanings of the specific singer, in this case Grey, though this tune seems to lean more heavily on her inheritance rather than personal influences.
Bally hymns are passed down generationally without the need of being taught. Rather, the songs—and the respect and deference to the natural world celebrated within them—are a part of the Edönic mantle impressed into daughters through the spiritual act of the bal-frue. Bally hymns seem to arrive in an Edön's heart when they are needed. Songs are an integral part of most Edönic practices as a way of deepening and celebrating an Edön's connection with the natural world. In the purest sense, Edönic hymns are songs of adoration that border on worship.

STORM IN A TEACUP
OCEAN IN A SHELL
DESERT RAIN
A SONG SUNG WELL

LIGHTNING IN A BOTTLE
CONSTELLATIONS IN AN EYE
THE MOMENT OF LAUGHTER
WHERE SEA MEETS SKY

Kiss of dew wet roses
Bright morning sings her tune
Midday lulls the heavens
With eye's of endless blue

Swift dusk falls earthward
Dawn's dancing son
Eventide tells his secrets with
Thunder's tragic tone

Lyrics whispered softly
In calm of middle night
Still the wild eruption
Of mountain's firelight

Music of the forest
Whole world hears you calling
You live where love is

Sing out your song
Let it ring
Give it wings

Sing out your song
The earth waits . . .
The sky waits . . .
Sing out your song
The earth is waiting . . .
The sky is waiting . . .

LADY, PARTED

BOOK THREE: *The Singing Bones*
CHAPTER TWENTY: Lest All Her Songs Take Flight

FOLKEN SONG

KEY: B flat

TEMPO: adagio, 69 bpm, ¾ time

ORIGIN: This is a song honoring the mythological figure, Fayelee Rose.

RUDDY SHADE, A FAIRLY BLOOM
OF LIGHT THAT SKIRTS THE NIGHT
TO CARRY ON OUR WAYWARD FRIEND,
SHE OF ROSE-FILLED LIGHT

CAST NOT AWAY THE MEM'RIES MADE
LEST ALL THE SONGS TAKE FLIGHT
COME FIND HER IN A SHADY GLADE
SHE OF ROSE-FILLED LIGHT

NOW ANTHEM RAISE
OUR PARTING SONG
FOR LOVELY MAID
TO SEND HER ON
MY FRIEND DO TASTE
THE FAIRY WAND
WE FIND THE LADY PARTED
MAY HER COURSE RING TRUE
WE FIND OUR LADY PARTED
SHE OF BRILLIANT HUE

NOT YET LOST, YOUR FRAGRANT LOOM
THAT WEAVES A ROSY SMILE

AND BEARS ALONG ON BLUSHING FLUME
TO CAST OFF SHADOW'S MIGHT

NOW LINGERS ON THE FAYELEE BRAID
THAT TOUCHES QUEENLY HEIGHT
AND BREAKS THE MOURNING BLADE
BETRAYED BY ROSE-FILLED LIGHT

WE FIND THE LADY PARTED
MAY HER COURSE RING TRUE
WE FIND OUR LADY PARTED
SHE OF BRILLIANT, ROSY HUE

Author's Note

This is a song version of a mythological story, one I would love to tell one day. It has a bit of an Irish lilt, though I always struggle to pin down the melody. It is a bit too free for all that, but it drips with melancholy. This song haunts me.

FLY HERE

BOOK THREE: *The Singing Bones*
CHAPTER THIRTY: Weeping Forest

EDÖNIC HYMN

KEY: A Major

TEMPO: andante, 76 bpm, 4/4 time

ORIGIN: This is an example of a combination of the two forms of Edönic hymns, bally and frulay. It is Grey's connection to Fenn that draws forth the elements of this song from within her Edönic inheritance to spin a tune specifically to honor her friend. This is the most common type of Edönic hymn, one that combines bally and frulay.

COME FLY HERE, RIGHT HERE
IN MY MIND HERE, A SKY FOR YOU
TO FLY HERE . . . . COME FLY

YOU CAN STAY HERE, RIGHT HERE
EVERY DAY HERE, A HOME FOR YOU
TO LIVE HERE, COME STAY

THE ROOM WE HAVE IS ENOUGH
AND WHAT WE DON'T, WE'LL MAKE UP
AND EVERY DAY WE'LL WAKE UP
AND SEE THE SUN . . . TOGETHER
WE'LL SEE THE SUN . . . TOGETHER

COME BE YOU, JUST YOU
IN EVERY WAY YOU, A HEART FOR ME
JUST FOR ME, JUST BE

Rest now, right now
Settle down now, a quiet place
To be still now, and sleep

You and me and you is enough
No matter what, it's just enough
And all the time I'll soak you up
We'll feel the sun . . . together
We'll feel the sun . . . together

FROM THE WORLD OF GLINT & SHADE:

A COLLECTION OF TERMS,
LORE, AND GEOGRAPHY

the
Forgotten
North

the
Grea
No

Goth

•BASTIAN
LE-

THE
BARREN

MALKET

THE DEAD MAN'S SPINE

THE
GRAY
LAKE

VALLEEN

•THROM

Earde-
Meridea

GAL-GAL

700

1400

2100

2800km

A COLLECTION OF TERMS

For a complete listing of terms, including all cross-referenced terms not included here, visit www.ericshanelove.com/glossary.

(A), B

bal-frue RELIGION AND BELIEF — A religious rite. **Bal-frue** is the Edönic practice of singing from one generation into the next their history and heritage. It is a sacred rite that typically takes place in wild areas of the forest, shore or other natural locations and is sometimes performed with one or more → *Edön* bearing witness. It is considered the → *Edöné's* most sacred act. It is the

transference of the potency of the Edön mother to her daughter
(or in rarer cases, her son) and is a literal activation of that power
(though the mantle does not manifest until puberty).

bally hymn RELIGION AND BELIEF — A religious song.
Bally hymns are one of two types of songs performed by the
→ *Edöné*. Bally hymns are inherited by the daughter during the
spiritual practice of the → *bal-frue*. Considered generational gifts,
bally hymns are not taught by mothers but rather are assimilated
by daughters as they come into their Edönic heritage. A phenom,
bally hymns seem to present themselves to the singer at the time
they are needed. Most songs performed by the → *Edön* are not
strictly bally hymns, but rather are a combination of both bally
and → *frulay hymns*. Song is often employed by Edöné, but not
always. In the cases where an Edön does not practice singing, the
hymns are spoken rather than sung.

→ *frulay hymn*

Brogden ETHNICITY — A tribe of giant-like people. **Brogden**
are a race of giant-like people, dark complected, with bright eyes
and hair (often gold, also green, blue or purple). Their eyes and
hair mirror each other. The hair, always a base shade between
blond and brown, has hues throughout that are similar to those
of the eyes. This feature is most pronounced with gold eyes. The
Brogden are most well-known for three reasons:

(1) Their size. With an average height of 9 feet, Brogden are also
very wide.

(2) Their stories. Storytelling is considered their religion,
especially telling stories to honor the dead, and is called in
their ancestral tongue sprechliif.

(3) Their purpose. Brogden are a race of hunters who track and
destroy → *rumenati*.

Brogden hail from the island Alabaster Kay in the Catcher's Sea, a day-long boat ride off the southernmost point (and least populated portion) of Ausrost. Brogden live to be several hundred years old.

C

cubare FAYE — A demon. A **cubare** is a type of → *shade*, specifically, a sex demon. They are known for having insatiable appetites. They may absorb other shades, assuming their power and/or magical properties, but they find most delight in inhabiting the physical body of a person or animal. Because they are sex demons, they may inhabit the body of an animal and use that body to copulate with other animals or even people. They can make psychic connections with people and → *faye*. The reason for their need for sex is unclear, though it is clear the act increases their power (particularly physical sex acts, as opposed to psychic sexual connections). Cubare may inhabit a host body and use it as their own until the body wears out, resulting in the death of the host. Depending on the specific cubare and their intentions, the host may or may not be aware of the possession.

D

dahnee RELIGION AND BELIEF — A religious order. **Dahnee** are members of an ancient order believed to be one of the earliest religious sects. Dahnee is a → *lynthian* term which means "Coming of the Light" and refers to the belief that the world was once shrouded in a type of darkness wherein the Coming of Light was prophesied and eventually fulfilled. Though not a belief system largely adopted by the → *folken*, there are pockets of the dahnee order which have survived and exist mostly in secret throughout Mor-Thandak. Among the order is believed to exist the most well-preserved → *scrips* from most of the known spiritual tribes.

→ *Order of Light*

Dragon, the MYTHOLOGY — A mythological creature. **The Dragon**, known as Gothro, is a mythological creature who was defeated and subsequently exiled by the → *Great Witch*, → *Dal-Reeahs*. Iterations of the tale vary, and specific details change depending on who is telling. Ancient → *scrips* do exist which outline a fuller narrative of the event, though these exist only within secret, spiritual orders. The → *Skree* and → *Quid* are believed to be descendants of the followers who served the Dragon, and the Dragon still plays a large part in the spiritual rites and observances of the Skree.

dumas RELIGION AND BELIEF — Druidic priests. **Dumas** are a type of druidic priest whose task is to perform ritualistic rites and sacrifices, often human. The dumas were found among nearly all the ancient religious sects, so the term refers less to a specific belief system and more to the actual duties specific to their most striking office—sacrifice. Though an archaic term, some lower religious sects still claim some form of dumas, though rarely do these perform human sacrifices.

Dun-twille GEOGRAPHY, RELIGION AND BELIEF — An area of ritualistic magic. **Dun-twille** is the → *lynthian* term for a → *Place of Skulls.*

→ *Place of Skulls*

E

Edöné RELIGION AND BELIEF — A religious order. The **Edöné** are a line of people who have a deep and natural bond with the greater connectivity of all things in nature. This bond allows open communication between them and the natural world even to the point of having limited influence over the elements and natural things — i.e., wind, rain, plants, animals, etc. This ability is usually manifested only in females but is passed down from parent to child; male children have shown signs of this ability but usually with less intensity than their female relatives, and generally, though not always, when such a male child, has no living mother or sisters or in cases where the women → *folken* have failed to either bear signs of the → *Edön* or simply resisted its power. The term Edön is often used before a person's name who is believed to be an Edöné, though few people actually know or understand its meaning. The Edöné are largely a private group, are not self seeking, and tend to avoid making themselves known to other folken to avoid attempts on their part to utilize the → *Edönic* gifts. They do not collect in like groups but generally live interspersed within larger communities, villages and cities, or occasionally as hermits. However, in times of great need, they have been known to band together for the service of the greater good.

ehwain RELIGION AND BELIEF — The essence of someone's vitality. A → *folken's* **ehwain** is the essence of their (or any living creature's) vitality, or their life energy. Believed to be visible to some as color and mist, especially during times of heightened emotion, stress, or vigor, it is most often something felt or sensed rather than seen. When it is seen, it is only by those who are keen on the spiritual elements. Only those with a seeing gift can see it. Regardless of how it is perceived, a person's ehwain can give insight into their intentions, mental state, physical condition and, to a lesser degree, their future. However, the degree to which someone can read and understand another's life energy depends on their innate skill and/or training in the spiritual arts.

elhwith RELIGION AND BELIEF — The ethereal plane. The **elhwith** refers to the ethereal plane, also known as the → *other.*

F, (G)

faye FAYE — A collective term for magic beings. **Faye** are those creatures who exist as a natural part of the world and do not practice magic so much as be magic. Examples include fairies, sprites and → *listeners.* Other creatures may be considered faye in some cultures while only fauna in others (an example of this is calamity fish). Faye can also refer to geography or flora. Faye do not seek magic or develop magical properties. Rather, magic is a basis of their fundamental makeup. This is the primary way they differ from the → *sōklyn* (seekers of magic) in that faye are born/ spawned with magical abilities.

fayelee FAYE — Someone who has faye-like traits. **Fayelee** refers to any natural creature, whether human or animal (and more rarely vegetation) which is imbued with faye-like characteristics, powers, instincts or sight (even the ability to see or be seen by → *faye* creatures) either through mixed blood line, exposure to or training in faye-related magical arts, an → *ehwain branding* (or → *staining*) by a higher magic (whether dark or light), or any other means by which the creature or person is marked as being separate from non-magic → *folken.* A → *sōklyn* (seeker of magic) may be fayelee but seeking magic alone does not make one fayelee.

Fayelee Rose MYTHOLOGY — A mythological queen. **Fayelee Rose,** also known as the → *Fayelee Queen,* was said to be an enchanted forest queen whose long braids of auburn hair were imbued with a magical light, allowing her to rule her kingdom for many ages in peace. However, an evil Shadow Lord eventually conspired to rid her of her hair and, after succeeding in doing so, bound her with leather straps from an → auroch's back and threw her into the sea (some versions, a large lake) to drown. All hope seemed lost as the Shadow Lord assumed her throne. Depending on the telling, what followed either happened soon after or did so many years later after the land had been ravaged by the dark ruler. However, most accounts say the queen came back from the depths, her very body filled with the magical light, and banished the Shadow Lord on a bridge of rose-colored light. The bridge is often referred to as the → *fayelee wand*. It speaks of the irony of darkness being exiled onto a shaft of light, on which shadows cannot exist, thus reducing the darkness to a state of nonexistence.

Fayelee Queen MYTHOLOGY — A mythological queen.

→ *Fayelee Rose*

fayelee wand MYTHOLOGY — A mythological bridge. The **fayelee wand** refers to the bridge of rose-colored light on which a Shadow Lord was banished upon the return of the → *Fayelee Queen*. It speaks of the irony of darkness being exiled onto a shaft of light, on which shadows cannot exist, thus reducing the darkness to a state of nonexistence. The fayelee wand is often invoked as a blessing before long journeys, especially if the journey may be dangerous. In some cultures, the fayelee wand is invoked as the path by which a dying person may reach → *the pasture next*, considered by the majority of folken in Mor-Thandak to represent the afterlife.

Feilebroc CULTURE — A festival. **Feilebroc** is one of four → *Hidain* (or Holy Days)—the festival of low winter. It falls on the first day of the second month and marks the coming of spring (is believed to conjure spring in many cultures). Life-size dolls ("goddess dolls" fashioned to represent the Goddess of Spring, Homůnre) are prepared and decorated with bright colors and winter's bane (when available; in warmer climates, → *dragonferns* are used) and are paraded from house to house until ultimately brought to the center of the village or city and burned. This burning is thought to light the way for the Goddess Homůnre (the incarnation of Spring). Feilebroc is a time of divination that heralds the coming of the end of winter and the beginning of spring. It is a festival of hope since it celebrates the coming of new life (spring) in the dead (or center) of winter. It is also characterized by giving gifts and keeping an → *embers pot* burning. Its twin Hidain is → *Tanneibel,* which is the festival of low summer and marks the beginning of the harvest season (the first day of the eighth month).

firesprite FAYE — A → *faye* forest creature. Believed to be a type of faye that live among the trees and rivers of the forests, **firesprites** aren't intelligent beings like → *fairies,* though perhaps they are distantly related. Instead, they are uncomplicated creatures whose actions are dictated by instinct (similar to bees or birds). When fully grown, they are roughly the size of a man's hand. Though their colors may vary, most are red or have a reddish hue. Their heads, hands and feet have glowing, fibrous threads (resembling hair) that give them the appearance of fire. They are birthed from the forest as glowing orbs (spores) and float in the forest for approximately two weeks before "lighting" (setting down upon a physical object to pupate). They take on the substance of that physical thing as they draw from the energy of the forest around them. Once lit, a crystal chrysalis forms and the firesprite pupates for one year. When it hatches, its lifespan is also approximately one year. → *Khamun* and others who know how to commune with the forest may call on firesprites for protection, though the protection they offer is instinctive in nature.

frulay hymn RELIGION AND BELIEF — A religious song. **Frulay hymns** are one of two types of songs performed by the → *Edöné.* Frulay hymns are very specific to the singer, often being birthed from that specific element with which the → *Edön* most identifies—these elements are sometimes called an Edön's "token" element. Most Edön identify with one or more natural elements on a deeper, more personal level than the rest. The result is a familiarity with that element which allows the Edön a swifter connection with it as needed. Frulay hymns often highlight such token connections. It is common for an Edön to develop an anthem over the course of their life which celebrates this token connection. However, frulay hymns are not limited to such connections; they may also come from specific connections to an event, location, person, element or other aspect of the natural world and the tapestry that makes up all things. Most songs performed by the Edön are not strictly frulay hymns, but rather are a combination of both bally and frulay hymns. Song is often employed by Edöné, but not always. In the cases where an Edön does not practice singing, the hymns are spoken rather than sung.

→ *bally hymn*

H, (I, J)

Hidain CULTURE — Festival days. **Hidain** are High Holy Days. There are four: → *Sauingrey,* → *Feilebroc,* → *Lunauinbroc,* and → *Tanneibel.*

Hidain lamp CULTURE — A religious object. **Hidain lamps,** also called → *tween lights,* are set during high festivals and serve a variety of purposes. Tween lights come in many different forms, but the most prevalent are any bucket or container that can be filled with burning candles, tallow or twigs. Common examples include hollowed-out gourds, clay pots, holes dug into the earth (generally surrounding a home or sacred place) and typically filled with burning logs, skulls (though these are reserved for the darker arts and are most often used during → *Sauingrey*).

K

khamun RELIGION AND BELIEF — Religious figures. **Khamun** are any holy → *folken*, mostly ascetic in nature (renouncing material comforts and leading a life of stern self-discipline out of religious devotion). Khamun may be men or women and the term is not specific to any one belief system, though it suggests believers who strive to be at one with nature (the → *Mother*), such as the → *Eri* or the → *Edöne*. Through the years, most belief systems have adopted the term.

kinnit LINGUISTICS, SOCIOLOGY — A respectful term. **Kinnit** is a term used to show respect to one in authority, to elders, or to anyone on whom a person wishes to bestow honor or respect. It is a formal term of honor, sometimes used before a person's name or in place of their given name.

kohlas CULTURE — A rite of passage. **Kohlas** is a → *cumatu*, or rite of passage, for boys of age seven that is peculiar to the rural regions of the Southerly Feet Mountains in the land of Carde, specifically the valley of Gal-Braith. A boy begins his kohlas on the morning of his seventh birthday. It is an adventure he must complete on his own without the aid of his father, mother, or any other adult or peer. It is believed to be the proper way a boy grows to become a man. In most regions, children take on adult responsibilities as early as age seven—a transition age viewed as the "sprout" of adulthood, but this rite is peculiar to the rural southwest. The boys of the kohlas are expected to leave home on a mysterious journey and remain gone for several years, returning only after they have reached full physical maturity. Wards who do not interfere with the boy's challenges accompany them on their quest. The kohlas is never spoken of openly as it is considered too sacred to do so. The kohlas is intrinsically tied to the valley's religion. Because of this, the kohlas is both revered and feared.

kolinga CULTURE — A rite of passage. **Kolinga** is a → *cumatu*, or rite of passage, for girls age thirteen that is peculiar to Lustrain and the surrounding mountains in Ausrost. The kolinga is a ceremony that marks a young woman's passage into adulthood. Origins of the rite are unknown, but historical records show the ceremony was once supervised by a particular sect of → *dumas* known as the → *Monkshood*. However, over time the Monkshood died out, and local → *khan* (in this case, elder women from among the → *cluster*) took over the Monkshood's duties. In older times, the girls would be given a sleeping tonic upon entering the ceremony and would often not wake for days after. The exact details of what transpired during the ceremony were never revealed beyond the dumas, and the girls themselves could offer no practical insight into the rite. The kolinga ended when the cluster grounds—along with its inhabitants—were obliterated during what is believed to have been an eruption of volatile steam from within the mountain on which the cluster was built.

L

leetide RELIGION AND BELIEF, CULTURE — The thinning of the membrane separating physical and spiritual planes. **Leetide** is a term that refers to the overlap of → *tweeny* times, places or → *folken* that increases the thinness between the worlds (that which is seen and those which are not). In extreme cases, a person can slip between the realms, even unintentionally. Because of this supreme thinness, and the relative unawareness of most folken to the spiritual world, a leetide can be highly dangerous, even for one who seeks knowledge of the spirit realm. The risk is almost exclusive to those folken who have → *fayelee* characteristics. Those who are unaware of their fayelee qualities are at the highest risk. Such extreme cases are rare.

Lunauinbroc CULTURE — A festival. One of four → *Hidain* (or Holy Days), **Lunauinbroc** is the last day of the fourth month of the year (or the eve of → *Summer Han*) and marks the beginning of summer. Special bonfires are kindled—flames, smoke and ashes are believed to have protective or destructive powers. In some regions, people leap over or pass between flames to signify prowess, strength or bravery, and this act is also considered lucky. The dew that falls on the morning following Lunauinbroc is believed to hold magical properties. Lunauinbroc also refers to midsummer festivals. It is a time of divination. In the northern hemisphere, it is celebrated at the other end of the year: the last day of the eleventh month. Its Hidain twin is → *Sauingrey* (celebrated on the eve of → *Winter Hu*); both are celebrated on the last day of the month preceding the seasonal turn.

lusts ECONOMY — A currency. Pronunciation: "loosts".

→ *tricks*

Lynth LINGUISTICS, RELIGION AND BELIEF —A language. **Lynth** is an ancient language spoken mostly by → *dumas*, → *khamun,* and other devout religious and spiritual followers. Mostly arcane, it was never widely spoken by the → *folken* but was reserved for religious rites and → *scrips* and is now nearly extinct. However, many lynthian terms (or variations of them) remain in the vernacular of the folken, particularly in religious terminology.

M, (N)

milk fern FLORA — A fruit-bearing plant. **Milk fern** is a rare fern that bears fruit that contains a milky white substance that can be extracted from the bulbs (called hearts). The milk is useful when administered to painful cuts, scrapes, and other external injuries for the reduction of pain. Though its medicinal uses are mostly limited to external pain relief, in some cases it may be taken orally in very small doses, but the application of such a use widely varies in purpose and effectiveness. One universal understanding of milk fern is that its milk is an effective poison: when ingested orally, it causes violent, painful death.

milly LINGUISTICS, SOCIOLOGY — A derogatory term. **Milly** is a derogatory term used to suggest someone is immature or otherwise inexperienced. It is often used by adults when speaking to youths, but it is particularly offensive when used to describe someone who considers themselves a peer or equal.

Monkshood RELIGION AND BELIEF — A religious group. The **Monkshood** are an ancient priesthood who myth suggests were originally followers of the witch → *Dal-Reeahs*, but they turned on her, leading to her exile. Legend also purports that some of the Monkshood who remained faithful to the witch were bound by her magic and turned to a human-animal hybrid called the → *wolfenkind*, though only the most superstitious → *folken* believe this to be true. Though their origins and purposes are widely debated, the Monkshood did indeed exist and may yet have followers.

Moon, Malkein ASTRONOMY, CULTURE — High moon. Malkein is an ancient → *lynthian* word meaning "magic." **Malkein Moon** refers to a period where the → *Sleeping Moon* (or → *Dead Moon*) "crests" on any of the four → *Hidain* (High Holy Days). It is believed to thin further the veil between realms, heightening the magical properties of the time. The exact meaning of a Malkein Moon is determined by which Hidain it falls upon: a Malkein Moon during → *Tanneibel* is a good omen, one during → *Feilebroc* is a bad omen, one falling on either → *Sauingrey* or → *Lunauinbroc* must be interpreted congruent to other factors. The "reading" of even the simplest Malkein Moon is complicated, as influential factors vary. Weather patterns, religious beliefs and regional superstitions play a role in the interpretation.

O

Order of Light (Order) RELIGION AND BELIEF — A religious order. Most commonly referred to as just the Order, **the Order of Light** is one of the oldest known religious sects. Members of this ancient order are called → *dahnee,* a → *lynthian* term which means "Coming of the Light" and refers to the belief that the world was once shrouded in a type of darkness wherein the Coming of Light was prophesied and eventually fulfilled. Though not a belief system largely held by the → *folken,* there are pockets of the dahnee Order which have survived and exist mostly in secret throughout Mor-Thandak. They are believed to own the largest and most well-preserved collection of → *scrips* of all known spiritual tribes. Their traditions are passed down secretly among those chosen to be part of their ranks. A person can choose to become part of the Order, but a rigorous series of tests (which require years) are necessary, and most do not pass these and are eventually expelled. If chosen for the Order, a person is chosen shortly after birth. The parents are given the choice of whether they will allow their child to become part of the Order (since once a child joins the Order's ranks, they never leave it). The basis for choosing members of the Order is known only to its members, though most who are chosen now are chosen from among villages and/or family groups who believe being chosen is a great honor. Members of the Order are considered wise and merciful and are occasionally sought to help resolve issues between warring peoples' groups. Their monastic communes are mostly hidden from the outside world and are protected by ancient magic.

P, (Q)

poke POLITICS — Hired fighters. **Pokes** are fighting men employed by → *regents* or other local officials and/or civic leaders to help govern. Because there is no standardized system of government, the role of pokes varies from village to village. Generally, they work to enforce local laws, may be hired out as fighting men or bounty hunters, and are either paid wages, given room and board in exchange for their work, or a combination of both. Pokes often have unsavory reputations, as there is a stigma associated with them of taking bribes. Those men most often attracted to the position often cannot find gainful employment through other means because of a history of violence or, ironically, breaking the law.

poobah LINGUISTICS, SOCIOLOGY — A form of address. **Poobah** is a familiar and affectionate term for grandfather or grandmother.

R

razor-bone FAUNA — A fish species. **Razor-bone** refers to a type of fish that has a fin that is a very strong and sharp extension of its spine. Due to this peculiarity, razor-bone fish are often captured for the sake of harvesting the blades of its dorsal and caudal fins for use as tools or weapons. A school of razor-bone can be deadly, though the fish themselves are not aggressive.

regent POLITICS — A political office. **Regent** (or the regentry) refers to any leadership or governing power in a village, region or city. Because governance varies throughout Mor-Thandak, there is no prescribed manner by which the regentry may govern. Equally, there is no standard for enforcing the regents' rule, but often fighting men, or → *pokes,* serve in the capacity of law enforcement. Regent (or the regentry) may also refer to any leadership or governing power.

→ *City Regent*

S

Sauingrey CULTURE — A festival. **Sauingrey** is one of the four → *Hidain* (Holy Days) and occurs on the last day of the 11th month of the year (or the eve of → *Winter Hu*). It signifies the end of harvest and the beginning of winter, or → *"the Darker Half."* During Sauingrey, special bonfires are lit. It is a liminal time when spirits and fairies are believed to move more easily in the world. Souls of the dead revisit homes. Divination rituals are common, often involving nuts and apples. In the northern hemisphere, Sauingrey is celebrated at the other end of the year: on the last day of the fourth month (→ *gu-delak*). Its Hidain twin is → *Lunauinbroc* (celebrated on the eve of → *Summer Han*); both are celebrated on the last day of the month preceding the seasonal turn.

scrip RELIGION AND BELIEF — A spiritual text. **Scrip** refers to any spiritual text but is most commonly associated with ancient writings of any sect.

seeing bowl RELIGION AND BELIEF — A religious object. A **seeing bowl** is used as a → *joiner* between people, objects, places or even realms. It allows the holder to see across space (and sometimes time), into the → *elhwith*, into the → *ehwain* of another person, and even multiple outcomes to situations by use of roleplay and/or magic. Seeing bowls may be formed from nearly any material but must be imbued with power and are most often plated with precious metal, like especially silver. The most potent seeing bowls are made from materials that were sacred to begin with, such as wood from an eldertree (→ *elderwood*) or altar stones (such as those used for → *cyth*).

shade FAYE — A → *faye* phenomenon. A **shade** is any spiritual being that once inhabited (or can inhabit) a physical body. Examples include ghosts, spirits and demons.

Skree, the ETHNICITY — A violent people group. **The Skree** come from the Kathian Mountains, sometimes referred to as the wilderness of the high county. They are a violent group of people who at various times send campaigns out for the sake of harvesting slaves from the eastern and southern regions of Ausrost and Carde. The Skree are cannibals, and a portion of their slaves are used for food (much like cattle with other people groups) while others are sold. The Skree's harvest season, a period of eight weeks believed to fall on the weeks leading up to → *Sauingrey* (the Skree's most sacred day of the year), involves the sacrificial offering of one Skree warrior (male or female) per day. Considered a high honor to be chosen for the offering, the chosen Skree's body is eaten by their kinsmen. The Skree's home base and temple are in the heart of the → *Mountain of the Dragon,* found in the uppermost range of the Kathian Mountains. Because their homeland is almost unreachable by the → *folken* of the southern lands, due primarily to the treacherous northern mountains, the Barren, or Lost Lake, and the ferocity of the Skree themselves, not much is known about daily Skree life in the Kathians other than their reputation for being merciless murderers and slave traders. However, the Skree are believed to descend from the followers of the → *Dragon* Gothro (a mythological deity figure believing to have come to this world following the witch → *Dal-Reeahs*) and are believed to continue serving him still. The Skree's two sigils include the burning of a fine powder specific to the Kathian Mountains that release billows of thick, red smoke into the sky, known as the → *Red Death,* and the wailing of the → *Criers,* Skree chosen at birth and subjected to a series of mutilations to the larynx to give them the ability to screech in an inhuman and unnatural way. By these means, and through the small amount of information known about the Skree and the legends surrounding them, the Skree instill fear in others. The Skree are albino and shave most of their hair, which is so light blond it appears white. The men often wear long, pointed beards or goatees, the women (who fight alongside the men) often have a single braid growing from the base of their skull. During campaigns they smear intricate patterns on their bodies with the Red Death powder, their skin layered with heavy scars due to the burning nature of the caustic powder, and use slivers of bone to pierce themselves on their ears, face, chest and torso, leaving only their arms and legs unadorned. They fight naked to the waist, even in winter and even the women. Many sharpen some or all of their teeth into points. The desired effect is for the very sight of them to instill poignant fear in their beholders even as their sigils and reputation have much the same effect. The Skree's weapons usually consist of broad knives, for close fighting, and spears, about four feet, with a sharp blade fixed to one end and a hook on the other.

söklyn CULTURE — A seeker of magic. **Söklyn** is a term which refers to any person who seeks magical abilities or power, whether through the discipline of a specific religious or cultural order or simply as a means to an end. The term is broadly used.

switch CULTURE, LINGUISTICS — A derogatory term. **Switch** is an extremely derogatory word for a woman's genitals that is used as a term of disparagement for women (often suggesting they are being difficult or dramatic) or men (often suggesting they are weak or have feminine characteristics, specifically emotionally).

T, (U)

Tanneibel CULTURE — A festival. **Tanneibel** is the festival of low summer and one of four → *Hidain* (or High Holy Days). Tanneibel takes place on the first of the eighth month of the year and marks the beginning of the harvest season. Traditionally, Tanneibel was celebrated with ritualistic athletic competitions (often to the death), feasting, matchmaking and trade. Tanneibel still offers athletic competitions, but in a lighthearted, festive way. Feasting, matchmaking and trade continue to be part of the festivities. An offering (or sacrifice) of the first fruits of the field is often made, though to which deity(s) depends on the region. Much of the festival, especially the rituals and offerings, takes place on the top of hills or mountains. Tanneibel, like its Hidain twin, → *Feilebroc* (low winter, celebrated on the first day of the second month), is a time of divination.

teeg ECONOMY — A currency. **Teegs** are coins universally accepted throughout Mor-Thandak. Their value, however, is not universal.

trap CULTURE, LINGUISTICS — A derogatory term. **Trap** is a derogatory term used to describe a person who is perceived to be immature, helpless, defenseless, or otherwise useless. It suggests inferiority that is derived from being overly complicated, childish or dependent on others.

tweeny RELIGION AND BELIEF, CULTURE — Referring to transitional times. **Tweeny** is a → *lynthian* term which refers to the "time between times" that is believed to hold magical properties. Daily examples are sunrise, sunset, and the time between wakefulness and sleep. In a broader sense, a tweeny time is any time of transition: between seasons, at the beginning or ending of a storm, puberty, life to death, etc. Though the concept's origins are lynthian, it is widely adopted throughout most regions and religious systems.

V, (W, X, Y, Z)

Valleen GEOGRAPHY — A village. **Valleen** is a port village on the Ausrost side of the Snake River. It is considered a → *ways place* and is one of the largest ports of trade between Carde and Ausrost.

vaultine FAYE, GEOGRAPHY — A place with magical properties. **Vaultine** refers to a geographical area where magical properties have pooled to create a potent region where ethereal sensibilities are heightened and the separation between spiritual and physical plains is lessened. A → *low place* would technically be considered a vaultine; however, the two are often considered opposites. Vaultines are often associated with positive energy or good magic, but they are yet wild and magical in inception and nature and must be treated with utmost respect and care. Vaultines are also referred to as → *vaults* and, occasionally, → *high places.*

AFTERWORD AND ACKNOWLEDGEMENTS

Because so much of this book has been my personal reflections, I will not include much here. However, I do want to thank two people for helping me catch the vision for this anthology. In 2020, I hired a marketing consultant to help me develop a launch plan. Mike and I have collaborated a handful of times since, and Mike always seemed to get this series. When I told him I had additional scenes and stories that would not be included in the main books, he suggested I collect those in an anthology. Almost immediately I began following his advice, and I am grateful for his nudge.

I must also thank my editor, Parisa. When I sent her this manuscript for a copy edit, she saw something in it I had yet to see. In a strange way, she shined a light on these pages and revealed to me the potential for a great book...only it was not yet great. You can thank Parisa for the ability to spend time with Leah and her grandmother, and for Roland introducing us to Tig and Janith. I knew those scenes, but it was not until Parisa suggested it that I began putting those words on the page.

I am thrilled with how far this anthology has come since its original inception. As the world of the Glint expands for you, I hope you find this and future anthologies fascinating safaris you can explore off the beaten path. As always, thank you for joining us.

—Eric Shane Love—

January 22, 2023

ABOUT THE AUTHOR

Since January 2016, I've been a freelance videographer, photographer and graphic designer. I live in a rural Georgia town about an hour and a half inland from Savannah. Before 2016, I worked nearly fifteen years at a small, non-profit youth home for troubled teenage boys. I was a mentor, educator and the creative director during that time. I've always had a love of writing. As early as sixth grade, I wrote stories about my classmates, passing them around the room to get feedback.

A few random, interesting and trivial things to know about me: I'm in a band with my brother, Brian, called Tiger Creek. I sing and play keys. I am a classically trained vocalist, though that has almost no bearing on the classic and 80s rock, and, less fortunately, the spattering of country songs we perform in the band. Halloween is my favorite holiday. Christmas is a close second. I have two dogs and a cat: Bella, a mutt who gives me the best cuddles, and Hot Breath Eugene, an enormous pit bull/mastiff mix whose head looks like a basketball with eyes. For those who have read my author bio in the first two books, you may remember Queen Maddie. Maddie, a 150-year-old basset hound, left us last year. She is now chasing rabbits in the pasture next. Bella has now assumed the role of Queen, and Eugene yet alternates between being the Court Jester and the Village Idiot. The cat's name is Chuck, and he is irreparably deranged. That's why we love each other. In keeping with our fantastical metaphor, Chuck is the Crazy Witch who lives in the forest outside the city walls, so to speak. All my pets are rescues. I also have about fifty plants in my house. I have a tendency to take much longer to tell a story than is necessarily required, and sometimes those stories don't have endings. I get that from Debbie, my mom. Also, I hate most modern technology.

Sign up for my newsletter and have access to a behind-the-scenes look at my writing process, read exclusive content, and learn about the lore and geography of Eliot's world at my website: ericshanelove.com.

ABOUT THE ILLUSTRATOR

A connoisseur of art, athletics, philosophies, and exotic fungus, I appreciate the ability to express the universe currently taking form as myself in an eclectic variety of ways, but visual art seems to be the one that grabs me the most. My current body was born in the high desert of Southern Idaho, right next to the canyon Evel Knievel failed to jump. I hope you appreciate the strangeness of my work. Thank you for joining us on the journey that is *Glint & Shade*.

—*Logan Peyman*—
September 12, 2022

MORE FROM THE GLINT & SHADE SERIES

The Scarecrow Hunters (2022)

A Greedy Shadow (2022)

COMING SOON

The Singing Bones

The Gathering Grim

www.ingramcontent.com/pod-product-compliance
Lightning Source LLC
Chambersburg PA
CBHW071135260626
47162CB00003B/795

9 798985 317367